JJ Hutton is married with three grown-up sons and lives in North Yorkshire, England and served as a senior Officer within the UK Special Forces group (Reserves). He combines his passion for history with an equal passion for writing, the combination of the two is intriguing for his readers. When he is not walking or writing, he is a mentor to schoolchildren facing personal challenges and is an active supporter of several British Army Veterans charities.

JJ Hutton

MILLER

Collusion is no illusion

AUSTIN MACAULEY PUBLISHERS™

LONDON • CAMBRIDGE • NEW YORK • SHARJAH

A CIP catalogue record for this title is available from the British Library.

ISBN 9781528938020 (Paperback)
ISBN 9781528942416 (ePub e-book)

www.austinmacauley.com

First Published (2020)
Austin Macauley Publishers Ltd
25 Canada Square
Canary Wharf
London
E14 5LQ

Collusion Is Not an Illusion

Historical Context:

In 1922, after the Irish War of Independence and the Anglo-Irish Treaty, most of Ireland seceded from the United Kingdom to become the independent Irish Free State, which, after the 1937 constitution, began to call itself Ireland. However, the six north-eastern counties, known as Northern Ireland, remained within the United Kingdom. The history of Northern Ireland has since been plagued by sectarian conflict between (mainly Catholic) Irish nationalists and (mainly Protestant) unionists. This conflict erupted into the *Troubles*.

The *Troubles* were an armed conflict in Northern Ireland which began in 1969 and ended with the Good Friday Agreement of 1998. Although the *Troubles* mainly took place in Northern Ireland, at times the violence spilled over into parts of the Republic of Ireland, England and parts of Europe. Miller (book one) is set in the period 1970–1972. Unionists (loyalists) who are mostly Protestants want Northern Ireland to remain within the UK. Irish Nationalists, who are mostly Catholics, want Northern Ireland to leave the UK and join a united Ireland.

The *Troubles* began during a campaign to end discrimination against the Catholic minority by the protestant/unionist government and police force. This protest campaign was met with violence by loyalists. This eventually led to the deployment of British troops, initially to support the police and protect Catholic civilians. After that, battle lines were drawn, and the violence spread far and wide.

The main protagonists were Republican paramilitaries such as the IRA and its derivatives, Loyalist paramilitaries such as the Ulster Volunteer Force and the Ulster Defence Association; the British security forces – Army and police (Royal Ulster Constabulary). Much of the conflict was fought by clandestine/secret forces from all sides and many murders remain unsolved to this day.

During the conflict in Northern Ireland, the violence never reached the agreed threshold to be called a "war". Nevertheless, its impact on the society of Northern Ireland with a population of about 1.5 million was profound, with over 3,500 killed and over 50,000 injured over a thirty-year period.

Chapter 1:
Manchester 1971

It was just another of those ordinary grey, overcast autumnal days in Manchester when unbeknown to Miller, his life was about to change forever, dramatically.

He entered the shop near to the Levenshume rail station in the suburbs. He bought a box of Iams biscuits for his dog Pilgrim and some baccy papers for his roll ups. This morning, the two shopkeepers of Pakistani descent eyed him in a suspicious and hostile way.

'Money!' the shopkeeper demanded. Miller stood there, and slowly counted out the small loose change he held in the palm of his right hand.

'Come on, we haven't got all day,' he demanded with irritation and impatience.

From off to the right the older of the two shopkeepers interjected.

'We have our eye on you, someone is stealing from our shop and we think it's you!'

Miller looked up and glared but didn't answer. He counted out the remaining coins for the biscuits onto the counter and turned. As he did so, the older brother blocked his way by grabbing his arm and retorted, 'We don't like your type, bums you are, you smell, always drunk, never work, always high on drugs. You are just a scum beggar and a scourge on society, don't ever come into our shop again, do you hear me?' His voice was venomous.

Miller just ignored the man and his insults and walked towards the door.

At the lack of any reaction, the shop owner turned even more aggressive and pulled again on Miller's elbow this time with enough force to spin his body around.

'Don't you ignore me, are you listening, you scum?' The storekeeper was shouting now.

Miller's training and instincts took over. Unfortunately.

He'd only been sitting at his regular spot for 90 minutes at the station along from the taxi stand when the tactical police unit came to lift him. The unit used no subtleties; they turned him forcibly onto his front on the floor and used durable plastic cable ties to secure both his arms around his back. They pulled him upright and shoved him into the back of the large van; he didn't offer any resistance. He just looked over his shoulder and asked, 'What about my dog?'

'Not our problem, we'll send the council out to pick it up and take it to the compound.'

After two hours in the cell, he was escorted into the interview room and the two detectives who sat there began questioning him. They weren't going to get far with that; unbeknown to them, he'd been trained well in the art of "resistance to interrogation".

He was being charged with causing "grievous bodily harm", a lesser charge than the one sought by the shop owner's lawyer who had accused the vagrant of "attempted murder and a hate crime" against his clients. The lawyer probably reasoned that the victim's compensation pay-out would be greater if the charges were greater. After a frustrating hour, the detectives left the room and gave instructions for him to be moved to prison to await trial. Even with no confession from the vagrant, he was clearly guilty: it was an open and shut case.

Miller had been in a cell previously, it was quite common for vagrants to be placed in custody occasionally, but he'd never been to prison before; he was looking forward to the challenge it offered to him. He smiled to himself. He was to be transferred into remand to await trial into the north of England's infamous Victorian prison, Strangeways, Manchester.

Chapter 2:
Release into the Unknown

Two months behind bars, one vicious riot and a visit from the Intelligence services had all created the potential to thrust Miller into a new world. He felt both a degree of trepidation and anticipation at the same time.

The early morning sun shone brightly as it climbed over the terraced houses that surrounded the prison in the Cheetham district of Manchester, and its glare caused Miller to squint. He stood there momentarily; the small wooden pedestrian gate to Strangeways was already shut and bolted from within. He was outside, a free man again. He breathed in deeply; the air was moist but smelt clean after the disinfected air offered by the prison. It washed over him like a small waterfall.

His moment of meditation was interrupted by two toots on a car horn, as Miller looked up, a hand from a driver's side window gesticulated to him to come over. A head popped out of the open driver's window.

'Miller, is it? Yeah, you must be, jump in then.'

Miller, never thought to question who the man was and simply climbed into the passenger seat, pushing it as far back as it would go to maximise the leg room for his particularly large frame.

The driver was balding, overweight and about 60 years old.

After driving in complete silence through the heavy Manchester traffic for about 40 minutes, the car joined the motorway to head south. The M6. The driver was the first to break the ice.

'Not being unsociable like, being doing this a long time now and I stick to my brief, no chit chat, no questions, just pick up the parcel and deliver in one piece.'

Miller turned to look at the driver and turned his head forward again before responding.

'Suits me, where is it we are going?'

'Walsall, take about an hour, I am to drop you off there and then that's me done for the day.'

'What's at Walsall?'

'No idea, just have an address that's all.'

The car, about five years old, was a Ford of some sort, non-descript model, and the driver was careful to keep it just under the 70 mph speed limit. Miller sat in total silence watching the busy traffic ebb and flow alongside them. Their destination turned out to be a large house in the suburbs, Victorian probably, with a short private gravel drive which led to a set of double gates with black painted railings. Quite ordinary really. That is except for the pole mounted camera adjacent to the gates, which had two lights on either side, one of which was infrared to allow the camera to function at night. A dead giveaway for MOD property.

Another man, also in his early sixties, stepped out of a side door in the gravel courtyard, and the driver encouraged his package to leave the car – the journey was over.

'Hello, I am Geordie,' the stranger offered an outstretched hand to Miller and the two men shook. The car turned and exited the gates of the house. A black oily plume from the exhaust drifted into the sky, temporarily polluting the courtyard.

'I've got a nice surprise for you, Miller,' offered Geordie, 'someone will be excited to see you, follow me.'

The mysterious, but friendly stranger, turned and walked back in the direction of the house.

Miller was somewhat intrigued, and as the two men entered the wooden floored corridor of the building, the quiet was suddenly broken, noise erupted, and an excited bark greeted them both. Slipping and scampering down the corridor like an express train ran a small mongrel dog. Miller couldn't believe his eyes; he immediately dropped to his knees as the dog barked, jumped up at him and licked his face profusely.

It was his dog. It was Pilgrim.

He allowed himself to smile, on the inside as well as the outside. He had thought he would never have seen his dog again.

Geordie explained that he and his wife had taken care of the little mongrel for the past few weeks. 'We are going to miss him, but we knew it was temporary like, we were just asked to look after it for you, now of course, she's pleading with me to get our own! Come on, 'er's your digs.'

Geordie had lost none of his accent and somehow it was reassuring to Miller. Hartlepool was some 50 miles south of "Geordieland", that is Newcastle, but the accent was welcoming, something he could identify with.

'I expect you two might want to get reacquainted, so I'll leave you be now. They'll be down to see you in about half an hour, just finishing off some meeting upstairs. Feel free to wander in the garden; its private enough and it's not a bad morning.'

Miller was nonplussed, it was all surreal and it was like he was floating along in someone else's dream. He exited the French windows and threw a small stick in different directions; Pilgrim was off after them quick as a flash, happy to be playing the game. It was as if they had never been apart these past months. He had wondered what had become of his dog after he was arrested, and no one had been able to tell him. Perhaps, there was a God after all. Their play time was interrupted when Geordie whistled from the doorway to attract his attention and beckoned him to come back in. He was shown to another room in which there was already a grey haired somewhat weedy man, and a curvy, overweight woman in her mid-forties.

'I expected you will be wondering what this is all about, Miller. Let me introduce myself, I am Lt Colonel Gilbert, I commanded D squadron in the late sixties, moved across to Intelligence Corp for a couple of years and now I am working for the Intelligence services, MI6 to be exact. As for this lady, you will get to know her as Rosie. We have a proposal, a job for you.'

'I don't need a job, and more importantly, I don't want a job. Thank you, sir,' Miller replied.

'Well, be that as it may, but we need you, Miller; your country needs you.' A silence followed for several moments.

'Look,' the Colonel opened. 'We know that after over three years on the streets, you will have changed, a lot, no doubt. However, hear us out; what we've got to say isn't too different from that life either.'

Miller, in his usual manner, was economical with his words and just responded, 'And?'

'Well, Miller, we want you to go back to how you were, that is living on the street with your dog. Pilgrim, isn't it? How ironic.'

Members of their Regiment were known to other British Army units as the Pilgrims, taken from a poem by an English poet called James Flecker.

'You've lost me,' countered Miller.

Col Gilbert laid out his plan. 'Did you know your case made the Manchester Evening News? The two shopkeepers were outraged at the leniency of your sentence, accusing the judge of racism for not sending you down for your unprovoked attack on them. It was picked up by an equal rights organisation, too, so I guess you can say you have had your five minutes of fame. More importantly, that's what we wanted to happen, you now have a record, a past. You are traceable, not as Sgt Burke but as a violent street person known as Miller.

'Look Burke, until recently, our enemies were people of a different colour, skin and culture, like those you fought in Aden or in Borneo. It was us against them, the sides were obvious, and soldiers knew who to take the fight to. Well, all that's changed. We find ourselves in challenging territory these days. Regrettably. By August, we fully expect to have the largest deployment of British troops anywhere outside of the UK since the end of WW2. Do you know where these troops will be? Bloody Ulster, that's where.

'We are fighting a civil war, Burke, and it's messy. The politicians like to call it the Troubles they are hiding away from the fact that hundreds of innocent people have already died, and the body count of our troops rises daily.

It's not like anything we have encountered in our recent history. Not the Malay crises or Cyprus or Kenya, no this is even more evil. It's against our former people from the Republic of Ireland. We have over 25,000 soldiers stationed over there, and the bloody IRA is running rings around us. The Irish have never forgotten or forgiven us for Cromwell, and they want their island back, all of it.'

'Sir, you have completely lost me now; if you think I am re-enlisting, forget it. Seeing a picture of my best mate's head on a spike did it for me. And what exactly were we fighting for in Aden? Bloody rag heads the lot of 'em if you ask me. They were not worth it, and I lost several good mates fighting for their Queen and country for who knows what reason. As poor a country as any on this planet and we chose to fight and die over that bit of sandy desert. Stupid, if you ask me.'

'Burke, listen to me. We are on the back foot here, totally, and we need to make big changes to our tactics if we are going to get on top of things. That is where you come in. We are not asking you to go back to your old regiment, even assuming they would take you back, you're too old for that. No, we want you to become our eyes and ears on the ground. We want you and your dog to go back to living on the streets again; we just want you to swap Manchester for Dublin, that's all.'

'Dublin! And what exactly do you expect me to see from my perch on a piece of damp cardboard outside a post office, might I ask?'

The Colonels' eyes diverted to cue in the woman who until this time had remained completely silent.

'You will be working for me, Miller.'

Her strong Northern Irish brogue could be cut with a knife.

'I am going to be your case officer. I will direct you as the need arises to seek out information on our behalf from the streets of Dublin, the Mountjoy area to be precise. You are a proven patriot, you have a readymade cover story, it can be easily checked if anyone, for any reason, wanted to do so. Oh, and you signed two important papers when you joined the regiment, one was an oath of allegiance to Her Majesty, her heirs and her successors and secondly, the Official Secrets Act. They are both life-long solemn oaths.'

The colonel interceded back into the conversation.

'You will be paid, of course, Burke. We have opened an account in your real, given name and a monthly dispensation which is to be forward to you. Quite generous too, not quite the level of pay as a Sergeant but it will soon add up and as you're living as a beggar you don't need it as your running expenses will be negligible so to speak. On top of that, we have arranged a standing order to be transferred to the post office account of your parents, not a lot, 20 pounds a month, but from the first telegram they received from you that you were now working overseas in a good job and could afford to send them a few bob on a regular basis, they have been thrilled. You came through for them, just like they always knew you would. You have two proud parents, Burke.'

'You have already told my mother I am working? How dare you!' Miller's head was reeling, so much to take in, so much manipulation, he felt like he was a pawn in another man's war.

'Listen, Colonel Gilbert, if I wanted to be somebody's puppet, I would have changed my name to Pinocchio!'

'Oh, I know it's a lot to take in, Miller, feel free to have a think about it, but you haven't got long. We would like you over in Dublin by the end of next month.'

At that, the two of them exited the room, leaving Miller alone to stare down at the floor.

'Do you think he will take the bait?' asked Rosie.

'Hmm, 50/50, hard to say really, what possesses a career soldier of his ability to choose a life he has been living, it's beside me. That said, he's not alone, over 15% of all homeless people in the UK served in the Armed Forces at some time, I am reliably informed. Let him sleep on it and we will meet again in the morning, I have matters to attend, too, which are more pressing. Geordie will see he is fed and watered.'

Miller fussed his only true friend in the world, Pilgrim.

A person can learn a lot from a dog, he thought to himself. Pilgrim had helped him to appreciate the simple things in life, loyalty, friendship and devotion. Oh, and other things too. The glory a shaft of winter sunlight, the smell of new rain, the unconditional love a pet has for its master. Moreover, his dog had taught him about optimism in the face of adversity and now they were reunited. He felt uplifted and more positive than he'd felt for a long time.

After a sound night's sleep, he went downstairs.

Breakfast had been wholesome; Geordie cooked tasty English and Pilgrim had enjoyed the rashes of bacon he had fed him. They were both in the garden when the Colonel returned with a file under his arm.

'Come inside, Burke, you can bring the mutt if you like.'

The Colonel reached into his worn leather briefcase embossed with the coat of arms of the Queen and pulled out a laced manila folder on the table. On the top, in bold font, it read: "Top Secret (UK) only".

The Colonel flicked it open and offered the first few pages from the file.

'This is your cover story, Burke, from now on you are only to be known as Miller. The story is pretty much true to life, we have left in your service, except not with the para's but the Green Howards and totally omitted your time with the Regiment, that's all. Oh, and of course, we have used Miller as your new name. The next pages are Maps of Dublin, with more detailed street maps around your new home. We want you to study these. As for contact with your handler, this will be all brought out in your training down at Hythe and Lydd.'

'Where is that? I've never heard of it,' offered Miller. 'Oh, and when did I say I would do this, exactly?'

'Well, you are still here, and you haven't said you won't do it, so I have assumed you're in. Are you?'

Miller never answered, and the Col continued his briefing.

'We have built a complete mock town, modelled on an area of west Belfast on the old ranges down in Kent. It's state of the art. All Battalions deploying into Ulster have a six-week programme down there. As I said, it truly is exceptional, quite simply the best in the world, and has even been used by the FBI and only recently the Sayret Matkal had been stationed there.'

16

Miller had come across the Israeli Special Forces unit in his time in Radfan.

'You will be joining a cadre of intelligence officers and will be given training in the use of dead letter boxes; agent contact and a refresher in weapons. They won't know your role, and you will be expected not to ask any questions of them either. Oh, and instead of the normal six weeks, you will be accelerated to complete the training in two.'

Something inside of Miller re-awakened the warrior in him, and he sat up straight.

'Happy to be of service again, sir. You can count on me.' It was like turning the clock back for him.

'After Kent, you will be moved to another training area close by. There, Rosie will oversee your orientation on Dublin and its many tripping hazards. She is switched on, with bags of live operational experience, she can help you a lot so take note of all she tells you, Miller.'

Chapter 3:
Dublin

The fake driving licence in the name of Algernon Miller was the only ID he needed. The custom official barely offered it a cursory glance. The free movement of folk was commonplace, as tens of thousands of Irishmen and women travelled across to England in search of employment. Of course, he was travelling in the opposite direction. He sauntered down the gangplank of ferry, the gloomy clouds of Dublin and light drizzle of an autumnal day seemed to offer him a hostile welcome. It could have been Manchester; they shared the same grim damp weather. Miller was back in his old clothes, unwashed now for a long time, their aroma was off putting, even to him, and it would take time to readjust. He felt vulnerable. No radio to contact anyone, no money, no weapon, no buddy…he was, as they say, "up the creek without a paddle".

In the past two months, he had been briefed and trained rigorously for the mission ahead, it was now time to see if he could pull it off.

The four miles walk into the city took him over three hours. Pilgrim looked forlorn too, its coat matted with the steady incessant rain they needed to endure. It was now 6 pm, and it was time to start looking for some bedding and a place to sleep. On reaching the Mountjoy area, he set to find lodging for the night. Behind a small convenience store was a large wire skip into which was packed all the collapsed cardboard boxes of the last few days of deliveries. Miller climbed easily to the top and pulled out those boxes which looked the driest.

Bundling them under his arm, he slipped down the alley until he found a wooden door which was hanging from its hinge. It led to a small yard of a disused shop. *Perfect*, he thought. A rusting steel staircase pretending to be a fire escape from the two floors above offered a little respite from the rain. Miller arranged the boxes through the treads from the first landing to provide a makeshift roof and one wall. The rest he folded into a rectangle of three feet by four feet, onto which he could lay on. Well, at least his shoulders and main frame would have some insulation from the wet floor. Now as his bed was prepared, he went off scavenging for something to use for a drinking bowl for Pilgrim. Using a small, three-inch blade knife, he cut off the top of a milk carton to use as a drinking receptacle for his loving pet and filled it with rainwater from a leaking drainpipe. It was his personal choice to live rough; Pilgrim just chose to be with his master.

The first night in this city was uneventful, save for the lack of any sleep and the chill which permutated his skinny, tall frame. Irish weather was as grim as Manchester.

The next morning, with the remaining few coins in his possession, Miller bought some dry biscuits for Pilgrim and a packet of digestives for himself. They would have to last for, well, who knew? It was time to look for the neighbourhood to get to know them both. Miller shuffled down the street as locals, earnest in their intent, went about their business and hurried to their lowly paid unskilled jobs. Just up from the disused shop that he was now prepared to call "home", there was a busy junction where two roads intersected and a bridge over the river Tolka slowed the traffic. Perfect.

He had only sat there on his cardboard seat for less than twenty minutes before the first coin was dropped into the cloth. How was it that folk who had the least were always the most generous? Perhaps, it was the fact wired into an Irish man and women's DNA that they had known famine on a biblical scale. After all, the population of this small island had halved during the potato blight in the middle of the 19th century.

Eating so little meant that it was seldom necessary to defecate, and the alley 30 yards away afforded Miller enough privacy to pee without the risk of being arrested for it.

At 8 pm, after a long day, Miller stood, stretched and sauntered back in the direction of the disused shop to spend his second night under the stairwell. The chip shop was enroute, Miller watched from the other side of the road until there was only one solitary customer before he entered. Whilst he was waiting to be given his chips, they had picked up on his strong Northern English accent to enquire if he was a Geordie but didn't pry beyond this basic pleasantry. The shop owner shared he was a Newcastle United fan and had recognised the dulcet tones on Miller's home area. The owner stared as he waited for the chips to cook and thought to himself how Miller's wrinkled, lived in face and crooked nose spoke of life challenges. Even though he paid for a single bag of chips, when Miller unwrapped them from the newspaper packing further down the street, there was a small piece of fish placed in there, too. He was a little moved; the kind gesture spoke of the empathy of the lowly classes.

On the fifth day at the junction, the owner of the newsagent on the opposite side of the road left his shop and strode over to engage him. Miller was neither rude nor forthcoming.

'Staying for long?' He was asked. 'Ever been over to the west, Galway city was the place to be,' was the suggestion.

'I am fine here, I'm a home bird,' answered Miller.

'Home bird, you say? So, what brings a Brit to beg on the streets of Dublin's fine city, we have our own pikeys here and only God knows what trouble they bring with their thievery.'

'I'm not a thief, never have been,' answered Miller.

'OK, then let me give you some advice: you are in the wrong spot. 500 yards down the road is a busy pub, Fagin's is its name. Folk there are generous to the likes of you and to sweeten the deal, here is two quid if you at least give it a try?'

Miller looked at the money and was quick to seize the opportunity. Climbing up onto his feet, he stuffed the notes and a couple of coins into his pocket, placed the cardboard under his arm and shuffled off in the direction suggested by the shop owner. Was it to be a good move or a bad move? Both as it turned out.

Miller's new pitch was outside of Fagin's pub which was just down the road. Close by was the beating heart of Irish Republicanism, Crooke park, the home of the GAA, the Gaelic Athletic Association.

It was more than just a sport; it was the native Irish game of hurling and Gaelic football. It had been established to nurture traditionalism and create a truly indigenous amateur sport. Its political aim embedded into its written charter was to strive for a 32 county all Ireland, united under the Tricolour. Crooke park stadium was also the scene of an infamous massacre of spectators by British soldiers.

It was early one November morning in 1920 that members of the IRA, organised by their hero, Michael Collins, coordinated and carried out the assassination of a team of undercover British intelligence agents. 14 in total were shot dead at addresses all over Dublin in one single operation. Inflamed by this attack, later in the same afternoon, the Royal Irish Constabulary aided by soldiers of the British auxiliary division entered the packed Crooke Park Stadium, where a match was being played. They fired wildly on the assembled crowd, causing widespread panic, injuring over sixty spectators, 14 of them fatally. Later in the same evening, three IRA prisoners, held in Dublin Castle prison were also beaten to death by their captors. Their crime? Allegedly for trying to escape. Revenge had been brutal, and the authorities were totally out of control.

Such was the public outrage at these atrocities, the event was seen by the leaders of the IRA as a huge victory. Not only did they succeed in destroying the British spy cell known as the "Cairo gang", but due to the wanton brutality of the authorities they also enrolled the support of millions of Irish men and women around the world to their cause: separation from the old Colonial enemy, the British Crown. It was a huge tipping point in the history of their struggles. They were to be rewarded a year later, first with a truce followed by total independence, at least for the southern counties. But not the six counties in the north, known as Ulster, they were to remain part of Great Britain.

Miller was only vaguely aware of the history of the G.A.A. but he did understand the importance put on it by the Irish people.
Today at the stadium the All Ireland final was to be contested by teams from Offaly and Kerry and their prize? The Sam Maguire cup named after an illustrious republican rebel. Yet another link between the sport and Republicism.

Fagan's pub was so full that the street outside was packed too with high spirited men of all ages from as young as 10 to over 90 from all over Ireland. many didn't have tickets for the sell out game; they simply came to Fagin's to savour the craic of the final.

Today, due to the crowds, Miller had moved his pitch to the other side of the road. Occasionally, someone would break from the crowd, pat Pilgrim on the head, nod and drop a few coins in the hat. On these grounds, it was a good day. He watched intently at the throng of men folk who had gathered there, it was so busy he couldn't be definite, but he thought he recognised several of the players he had been practiced in identifying. There was one for certain, the target, Tom McGoldrick, he had come out onto the street to talk with another man for several minutes before diving back into the pub. As kick-off time approached, the crowds began to drift off towards the stadium, expectant of the spectacle which was about to unfold. Despite this migration, the pub remained relatively busy with the remaining ticketless folk.

The three Travelers sauntered down the road along the canal with their Kerry blue terrier straining on its leash in front of them dragging its master with it. Travelers have been part of Irish society for centuries. They have their own distinctive identity and culture, based on a nomadic lifestyle and this sets them apart from the settled people. Folk often referred to them as tinkers, pikeys, and gypsies. They have a reputation for living outside of the law and are labelled as brawlers and petty thieves. This reputation made for their general dislike by the common settled Irish folk.

The terrier which accompanied them stood tall with a long head, flat skull, deep chest; as a breed, they are strong-headed and highly spirited. The dog was known to be downright mean toward other animals, including other dogs. Miller became alert to the threat the dog offered by Pilgrim who stood erect, looking down the street. He was proven correct to be so. This Kerry blue had been bred to be vicious, and as it closed to Miller, it slipped its lead easily and charged at Pilgrim.

Its teeth bared, and its growl menacing, Pilgrim was easy meat for the vicious and aggressive dog.

Miller rose to his feet quickly and set to pull the dogs apart, the terrier was now in a blind rage, frothing at the mouth, and poor Pilgrim was being mauled badly by the larger and more powerful animal. Miller, frustrated he could not get hold of the terrier with his hand, swung his foot and connected, temporarily winding the dog sufficiently long enough for him to grab it by the scruff of its neck and fling it several feet to one side. No sooner had the dog had left his grip, the first heavy blow reined in on him.

It caught him completely by surprise as the fist connected with the back of his head and neck causing him to see stars but not to black out. It was quickly followed by several other heavy blows in quick succession from someone who was clearly well versed in using their fists. As the blows rained in on him, Miller turned, blocked with his left forearm, pulled back his right arm and with his two fingers splayed two inches apart released the coil and struck his assailant forcefully in both eyes. A loud blood curdled scream filled the air and the assailant dropped like a stone to the pavement.

Someone else grabbed Miller's arm and a fist hammered into his face. He was conscious of shouting but couldn't understand a word. His pulled his arm free and swung both his fists as fast and as furiously as he could in retaliation. A kick to the back of his knees caused him to fall backwards onto the floor. A man now stood over him, pummelling his face with ferocious blows. Miller's right shoulder was pinned to the pavement with someone's knee. He knew he had to do something quickly. He was being beaten badly. Summoning up all his remaining strength, he managed to turn his body in the direction of the pinned shoulder so that the blows could no longer impact with his bloodied face. Several more blows struck the back of his head and then after more shouting they suddenly stopped.

He was pulled to his feet by two men, Miller's head by now was bowed and bloody, his nose broken and torn, and he couldn't see anything out of either of his eyes due to the heavy swelling. He was helped into a chair and reassured. A woman proceeded to mop the blood from his face with her apron. She explained that she was a barmaid from the pub and that her name was Catriona. She dabbed his face softly and carefully, but each movement caused him to wince with pain such was the tenderness of his skin. As she tended to him, she gagged at the smell from the homeless man, it was revolting. She shared that it was her who had demanded a couple of local men broke up the one-sided fight. When the ambulance arrived from Mater hospital close by, a young teenage boy called Enda was instructed to accompany Miller to the A&E. Catriona assured Miller that his dog would be taken good care of until his return.

It was much later in the evening when a local man, Enda returned with Miller back to Fagin's. Miller could clearly hear the melodious sounds from inside the pub as the revellers, returned from the game sang with all their heart the Fields of Athlone. Enda led Miller by the arm and beckoned him to stand still in the doorway whilst he popped inside to see what was to be done. Both of Miller's eyes were still closed with the heavy swelling and he ached across his body with the bruising he'd suffered at the hand of the travellers.

Enda stood at the end of the crowded bar and explained to Catriona that the hospital wanted to keep him in overnight due to the bruising on his skull but that he would have nothing to do with it. The doctors didn't argue for long, there were too few beds as it was, and they were used to dealing with the aftermath of brawls: it was Dublin on a Saturday night, after all.

After a few minutes, a tall mature man approached with a strong voice which came clearly from a height above Miller.

'I hear you're living rough? Well, you're not in a fit state to look after yourself for a couple of days, so, we're going to give you a roof over your head until you can see out those eyes again. Oh, and as for the scrap, don't be too disappointed, by all accounts you gave as good as you got despite the odds of 3:1. The man you floored was a bad un, Andy Connor is his name. He is a cheap bullying gangster and he's not in a fit state to leave the hospital after what you'd done to him,' a chuckle followed. 'I hear he may lose sight in at least one of his eyes, just wish I'd been around to see it.'

'me dog?' responded Miller.

At that, he could hear the familiar bark as Pilgrim was brought out from the pub.

'There you go, all safe and sound, your dog likes the black stuff for sure.'

Miller, unable to see anything except blurred outlines was totally at their mercy, he was bundled into the back of a car and instead of Enda accompanying him, it was Catriona, the barmaid who climbed in next to him.

'Where is it you're from then?' she asked.

Head bowed and still thumping painfully, Miller answered.

'Originally the north east, Hartlepool to be exact, though I haven't lived there for many years now.'

'And your dog?' she countered.

'me dog is called Pilgrim, she's a loyal thing, though sometimes I wonder why.'

'Well listen, I am taking you and your dog to my aunt's house. She's quite old, 71, but still got all her marbles, lives there with my uncle, Sean. Their daughter, my cousin, Ciara lives in Boston. You can take a bath there and we'll fix you up with some new clothes and you can rest for a few days until you recover.'

'No thanks' answered Miller. 'If you can drop me off somewhere quiet, a park perhaps, that will do for me.'

'Nonsense and you have no say in it. It's to Mrs Corcoran's for you, direct instructions from the big man.'

Miller's face was covered side to side with a large stick plaster which covered the now stitched nose, still sore from the break it had received. He was just too exhausted to argue further.

The Corcoran's were expecting him, and Catriona helped him up the stairs first to the bathroom to allow him to clean himself up. The bath was already drawn; it was nice and warm, not hot and the soap smelt perfumed. Roses, no doubt, a present from a family member. The swelling in his right eye had receded enough for him to at least partially see through a faint squint.

After his bath, he wrapped a towel around his midriff and wandered down to the only open door which signalled his sleeping quarter. The room was a small box room at the front of the house with an iron framed single bed, a small three draw pine chest of drawers stood sentry like next to it, an eight-inch brass crucifix stood on top, strategically place in the middle. It smelt a little damp and unused but compared to his place of rest the previous weeks, this was bliss. Miller eased himself gingerly into the bed; his ribs were so badly bruised, to turn on his side was excruciating, so he lay on his back gazing in the direction of the ceiling.

Chapter 4:
Bathroom Encounter

In the little local cafe, the reading glasses perched precariously on the end of Mae's nose as she flicked through the paper and at the same time she sipped on her tea. She was waiting for her friend Mary; it was Wednesday, and of course, that meant parish bingo afternoon. Suddenly, Mae felt two warm dainty hands press on to her eyes, blocking her vision.

'Who is it?' she asked.

'Guess?' Was the gruff, muffled answer. The hands then dropped away and as she turned Mae's face lit up.

'Jesus Mary and Joseph, is that you, our Ciara?'

Ciara wrapped both arms around her mother in a warm embrace.

'I wanted to surprise you, ma.'

'Why b'Jesus you did that an'al.'

Mae made the sign of the cross to admonish herself for cursing.

The other ladies and one man in the café all looked in at them; the place was joy itself. All the folk in the café knew what it was to have a loved one live away from home. This was, after all, Ireland. Ciara and her mum sat looking into each other's eyes, catching up on the news. They were joined a few minutes later by her friend, Mary. It was hugs, all around again.

'Oh, the bingo can wait. Let's go home, you must be starving, our Ciara.'

'No, I'm not at all, you get yourself off to St Mary's; it's your lucky day. That jackpot has got your name on it. Is me daddy in?'

'Oh, I expect so, if not, he'll be at the allotment seeing to his spuds as usual. The key is under the plant pot. Now, are you sure you'll be all right. We can always miss the bingo?'

'Now away with ye, I will see you in a couple of hours. I have a couple of messages to run anyway.'

Ciara picked up a small suitcase, waved to the coffee owner and left to walk the few minutes back to her parents' house. She was smiling to herself, happy to be home and amongst her kin. The Corcoran's lived in a modern three-bedroom unit situated in the corner of a cul-de-sac. The front door wasn't locked at all and there was no sign of her father. Taking the stairs quickly, she started to hitch up her dress, placing her thumbs under the elastic of her panties, she was desperate to pee. She made the last few steps to the bathroom; her pants were pushed off the cheeks of her buttocks, so she could be ready to relieve herself quickly. As she approached the bathroom door, it suddenly opened inwards and staring at her from less than a foot from her face was a tall semi naked man with a small towel wrapped around his middle. An intruder.

With instantaneous reaction, she struck out with her right hand, her fist connecting somewhere in the middle of his chest. She didn't get chance for a second blow, the stranger caught a hold of her wrist, and as he did so, his towel dropped to the floor so that he was no longer covered and was now totally naked.

Ciara found herself being spun quickly around and the naked man was now behind her and she could clearly feel his appendage on her bare buttock. A moment later she was spun again and propelled headfirst into the bathroom. The door pulled close behind her as a barrier, then a voice boomed out:

'I live here,' the gruff heavily accented voice announced. 'You must be Ciara, your cousin works in the pub, your mum is at the bingo, Sean, your dad that is, is working down his allotment.'

Bugger, thought Ciara, remembering what she needed desperately to do, squatted over the pot; she was in full flow now. She pulled a few leaves of the tissue off the roll and dabbed herself dry. Washing her hands, she gazed into the mirror, her head was full of questions: who is this stranger? A bloody Brit to boot. Why had my mammy not thought to mention him, what was he doing here, where was he sleeping? After several moments of trying to compose herself and arranging her hair as best she could, she exited the bathroom. Complete silence. Retracing her steps down the stairs, she could hear some movement coming from the kitchen.

'Thought you might appreciate a cuppa milk?'

Ciara sat down at the small square kitchen table. 'Yes please.'

'OK,' she said, 'can we start again, like, just who are you?'

'I'm Miller.'

He offered his hand, which she accepted, shook limply before saying, 'And?'

'I was living on the streets, I got into a bit of bother. The English guy from Fagin's pub insisted I stay here, it wasn't my choice, I can assure you.'

'English man?' she inquired.

'Well sort of, his accent changes with the wind. Mac is his name.'

Bloody Mac Stiofain, thought Ciara, *he must have some private agenda.*

'OK, next up, so where exactly are you sleeping? This is not a big house, though it has been my home all my life.'

'The small box room at the front; your things are in the back bedroom. I moved some boxes into the loft for your mum the other day and access is from your room. She keeps it for you. She expects you back any day,' added Miller. 'She will be thrilled.'

'This is just a short visit, five days, seven max. I've got a lot going on in my job.'

'Your mam said you are the area manager for a group of Irish pubs in Boston.'

'Yeah something like that.'

'Well, she is so proud of you, several promotions in a few short years, you know.'

'Ha! mammy's like that. She will be telling folk I'm running for mayor of Boston next.' Ciara's adrenaline had run its course and she felt relaxed, even comfortable in this stranger's company. Despite the obvious bruises, he was ruggedly handsome, tall and he had the most piercing blue eyes.

'So, tell me, who decided you needed your face rearranged?'

'Ah, some pikey's dog attacked Pilgrim and one thing led to another.'

'Pilgrim?'

Without any further verbal response, Miller stood, opened the back door and let out a low whistle. Tail wagging, a small mongrel, quite heavily bandaged, padded into the kitchen.

'Oh, like father like son.' Ciara offered.

'He's had a few stitches granted and most of his left ear is lost. Mac paid for its vet's bills. I owe him for that.'

Pilgrim padded over to Ciara as if to say hi.

'Well, I suppose he's cute in an ugly sort of way.' Ciara lightly patted the dog.

Millar never answered but responded with a broad endearing smile. He was clearly attached to the dog. 'I will take your bag up to your room.'

Without waiting for any answer, he exited the kitchen, collected the small red suitcase from next to the front door and carried it up to Ciara's bedroom. As he descended, they were about to pass on the stairs when Ciara checked and walked back down.

'Seven year's bad luck and we don't want that,' she said.

Irish – bloody superstitious lot, thought Miller.

An hour or so had passed, Ciara had showered and changed into fresh clothes and descended the stairs once again. This time, there was no stranger in the kitchen, just her dear old pa. She flung her arms around him, giving him a hug and a kiss at the same time. This was one man she loved deeply with all her heart.

'I hear you met our lodger already,' suggested Mr Corcoran.

'Yes, and I don't mind telling you it was a big surprise, mammy never mentioned it earlier.'

'Oh well, I guess she overlooked it in all the excitement. He is a bit of a loner; was living rough on the streets near Mount Joy and got a bad beating outside Fagin's from that bully Andy Conners and his lackeys. Mac asked us if we put them up. We said no, of course, but he offered us twenty quid a week and the truth is that we could do with the money, love. And is it turns out, he's no bother, hardly get a word out of him. He talks to that dog more than he does to anyone else. It's his only friend in the world, poor bugger; we've got the wee doggy sleeping in a box in the coal house. He seems comfortable enough, and I'm sure it's better than where they have been living, sleeping rough in all weathers by all accounts.'

'Oh, pa, if you need money, you've only got to ask. I don't spend a thing, you know that. I will transfer you some money over as soon as I get back.'

Chapter 5:
Fagin's pub Drumcondra Dublin

Tom Cullen, the barman of Fagin's, beckoned Miller through to the back room. As he entered the smoky, dimly-lit snug, the man sat next to Mac stood up, looked at Miller in a sort of hostile way, and without speaking a greeting, promptly left.

'You asked to see me?'

'Sit down and have a wee glass.'

'Water's just fine, I don't drink.'

'I don't much care for a man that doesn't drink, it's an insult.'

The man, clearly important in these parts was in his late forties with heavy set, thick dark hair. Miller receded to the request, and for the first time in many years, sipped on the black liquid.

'Thank you for taking care of Pilgrim's vet bill, if you let me know how much I owe you?'

'And you'll what?' countered Mac.

'And just how many weeks begging on the streets will it take you to pay that bill, lad?'

Miller shuffled in his chair clearly uncomfortable.

'That's for you,' said Mac counting out five crisp, five-pound notes.

'For me? For what exactly?'

'Gifts, a token of esteem from certain families.'

Miller looked at the man opposite him with a puzzled expression.

'The man you fought is a petty gangster and a bully in these parts, a pikey from Kerry. Andy Connors is his name, he's not liked by anyone. So, when it was learned he's lost an eye on account of you, they stopped by with, well, a reward, if you like. You're the talk of Dublin, me lad.

'However, a coin has two sides, you are also a wanted man. There are a 100 guineas on your head for the man who brings you to him. Your days of begging on the streets of Mountjoy are finished.'

Miller stared; it had been a bit to take in.

'So, why don't you cash in on the bounty?'

'me? I can't stand the petty crook either; if I choose to, I could swat him like a fly.'

'Anyway, how are the digs?'

'Just fine, Mr and Mrs Corcoran are fine, kindly folk, I like them.'

'Yes, they are, where are your parents, lad?'

'passed. Father worked in the steel mills and the dust got to his chest. Only 56 when he died. ma lived a while longer but didn't take care of herself and died of pneumonia, the damp house and smoking didn't help.'

'No siblings?'

'None.' He was lying, of course.

'You did time with the British Army.' It was a statement not a question.

Miller looked up. 'So? Where I lived, you only had three career choices, the steelworks, ICI or the Army. Suffer the pollution or travel. It wasn't such a hard choice.'

Miller's brain raced. He knew it was futile to deny his military service and his handler had gone through his cover story with him many times.

'Which Regiment?'

Miller reasoned this wasn't a cosy chat over a glass of beer, it was a mild interrogation. *No problem, I can handle it*, he thought to himself. 'Local County Regiment, the Green Howards.'

'Serve up north?'

'Hardly, I've been out more than five years. Sweeping leaves in Germany and a couple of trips to Cyprus, that was my lot. I did like Germany though; it's so clean and orderly.'

'So why did you leave?'

'I didn't. I was kicked out. Got into a brawl in Hannover, a bar got wrecked and I carried the can. SNLR. Services no longer required. So, is my interrogation over yet?'

Miller's eyes met Mac's and there was complete silence for almost a minute.

'RAF myself,' offered Mac. 'National Service after the War. Quite enjoyed it, too.'

'How's that?'

'Well, I'm from London originally, moved over here years back. I can't say I care for the Brit establishment myself bunch of landed gentry lording it over the masses if you ask me.'

'But your accent and the Gaelic you speak?'

'Self-taught. Helped me too, well, gain acceptance, fit in if you like.'

'So, are we done here?'

'Yes sure.'

'Well there is just one more thing. Why are you here? Why Dublin? You're from the north, aren't you?'

Miller just shrugged his shoulders. 'Never been here before, thought I would give it a try and it was easy enough to nick on the ferry, even with me dog.'

'Really?' Mac countered.

He pushed over the newspaper cutting from the Manchester Evening News. It read:

Ex-soldier given a three-year suspended sentence for brutally attacking two Asian shop keepers, pillars of the community.

No picture, just a name: Miller.

Silence.

'Seems you are bit too quick with your fists, Miller. You should try and calm down a bit, you're not exactly a young man, now are you? Anyway, enough of the small talk, I have an errand I want you to run. Do you have a driver's licence, Miller?'

'As a matter of fact, it's all I have,' Miller reached into his pocket and flashed his UK licence.

'Good. Let me explain what it is I want.'

Miller sat listening for several minutes whilst the older man explained the details of the errand. He nodded in acknowledgement and took the final gulp of his beer, turned and left without further reply.

Exiting the main bar onto the street, he untied his dog from a railing and walked slowly down the road. He fully expected that at any moment a car would screech to a halt, bundle him into it and whisk him off to a shallow grave.

Nothing.

After several minutes, the suspension had eased, and he tied his dog up once again. Popping into the corner shop, he bought the daily paper.

Crossing the bridge, he espied a bench overlooking the canal, sat down and began to read.

Tomorrow would be the agreed meet. At 1 am, he was due to make his first encounter with his handler since his deployment into active service. So far so good.

Chapter 6:
Clearing the Air

'So, would you like to tell me what's going on, Mac?' asked Ciara.

Mac gave a puzzled look; Father Treahy was waiting outside the archway of the church.

Mr and Mrs Corcoran had already walked through the door into the hall where tea and biscuits awaited the parish faithful. Mac glowered and barked, 'Be quiet, girl. Drop around to the pub tonight at 7 sharp. I have some errands for this man Miller.'

'But,' challenged Ciara. The look he gave her told her it was best to drop it and just do as he bid.

Ciara watched as Mac and Father Treahy chatted about the sermon whilst holding a firm handshake. Sean MacStiofain was a devout Catholic and it was clear the two men had a great deal of mutual respect. These were the two most influential men of the district, one a man of the cloth, the other a feared extremist of the Irish Republican Army. No less than its Chief of Staff.

One of Mac's enforcers was never far away and today was no exception. He looked on vigilantly; Mac was after all, a target for those who opposed one Ireland, both in Ulster and on the mainland.

Chapter 7:
Anyone for Tea?

Miller was a little uncomfortable; it hadn't been the deal that he would eat with the family, he was staying on a strictly room only basis.

Mae, Mrs Corcoran that is, had insisted. This Sunday was special; Ciara was home, slow cooked roast lamb, green beans, peas, carrots and home-grown Irish potatoes, courtesy of Sean's allotment. Mrs Corcoran could certainly cook a wholesome Sunday dinner. *It was a privilege to be asked to join them*, thought Miller to himself. He'd never sat down to a family dinner for more years than he cared to remember.

'Have you thought about getting yourself a job?' asked Sean.

'Doing what, exactly?' countered Miller, slightly embarrassed by the question posed. 'I don't have any trade or skill or much of an education.'

'Hmm, I suppose so. Couldn't Mac fix you up with something? He's lots of connections, you know.'

Ciara cut in. 'Leave our guest be, pa. I expect once he's feeling better and all the bruising has gone; he'll want to be on his way.'

The words were easy, but she neither believed it, nor wanted it to be that way. She couldn't explain it but there was something about this Brit which she found appealing, mysterious, arousing her interest like no other suitor in Boston had been able to do these past three years.

Sensing the chemistry, Mae added her weight to the conversation. 'Ciara dear, why don't you take your pa's car and show Miller the Phoenix park? It's beautiful at this time of the year,' she added. 'It's a great place for the wee doggy to run free to, I would expect he enjoy it, after all what little doggy doesn't like to fetch?'

'Mr Miller has his own life to lead, ma. Don't interfere.'

'Well, actually,' Miller spoke softly, 'Pilgrim and I like open spaces.'

'Well, that's settled then, your pa and I will do the clearing up and you two can take a drive over to the park.' Mrs Corcoran was pleased with herself. She fretted constantly for her daughter and wanted her to settle down and marry.

Chapter 8:
Phoenix park

The car wasn't really a car.

It was a three-wheeler van with a fiberglass body and a small 850CC engine. In truth, it was more like an oversized pencil sharpener. The car maker, Reliant, had turned them out in their thousands. Their appeal? Cheap to buy, cheap to run and only needed a motorbike licence which was the easiest test to pass. In the back of the Reliant was a white enamel bucket with newly dug beetroot, some forks and hoe's and assorted bits of string, oh and damp sacks. These lent a distinctive aroma to the van. Earthy.

Owning the allotment gave Mr Corcoran a sense of being self-sufficient of providing food for his family. That was important to him, an imperative you might say. The spectra of the great famine haunted all Irish men and women. The population of the country had halved over a few short years. Folks either had starved to death or sought a new life in the overseas territories of the far flung former British Empire – America, Canada and Australia. many had perished during the journey. Even if they survived, the journey life was harsh in the new settlements and not person could thrive. All in all, Ireland had lost over two million of its people.

Mrs Corcoran had been correct. Miller had never seen Pilgrim so full of life and enjoying himself. And all because of a simple stick. The dog wasn't the only one enjoying the fresh air and the greenery of Phoenix park.

Ciara was, too. Her smile stretched from ear to ear and lit up her face, and her green eyes flashed like emeralds. The tiredness from her journey had gone away and she was wearing a little makeup. Not a lot, just a little blusher and some lip gloss, but she looked all woman.

'What's Boston like?' asked Miller, as they strolled together over the vast open space of the park.

'I like it, a lot actually. I've lived away from home for so long; I was 22 when I left, so I guess you get used to calling different places home.'

'22? That was young to go to America on your own.'

'I didn't.'

'So? What did you do back then?'

'Well, I left school at 16, as did all my friends except Mary. I worked in a chemist's shop on Grafton Street, then I applied to do nursing at Rotunda Hospital on Parnell Square. That was a real hoot! I was 18 and lived in the nurse's halls with about 40 other wild feckless Irish lasses.

'Boy did we know how to party. You'll have to wait for my book to come out before I can share any of those stories!' Ciara laughed out loud as she clearly reminisced over happy times.

Her voice lowered.

'I took off to Spain after I qualified. Waited on rich Brits in Benidorm, tight wads, never left more than a few pesetas as tips.'

'Why did you leave nursing to go to Spain?'

She hesitated. 'Boyfriend trouble. I rather not go into it, if you don't mind.'

Ciara didn't want to share with this stranger that she had been engaged and then jilted.

'OK, so go on,' Miller encouraged her.

'That's when I met MacStiofain. I thought he was a local at first as he was out to dinner with a large group of Spanish men.'

'He took a fancy to you then?'

'No, don't be stupid. He's old enough to be my dad. He's also a devout Catholic and a family man so don't you ever forget that. He can also be an unforgiving man. My advice to you is stay on his good side.' Ciara stalled now in uncomfortable territory. She wasn't about to disclose who her boss really was.

'He complimented on my waiting and said that if I was interested, he could fix me up with a job in Boston. He knew some folk over there.

'When he eventually left the bar that evening, he also left his wallet. Rather than hand it in to the bar owner, I took it on myself to track him down; he was Irish, after all. Apart from that, it had a lot of money in it, more than I had ever seen in my life.

'So, I spent the next day tracking him down to the usual hotels where I could expect him to stay. Funny thing was no-one had heard of him. Then fate lent a hand and as I was walking down a street, I spied him in a café reading a paper enjoying the afternoon sun. It was quite by chance, really. He was extremely grateful and impressed with my honesty. And sure enough, he kept his word. I now live in Boston and we've been the best of friends ever since.'

'As for Boston, New York and Chicago might have more Irish folk living there but Boston is where we are the most dominant. Such is the Irish presence there you could mistake it for a town in Ireland,' she laughed again. 'The craic is excellent; it brings in folk from across America. In the bar I live, we even have a picture of JFK enjoying a glass of the black stuff.'

They had now crossed the open space and were entering in the old part of the forest. In these beautiful woods, the branches reached up to the sky and at the same time reached out for and wide.

'Watch this,' said Miller.

Picking up a short heavy stick, he allowed Pilgrim to chew on it and try to wrestle it from him for a few moments.

Taking a step back, he threw it high and long deep into the stand of trees. As he did so, Pilgrim gave chase. Turning to Ciara, he lifted her up onto a low bough of an old oak and urged her to climb quickly. He pulled himself up after her.

Pilgrim returned to the spot below a few moments later with the stick and dutifully dropped in on the ground. He looked around confused and puzzled at the same time. He ran off in one direction and then another and barked for its master, totally confused as to how they had disappeared. Miller pursed his lips and whistled. Pilgrim returned to the tree, no less confused. Looked around again and padded off.

'Stupid mutt,' laughed Miller. He whistled again but this time as Pilgrim returned, he dropped to the ground with a thud, the dog jumped with excitement.

'Heh, what about me? Care to rescue a damsel in distress?' pleaded Ciara.

Miller's outstretched arms caught her as she fell the last few feet to the ground.

Immediately, they were entwined, their faces only a few inches apart. Without hesitation, Miller closed in and kissed her on her ripe, full-bodied lips. She tasted good. Ciara closed her eyes and drank in the moment. Their lips stayed clasped together, seconds later she could feel his tongue as it explored her mouth and the French kissing caused her to stir in her loins. They kissed passionately in complete silence for several moments, oblivious as to where they were or their surroundings. Miller walked her gently back a few steps and as she did so, she stumbled on a root. He guided her until her back was leant against the trunk of this ancient tree. He took both her arms and placed them above her head and pinned her there. She was powerless to stop him as he moved in to kiss her passionately again. She was completely at his mercy. He was so strong, and in control. She was weak and submissive. Bliss.

He spun her around, so she was now facing the trunk, her cheek pressed against the sharp bark. He brushed her ebony hair away from the back of her neck and gently bit into her nape. As he ran his sharp teeth across the exposed flesh, electric currents coursed through her body. The shivers were sensational.

It was ecstasy.

He continued to draw his teeth up and down her neck all the while she panted. He raised her hands higher up the tree trunk and pinned them there with one of his own. He traced down her body with his free hand to her hip. Moving around to the front he freed the top button of her Levi's jeans and pulled down on the zip. The jeans were now gaping at the waist.

She offered no resistance. He licked his fingers, and his hand now returned to the back of the body and passed into the gap, down the arch of her back, slipping between the soft cheeks of her bum until his right index finger was far enough around to contact her woman hood.

These parts were already moist and soon became even more as he drew his finger across the entrance. He moved his finger backwards and forwards across the entrance of her vulva.

Then, as suddenly as it started, it stopped, the hand was removed, and she was spun around to face him eye to eye again. Still no words passed between them. They continued to kiss and as they did so, Miller's hand slipped down again, this time into the front of her panties. The jeans, now loosened, offered little obstruction. As his middle finger reached inside her quim to enter her, she gave out a gasp. Miller hooked his finger up inside her to massage her G spot expertly. There was just no feeling like it on earth. Slowly, he made circles inside her with his finger.

Miller continued to play, the pleasure and the sensations were so strong. Ciara knees were weak and about to buckle; they could no longer support her own weight, her body was in spasm, she was in complete ecstasy.

Her back slipped slowly and awkwardly down the trunk until she was lying on her back between two large tree roots. Miller pulled off her shoe and one leg of her jeans. She could feel the cold ground on her bare cheek now but didn't care. He unfastened his belt with one hand and after loosening his trousers his man hood was exposed. She gazed south, his penis was erect, like a baton and it was long, too. She watched as Miller licked his fingers to moisten the entrance once again and after an initial fumbled attempt, full penetration was achieved.

Ciara let out a gasp as she was filled. Using his elbows for leverage, Miller rocked, slowly and rhythmically. Carnal lust. Rutting in the woods, there was nothing in the world quite like it.

Their eyes met, and their gaze held as the rutting continued. She was moist, and it felt amazing. She arched her hips to match his stroke for maximum penetration.

Pulling her roughly away from the tree so her back was completely flat, Miller pulled up both her knees and climbed onto his haunches. Sitting on his heels, crouched, the thrusts became swifter, more powerful and much deeper. The pleasure became even more intense and she was aware of the noises she was making, animal-like, as they joined in their lovemaking. She couldn't stop herself from moaning aloud with pleasure as his hips thrust in and out. They looked into each other's eyes, scarcely believing what was happening to them. Exciting, it was his turn to make the noise now as he moved towards a climax. The pleasure she felt stopped before she wanted it to, and Miller rolled off and lay by her side.

Was that it? She thought for a second.

He wasn't ended, he was just changing positions. Without speaking, he swung her legs across his body and lifted her astride. She was now on top, in a classic cowgirl position; the man was not yet finished with her. She needed no instruction as to what to do.

Raising her hips and upper body, her right hand dropped to his penis and she guided it expertly to her waiting quim. Skilfully, she helped it force entry, and once again they were joined. As his penis entered, it pushed back the outer lips of her vulva and sent an immediate tingle into through her body once again. She was in full control now and she was liking it; she smiled as she pushed back his arms and rocked her hips back and forward. Miller's eyes were closed, he was savouring each thrust she made on him. The feeling was like no other and the two were now in unison making sweet music together.

His climax started in his toes.

The sensation was superb.

It travelled up both his legs joining forces somewhere in his groin until he could hold it no longer as he erupted.

Ciara could feel the hot sperm as it pulsed inside her.

Miller grabbed both of her hips and slowly pulled her forward to allow him to fully discharge his remaining load. After several thrusts his head dropped to the floor of the woods and his hands to his sides. Spent.

Ciara leaned in to kiss him and as she did his penis, now softening and shrinking fast plopped out of her. She allowed her face to drop to his and they lay there entwined. Ciara rolled off to one side and looking up at the grey sky above and the dark boughs of the oak. She was the first to speak.

'What just happened?' she asked.

'No idea. One minute we were throwing sticks and the next minute you threw yourself at me.' Ciara gave out a laugh as she thumped his chest with her fist.

'You forced yourself on me,' she said jokingly.

'Force?' responded Miller. 'Weren't you just on top of me a moment ago?'

They both laughed.

Miller couldn't remember the last time he had laughed out loud; it had been a long time; he knew that much.

'Shouldn't we both be smoking cigarettes now?' She enquired.

'Dunno, never have, never will.'

Ciara laughed again.

'What, never? A bit of a goody two shoes, are we?'

'No, not really, just never felt the need and the fact I grew up listening to my old man's hacking cough and him spitting gold watches into a bucket.'

'Oh, that's disgusting,' she scowled. 'Thanks for sharing, not! Come on, let's get our clothes on before someone sees us.'

'Someone already has,' replied Miller.

Pilgrim was sat, five metres away, happily resting and looking in.

'Bloody dog's a pervert,' laughed Ciara. 'Watching us do it!'

Chapter 9:
The Meet

Miller arrived a full hour before the pre-arranged rendezvous time.

He slowly drank in the surroundings, types of cars parked along the river, did they have anybody in them? What was the van, was it local, could it be occupied? Which shops were open, which were busy, who was walking up and down the road? He called into the newsagents for a daily paper, folded it neatly under his arm as he made the final approach to the bench and sat down. T-5.

At zero hour precisely, his handler, Rosie, sat down on the bench next to him. As she did so, she stooped down to pat Pilgrim innocently as if they had never met.

'Good morning,' she offered.

Miller looked up from his paper momentarily to acknowledge the greeting and then continued to read.

Rosie investigated her rather large handbag; and continued to speak.

'Nearly didn't stop,' she said.

'What the hell's happened to you? Clearly not living rough on the streets now, are we? Won the Pools, have we?'

'Finished?' He responded curtly.

'No, not quite, so are you going to tell me what's going on here? For instance, have you clocked any important players from our I.D. cards perchance?'

'No, not exactly. However, there is someone of interest to you if I'm not mistaken, but not from any of the cards.'

'So, what is this bloody quiz game, stop wasting my time Miller and get on with it?'

'That black and white picture of the two Irish guys which is hanging outside your office at the camp. The one with the moustache, would he be called Mac by chance?'

'Yes, that picture is of David O'Connor and Sean MacStiofain, Mac as you rightly say, is the Chief of Staff of the Irish Republican Army.'

Miller had figured he was a big cheese but had no idea just how big.

'Well, Mac likes me and has sort of taken me under his wing he has. In fact, I'm to run an errand for him in a few days. Ferry a couple of his guys to Belfast, seemingly neither of them drives.' Rosie broke with the drill; stared directly at Miller, mouth agape before saying.

'Bloody hell. The man is ruthless, you've hit the jackpot. This is not a wind up, is it? You're playing taxi driver for MacStiofain? Is this a soldier black humour perhaps?'

'No. He's acting like he's a kindly uncle to me. Even forked out for the vet bill for little Pilgrim here.'

At that, Miller bent down and run his fingers through the dog's coat.

'This is incredible news, outstanding work, Miller. He's got you running errands to Belfast, this could be just the break we were hoping for. He's not playing you, is he?'

'Nope, I don't think so, he knows I served in the Green Howards, that didn't bother him, and he knows of my little scrape in Manchester, had a paper clipping so he's done some homework on me. He seems OK with it all; even shared he'd done time in the RAF when he was younger.'

'Miller, this is unbelievable, I need to run this up the ladder and pretty damn quick. Extraordinary events call for a break in SOPs. Meet me again same time, same place next week.'

'No. Not here,' answered Miller.

'Same time, yes, but half a mile down the road there is a bench overlooking a park with a few swings, I'll be there.'

Rosie stood up and without saying anything else strode briskly off into the Dublin morning.

Miller reached into his pocket and pulled out a biscuit which he fed to a happy little Pilgrim.

Chapter 10: Whitehall

'I am here to see sir John; my appointment is for 10 am.'

'Please take a seat Madam, he is expecting you.'

In only a few moments, Rosie was shown into the cavernous office of sir John Rennie head of the British secret intelligence service more commonly known as Mi6, in inner circles it was known somewhat disingenuously as the "Circus". This nickname originated during the Second World War when one of its predecessor units, SOE, was housed in the same building in London as the Bertram Mills circus, 1 Dorset Square.

'This is a real breakthrough, great work, Rosie, well done. To have one of our own under the nose of that bloody hypocrite MacStiofain is a great coup. This source, can you elaborate a little? Can we truly trust him?'

'Yes, sir, we recruited him direct. He's a Brit, ex Hereford actually.'

'Really? Splendid, splendid. And how does he fit in then?'

'He was living rough on the streets around Mountjoy, got into a spot of bother with local pikeys and Mac took him in and is looking after him. We gave him a robust and believable cover and seemingly Mac has already had him vetted and he's still here to tell the tale. They know he was a former soldier from a County Regiment, that's all.'

'Rosie, I had a glass of vino with our cousins last night and they want to share him. Mi5 would value an asset like this greatly, too.'

'No, sir. That would be disastrous. We have him focused on the south, that's our patch, after all, and we must keep the number of people who know about him to as small a circle as we humanly can. The more agencies know about him, the greater chance of him being burnt. He must be our long-term strategic asset, low intensity, low profile, who knows where he might take us.'

'OK, I thought that be your response, let's leave it like that for the time being. He's hot property, actually he's included in the P.M.'s weekly brief, you know.'

'No, I don't know, sir, I wasn't aware of that, a bit early if I may say so.'

'We needed some good news, Rosie, we are under so much pressure from the bloody IRA, and they are running rings around us. However, that's all about to change; we are going on the front foot, Rosie.'

'sir?'

'MRF.'

'Yes, sir. I know of them, of course. What of it?

'We are going to unleash the mobile reaction force. As you appreciate it's outside of the Green Army' command structure and is working for Mi5, gathering intelligence on the players in the north, just as we are beginning to do in the south. It is, however, prepared to arrest, and when necessary, engage without having to run all decisions up the bureaucratic command of HQ NI and the Op Banner folk. The GOC, Harry Tuzo, is all for it, he's a great soldier, was born in India and served in Indonesia doing similar work. It's our response to this dirty war. We know who the players are, and we are weeding them out. We reckon that within two years, we could neutralise all the active units the IRA have operating in the north. The Green Army has their hands tied all the time; everything they do is beamed out onto TV each evening.

'Big boy's games call for big boy's rules, Rosie.' His voice trailed off. 'Right, I think we are done here.'

The two of them walked towards the large oak door. 'Oh, and the codename – Monkey, how was this determined?'

'Hartlepool, sir, our man is a Geordie.'

'So, Rosie, get your Monkey busy, I want a complete bio on Mac, what are his likes and dislikes and more importantly what that bloody man is up to.'

'Yes sir, of course sir, just one last thing, can I have your approval for direct access to the MRF, they could be useful.'

'Yes, yes, I suppose so.'

Rosie walked out from the Circus into the bustling street and blended in immediately with all the office workers and tourists that populated that part of London. Turning right, she walked up to access the tube at Charring cross.

She was pleased with herself; smug even, the meeting with the DG could not have gone better. It was time that those stuffy port swilling Etonians moved over and appreciated that intelligence work was the work of women, too. pay review and promotions were due in a couple of months and it all augured well for her. The light drizzle didn't dampen her spirits; although she was just a little peeved, she had left her brolly in the hallway of her apartment this morning.

This new unit offered great potential, too, she would have to get over to see the folk at "Box 500", Mi5 tomorrow, and break the news that she was to be given access to their assets without having to relinquish or share her own. *An excellent morning's work indeed*, she thought to herself.

Chapter 11:
Journey to Belfast

The traffic on the M1 up through Swords and Drogheda to Belfast was quite light for a mid-week and the route was straightforward enough. Miller never questioned Mac as to why the two men just couldn't get the train up to the north and just shrugged his shoulders and ceded to his request to be their driver. As they reached the outskirts of Newry, the traffic slowed and at Killeen it came to a standstill. As they edged forward toward the vehicle check point, Miller noticed in his mirror the two men in the back seat continued to read their newspapers and had barely spoke to each other for the whole journey. When they did speak to each other, it was in Gaelic.

Pilgrim, who up to now had occupied the front passenger seat, now crossed onto Miller's lap.

The beret was a dead giveaway. Northumberland Fusiliers, a white feather with a black tip protruded about their eye line.

'I.D,' demanded the corporal.

Miller handed over his licence and at the same time asked, 'Makum?'

The soldier looked up and answered, 'Yup, and you?'

'Smoggie, just up for the day.'

'Oh, OK, on your way, me lad.'

The Corporal waved his arm and the barrier lifted as Miller edged the car slowly through the chicane knowing that it would be covered with a GPMG, General Purpose Machine Gun. The Honda he was driving wasn't a big car or a new one either, but it wasn't bad as it had a radio fitted as standard, better than most of the cars rolling off the line of Dagenham or Halewood.

Miller couldn't be sure, but he thought he could see the two men in the rear steal a smile at each other. They hadn't even been asked for their I.D.

Forty minutes later, he parked the car in the Civic car park behind Belfast City Hall and waited for the two men to climb out before he locked it up.

'2 o'clock it is then,' Miller offered. 'Don't be late or I'll leave without you.'

The older of the two men nodded and they both walked off.

There was a couple of hours to wait and to kill time, Miller thought to himself, somewhere there was a café with a cup of tea and a bacon sandwich with his name on it.

He was no fool; despite the fact the two men looked respectable in their jackets and ties, it was clear to Miller that they were players of a sort. *I bet they were shitting themselves at the checkpoint*, he thought, wondering if he would turn them in.

Of course, he wouldn't, he knew that there were bigger fish to fry.

Having never been to Belfast in his life, Miller, for first impressions, thought it was a bizarre place. Women and children in pushchairs and others hanging onto coat tails pushed their way through the crowds whilst soldiers from the occupying British Army patrolled nervously, their distinctive black SLR rifles at the ready. A great weapon, and Miller knew from personal experience it certainly packed a punch. The soldiers looked young to Miller, babies in fact. Young kids off the council estates of Glasgow, Dundee and Aberdeen or perhaps, like himself, Hartlepool. The uniforms changed here from those at the border. Here they wore soft black caps with a checked badge of a red cross on a white background with black at its centre. Fusilier's from a Scottish regiment.

The town hall dominated the city. Constructed from white limestone quarried in Portland Dorset, the building was finished off with several green domes. It was magnificent. It had been built during Queen Victoria's reign when the whole of Ireland formed part of the vast and thriving British Empire.

In less than 25 years, all that had changed forever, and Ireland was now two countries, separated by religious bigotry and wanton nationalism. The two countries were now at war with themselves. Family against family, Catholic against Protestant. Northern Ireland was in the middle of a violent bloody war with itself, what a mess.

Chapter 12:
Belfast, Military patrol

There was a spring in the step of newly promoted Sergeant Neil MacDonald, recently returned from his senior Breckon course. He was like the cat with the cream. Mac was a 22-year-old man, that is he'd signed up with Royal Highland Fusiliers for the maximum extent possible. He knew that ensured him promotions, he needed to get some courses under his belt and keep his nose clean.

He knew that he couldn't stray off the path too. Or more precisely he didn't need to get caught doing something he shouldn't! Mac grew up in tenements of Irvin on the west coast of Scotland, a short train ride from Glasgow. From the age of 11, he would go up to the town to watch the "Gers", Glasgow Rangers, alongside over 80,000 patriots. Under the manager Jock Wallace, the Gers had been dominant in the Scottish football league with only their arch-rivals Celtic ever challenging them. The best thing about going to the games as a teenager was the street brawls they could get into. Fenian bashing, that is attacking the catholic Celtic fans was better sport than the footy. Mac despised the Micks. He loved the Gers.

Mac enlisted as a boy soldier at 16 like many of his countrymen, and at 25, he was now a highly experienced and a senior non-commissioned officer.

Today's patrol was to be a doddle. The young Lieutenant, barely 20 and from some privileged English public school, was leading a platoon to do a house search of Sandy Row, a staunch loyalist area. The officer was barking out orders left right and centre as if there were about to be attacked by thousands of Zulus at any moment, so nervous was he. Today it was house to house searches for concealed weapons or criminals or terrorists. Mac brayed on the door of the terraced house, opened it and ordered the four men under his immediate command to follow him in. The lady of the house stepped into the corridor arms folded across her chest. Mac leaned in and gave her a peck on the cheek.

'And how's the love of my life doing, Mrs McMichael, have you missed me?'

'Now get away with you cheeky, and what's with the braying at my door, young man?'

'Ah, we are breaking in a new Rupert, shitting himself so he is, Mrs McMichael. How's the big man?'

'My husband is where he should be, working down the docks, how else do you expect me to feed these five nippers?'

Mac reached inside his camouflage smock.

'Here, young Wille, I've a present for you.'

Mac bent down on one knee and offered the young lad hanging off his mother's leg two football programmes. The child hesitated. Mac then reached inside again to reveal a scarf, bright blue with a red stripe inside a blue one, the icon colours of Glasgow Rangers.

The young boy darted forward to collect his presents, it was if Christmas had come early. He wore a smile from ear to ear.

'You put the kettle on, and the lads will shoot upstairs as the Rupert will be waiting for our all clear from the bedroom to let him know the search is going OK.'

Mac dispatched two of his men upstairs to watch proceedings in the street and to signal to the command team that they were searching the thoroughly. Meanwhile Mac sat down in the parlour sipping his mug of tea and sharing all his news with the lady of the house.

Sandy Row was a traditional heartland of the paramilitary Ulster Defence Association (UDA) and the Orange Order. John McMichael, the big man and owner of the house, was the leader of the UDA in these parts. Feared and respected in equal measures. Helen McMichael listened to all the rumour and gossip shared by her army visitor and thanked him. The news of the new unit MSF in palace Barracks particularly caught her attention and she suggested the big man would like to chat more about this. Mac agreed to visit the local pub in a couple of nights as soon as he could slip away from the barracks. It was important for the Scottish soldiers to have allies in this God forsaken city, and what better than kindred spirits? Most of Ulster's protestants were originally from the west coast of Scotland and roots of Unionism ran deep. More importantly, they shared the common enemy, the Fenian Pope loving Republican bastards. Sharing intelligence ensured their safe passage in these parts of Belfast and made their patrolling a doddle. Unlike most other districts which were predominately Catholic and a different kettle of fish all together.

Helen passed over a parcel wrapped in a tea cloth. 'There is a tea loaf freshly baked for the lads in mess, oh, and before I forget, thanks for letting us know ahead about the search today, you can be assured we appreciate it.'

Sergeant MacDonald and his team continued down the terraced street pretending to be alert knowing all the time there was zero threat to them from this district.

Chapter 13:
Belfast, Military Rule

After an hour of admiring the wonderful architecture of the city buildings in the centre of Belfast, Miller decided it was time to find somewhere to eat. Close by, on Donegal square, he found what he was looking for. The café was nothing to write home about, but it was busy and that was always a good sign. The menu, laminated in plastic, had both a written description of the fare on offer and a picture. An easy decision was made in two seconds.

'Irish and a tea, please.' You just couldn't beat a full breakfast with all the trimmings and black pudding to boot.

'Not from these parts, are we?' It was both a statement and a question.

'Nope, up from Dublin for the day, first time actually.'

The café owner wiped the table, accepting the answer at face value and moved away.

From his vantage point in the café, Miller could see straight down Donegal square. It was quite wide, two lanes but could probably have fit in a third one, he became transfixed on the unfolding scene.

The view was surreal.

The large Army land rover moved slowly down the centre of the street towards the café. Its windscreen was covered with a wire mesh grill and two soldiers stood on the back-bumper bars, their rifles pointing at the first-floor windows at the ready for an engagement that never came.

75 metres in front of the vehicle, four men took short sprints between firing positions as they patrolled down the street. The land rover halted, and a young boy got out. 60kg maybe, slim and gangly, perhaps just 18, but looked so fresh faced he could have passed for 15. It was the Platoon commander, a single pip on his shoulder, 2Lt, fresh from Sandhurst, the officer academy of the British Army. Two of the squaddies had taken up firing positions in the petrol station, crouched behind the petrol pump. How unbelievably stupid. They were literally hiding behind an inflammable bomb, if by some chance there was a firefight

these two naïve soldiers would be blown to smithereens. *This must be the unit's 1st tour*, thought Miller, green horns.

What happened next brought Miller to his feet. The young rookie officer had stopped a young couple in their early twenties pushing a large pram. The man was moved off to one side and made to stand against a wall with his arms outstretched above his head. Whilst one soldier talked into his radio getting a "P-Check" on the man from base control, the other soldier searched the man from tip to toe. OK, fair doos with all of that, but what happened next was unbelievable.

Other soldiers in the unit clearly had explicit instructions from the rookie officer.

While one soldier pinned the arms of the now distraught screaming mother to her side, the other lifted the crying baby unceremoniously from the pram and swept it looking for what, God only knows.

Nothing was discovered, of course. The man on the wall clearly agitated to hear the cries of his wife and baby turned his body and pushed the soldier away. The butt of the rifle from the other soldier came quickly up to club him viciously in the side of the head causing him to drop like a stone to the pavement, blood could be immediately seen spreading across his now bruised face.

The diners in their café, regardless of their religious loyalties, voiced their disgust at the heavy-handed policing they were witnessing in real time outside. It had been a totally unnecessary use of force.

Miller sat back down at his table as one of the other diners looked across at him and said, 'Bloody disgrace.'

Miller nodded his head in agreement, he was as confused as they were.

As he sat staring at his tea, Miller mused to himself. Had they forgotten all the learnings from his time in Indonesia, the winning of hearts and minds of the locals. It was always ingrained into them. Be nice to the locals, feed them, set up clinics for health, be friendly, and play with their children, give them sweets. Wasn't that the reason why Malaysia and Indonesia conflicts had succeeded when Vietnam had failed? Miller knew that with behaviour as uncalled for and aggressive as he'd just witnessed, both sides of the divided community would see them as the enemy and act accordingly.

The breakfast had lost its appeal; discretely he fed the remainder of his sausage to his faithful companion. Pilgrim devoured it voraciously.

Miller and Pilgrim approached the door to leave; he nodded an acknowledgement to the café owner and turned out onto the streets of this besieged city.

He could still see the tail end Charlie of the Army patrol walking backwards down the road protecting the soldiers from any threat to their rear. It was an odd picture. Miller thought to himself, *how could this be the streets of Great Britain? How did it ever come to this?*

His mind drifted back to his schooling and geography with his teacher, Mr Atkinson, himself from the west coast of Ireland. Being a Catholic school, the consensus was supportive of the all Irish cause. Miller remembered how his short essay on Ireland had resonated with his teacher. In it, Miller had written as if he were an eagle flying high and looking down on that small Island below. This emperor of birds mused that the Island was just too small to be two countries; it was just that plain and simple. History, of course, had other opinions. Now fifty years after the south had gained independence, a bloody war was being fought out to determine the fate of the six counties of the north. A war where there could be no victory, just tragic loses.

Some refreshment was called for. Along the road known as the Cornmarket, Miller found a pub called Mooney's. It was a rounded façade being on a corner, its sign was a vertical one with an arrow pointing down to the door. Above the sign was a large clock, the hands were not working, and it showed 6:15 permanently. At least it would be correct twice a day.

Mooney's bar was quite busy and across the table from Miller sat three young boisterous Scottish lads, off duty soldiers, no doubt. Miller nodded in acknowledgement and then for some reason unbeknown to himself he walked over to say hello. Two of them were brothers, John and Joe, and the other a slightly older 23-year-old was called Doug. The younger of the brothers, John, was not even old enough to get served beer, being only 17. He was, however, old enough to serve in the Queens Army. They were joined by two local Irish girls, clearly attracted to the fit and handsome boys. They were in buoyant spirits and clearly great comrades.

Miller chatted with the young men for several minutes, indeed they were privates in the Highland Fusiliers, they reminded him of himself in days gone by, perhaps that's why he had been drawn to them, he yearned for the comradeship of those salad days as a junior soldier.

He finished his pint and offered them advice as he left.

'Watch out for each other lads, buddy-buddy style, the world can be a cruel place.' On that note, he left to return to the car, leaving the young soldiers to continue enjoying their day off.

Back at the car, Miller was resting his eye lids when suddenly he was aware of someone trying the locked door. Miller looked up as Pilgrim barked; he leaned across to the side door and let in his passenger.

'Having 40 winks, were you? Right boyo; let's be having you it's time to go.'

'What about your friend?' questioned Miller.

'Oh, he's OK, so he is, decided to stay over for a couple of nights or so. There's just the two of us, oh and your wee doggy, of course. What is it called?'

'Pilgrim,' answered Miller as he gunned the Honda to life and pulled out of the car park to commence the return journey back to Dublin.

Chapter 14:
Café Life Dublin

'So, what's the goss' from the ole' US of A, do tell, what's it like over there? I am so curious.'

'Then why don't you come over and visit me, Catriona, then you could see for yourself,' responded Ciara.

'Ah, 'cause I can't save two buttons to save me life, that why.'

'Maybe that's because you are always spending on yourself?'

Catriona beamed a warm radiant smile.

'Ah, a girl can never have too many shoes, can she? And as for makeup, it's only the best for me,' she laughed out loud.

Catriona and Ciara had been joined by their friend, Maria, for ladies who lunch afternoon in Dublin centre and a girlie catch up.

Brown Thomas luxury departmental store boasted a great classy restaurant as well as all the latest fashions from the top designers: Louis Vuitton, Gucci and Armani. The store was Ireland's own Harrods. It was situated on Grafton Street; Dublin's main shopping area, and it had been an institution to the Dublin upper classes since 1848.

The three friends shared several common bonds. They were all in their late 30s; unmarried, unattached and they all worked for Sean MacStiofain. Catriona helped Tom out in the pub which Sean owned, Ciara worked out in Boston as the bookkeeper for the chain of pubs he owned, and Maria; well she didn't do any real work. Maria, like Sean Mac, was a political activist, a staunch Republican with jaundiced anti-British views, entrenched, one might even say. She was good to have as a friend, for Marie was powerful in her own right and not one to get on the wrong side of. She was only 36, slim, if a little plain, and didn't dress to please anyone. She had been a teacher after qualifying from Trinity College for a few short years before giving up her job for the cause. Both her parents had disapproved, and she had little contact with either of them these past five years.

'So,' asked Marie, 'what's the news from the north-east?' She meant the Boston area, of course. 'Just the same really, I guess I am a bit of a saddo, keeping up with all that's going on is a 7-day-a-week job. Especially so, since the Council increased my responsibility.'

'Yes,' replied Marie, 'you've got New York and Chicago, too, haven't you?' Marie had not made a lot of effort and looked rather plain; she was wearing no makeup. She had tied her hair back into a bun, which made for a stern appearance and was not at all endearing. In fact, it reflected her character and disposition, stern.

'Ah, if I am honest, I haven't really got a handle on those two yet. New York is OK, we sort of hold our own, the Italians don't bother us but lately the Hispanics are flexing their muscle, especially the Columbians. There have been a few turf wars between them and the Ities. There is this man I've met, just the once, head of the Gandalfo family. He rules the other families with a rod of iron, he's not one to mess with, so we don't. He leaves us alone and we leave him alone and that's important, too.'

'Lower your voice, someone may be listening,' chastised Marie.

'I'm not interested in hearing about mobsters, what about the young bucks out there, are you doing anyone in particular?' laughed Catriona.

'I can always rely on my cousin to bring the conversation back to sex,' smiled Ciara.

'I don't like to disappoint you, but there is no-one on the scene, the only man I manage to spend any time within Boston is our Bishop Humbeto, and he's already married, to the church!'

'Oh, so do I hear you are turned on by a man of the cloth, our Ciara?'

'No, it's not like that, you have a dark mind. He just likes to help out with our fundraisers for NORAID. Even though he's Portuguese, he's happy to lean on the Diaspora who are affluent enough to throw a few bobs our way. He's influential too; he's a personal friend of the Kennedy family and often travels over to Martha's Vineyard to stay at a house they own over there. He's a great networker and so important to our cause.'

'Boring, boring,' interrupted Catriona. 'OK, so let's switch back closer to home. Pray, do tell me, how's that sexy lodger of yours?'

Ciara blushed involuntarily. Catriona picked up on this as quick as a flash.

'Oh my God, our Ciara, you've already done him, haven't you?'

'No!' Came the response. This time even her neck was red.

'Come on, girl, spill the beans, it's obvious you have.'

Marie sat quietly listening to the banter. She knew exactly who the girls were talking about, every member of the council knew about the Brit. A soldier Brit to boot.

'Come on Ciara, give it out, we all know about you two anyway.'

'Meaning what, exactly?'

'Let's start with your boss, Mac. I overheard Tom Cullen gossiping about you both; you were seen in Phoenix Park last Sunday, so you were.'

'Oh no, I'm mortified, it was…' she hesitated, 'a spur of the moment thing, that's all. It just sort of just happened.'

'Well if you hadn't done him, I would have,' answered Catriona. 'Even with his swollen face after that beating, he took, his eyes do it for me, piercing blue. At 6'3" he's a hunk, all silent and mysterious like, what a turn on. So, come on girl, do tell all, we can't wait to hear all about it and don't leave any detail out!'

Ciara knew her cousin well and there was to be no escaping until she confessed, so she explained to her lunch companions how they had first met outside of the bathroom and how they had taken a walk in the park and lastly how they both had enjoyed their spontaneous, passionate lovers' tryst in the woods in Phoenix park.

'Oh, al-fresco does it for me,' laughed Catriona as she knocked back the last of the Prosciutto in her glass.

Ciara's cheeks could not have been coloured even if she had rubbed tomato sauce onto them. The ladies were having fun.

'You do know he was a soldier,' chipped in Maria.

'Yeah, so what? Just about every Brit between the ages of 18–30 serves some time, they're all mad for it. Bloody savages, the lot of them if you ask me. Anyway, he's been out for years, he was living rough on the streets a few weeks ago. He's not a soldier now, is he?'

'That remains to be seen,' Maria's comments were cutting.

'Well, Mac seems to like him and trusted him enough for him to take McGoldrick up to the north.'

'Mac uses anyone, you of all people should know that. And as for taking McGoldrick to Belfast, that was a reckless thing to do.'

'Oh, really? Well why we are about Mac, he was also born in England and served in the bloody RAF, didn't he just? And what is he now? Only our boss and the bloody Chief of Staff of the IRA!'

Accidently, perhaps due to the amount of wine she had drunk, Ciara had spoken too loudly. The couple in their early 30s on the next table looked in and stared intently at the three ladies.

Marie didn't hesitate as she turned on them aggressively, 'You two, keep your noses out of our business. Right!' She added in a threatening way.

Sensing the three women spelt trouble, simultaneously they pushed their chairs away from the table and walked briskly across to the till to pay, ruffled, their lunchtime clearly spoiled.

'Let's get the bill and go onto Slattery's for a real drink,' it was Catriona who asserted control.

'We might even get lucky and score,' she laughed.

Splitting the bill three ways, as all girls do, they collected their coats and walked out into the chill air and onto Grafton Street to hail a cab for the short ride over to the pub.

Chapter 15:
The Tryst Continues

'Hi mam, hi daddy,' Ciara walked across the room and gave both her parents a warm hug.

'You're back late, how was lunch and how are the girls?' asked Mrs Corcoran.

'Oh, we had a fab time catching up, our Catriona's a hoot, Maria is as serious as ever, of course, but still we had a lovely time of it, how could we not enjoy Brown Thomas's, eh?'

Ciara's dad looked over his glasses, 'Yes, we can see that, a wee bit tipsy, are we?'

'What of it, not a crime now, daddy, is it?'

'Girls drinking on an afternoon…I don't know what the world is coming to, can't you find a nice Dublin man and settle down and give us some grandchildren?' Ciara's mum intervened and changed the subject.

'Can I get you some tea, our Ciara?'

'No thanks, I'm stuffed and tired, the jet lag is kicking in, I suppose, and I'm off to me bed.'

'Well, just keep the noise down, our lodger is resting, so be careful not to disturb him now.' Ciara pursed her lips and held her index finger over them.

'Yes, yes, I'll be quiet as a church mouse, in my own home, I promise!'

As Ciara turned on the landing, she could see a chink of light under the door to the box room. She first went into the bathroom. She was in a joyous mood. Wine does that.

As she made a gentle tap on the door to Miller's room, she opened it at the same time and in a low voice asked,

'Am I disturbing you?' She beamed a broad endearing smile.

Miller put down his book as Ciara sat on the edge of his single bed; one hand was behind her back.

'Nice lunch, I take it?' Miller could discern that she was a bit merry.

'Yes fab, just fab, a great girly catch-up. I've brought you a present,' she said.

'Oh?'

Ciara brought her hand from behind her back and pushed the red panties she had been wearing only a few minutes ago into his face, laughing all the while.

'You're a naught young lady, brazen in fact,' he said with a smile.

'Oh, and what are you going to do about it?'

Still wearing her clothes, she straddled across him on the bed, pinning his arms to the side. Leaning in she planted a wet kiss full onto his lips, there was no resistance from him. Miller was wearing shorts and a plain black T shirt. Ciara sat upright and pulled on the waist band to expose his already erect penis and without any prompting dropped her head immediately onto it. 'Whoa there, girl,' interrupted Miller, 'your parents are just below us; you know!'

Mischievously, Ciara responded with, 'Well, you'll just have to be quiet then, won't you?'

She flicked her jet-black hair over her right shoulder and dropped her mouth onto his penis again. Twisting with her left hand she used her tongue gently to run up and down. It sent a tingling sensation through the whole of Miller's body and it felt good.

Placing a spare pillow under the small of Miller's back caused him to arch his hips even further. Ciara now ran her tongue along the full length of his perineum. For Miller, it was sensational.

He tried in vain to remove Ciara's coat, but she wasn't having any of it. She was in charge tonight. She run her wet mouth up and down his manhood, and paused only to bury the shaft deep into her mouth until she could fit no more of in and was gagging.

As she came up for air and sat up right, Miller seized his opportunity and lifted her forcefully into the air whilst at the same time, he dropped his upper body slithering down the bed until his mouth was directly aligned with her quim. He lowered her onto his mouth and pushed the tip of his tongue forcefully into her wet vagina. As he did so, Ciara gave out a low growl. For the next ten minutes, he held the same position using his tongue expertly alternating between Ciara's clitoris and penetrating inside her vagina. It was the best ten minutes Ciara had experienced for a long time and even more sensuous than it had been in the woods. Ciara felt her body react. First, she stiffened completely and then quickly weakened as she climaxed and immediately after, her clitoris became sensitive. Miller, with both his hands on her hips, pushed her down his body until she was over his penis. Expertly, he entered her. Ciara's head tilted back as she rocked once again in the cowgirl position. Miller unbuttoned her blouse and released her fulsome breasts from the cups of her bra, and using one hand, pulled her right breast into his mouth, drawing his bottom teeth over the erect nipple like a nail file. Ciara moaned, partly of pleasure and partly as the sharpness of his teeth caused a tingling sensation down her body.

Miller groaned lowly then lifted her off as he ejected his hot sperm onto her legs and not inside her. His body spent, he looked directly into her green eyes and smiled, it felt natural to lay with her. He was in a good place.

Ciara sensed the intimacy of the moment, too, and dropped down to hug him.

Her girly lunch and gossiping about her sexual exploits had only served for her to desire more, much more. She rolled over to lie next to him, cramped together in the single bed.

She felt the happiest she had been for many years.

This man made no demands on her, made no false promises or tried to flatter her; he was just himself. He was raw, manly and yet at the same time a passionate lover. A giver, Ciara liked that.

'Wow,' Miller said in a low voice. 'When I was reading my book a few minutes ago I couldn't possibly have imagined this would happen.'

Ciara smiled, her cheeks a little flush, but she was glowing with contentment.

'Nice lodge, isn't it? 20 quid a week and free servicing thrown in, now that's what I call a bargain,' she laughed at her own comment. They lay entwined for several minutes, savouring the moment.

'I'd better go to my room; I've a busy day ahead, well at least up to tea-time. What are your plans tomorrow, Mr Miller?'

'None really, expect I'll do the usual, take Pilgrim out for a walk.'

'Can I buy you tea then?'

'Yes sure, if you want to, what time, where?'

'Meet me just after six at Slattery's. It's a pub on Landsdown Road, not far from Fagin's. Do you know it?'

'Yes, sure.'

Ciara, still wearing her skirt but with her blouse agape, breasts totally exposed, closed the door gently behind her and retired into her own room down the corridor.

Miller stared at the ceiling.

He did have plans tomorrow, but he wasn't about to share them with her, it was time to meet Rosie, his handler, again.

Chapter 16:
IRA Council of War

David O'Conner and Sean Mac sat together at the small wooden table at one end of the dimly lit smoky room. Down their right-hand side sat three men, all from Ulster's catholic community. On the left of them were two of Mac's lieutenants, the bank manager and the Quartermaster. Just behind them sat Marie, attentive and alert, the only female in the room. Tom, the landlord, sat close by to the door, controlling who came in and just as important who could leave.

It was the young Brigade commander from Derry who spoke next. He was barely 23, his hair was made up of a mop of tight ginger curls and his features were as sharp as his general demeanour.

'We are just not doing enough,' he pleaded. Two years ago, the Irish Army was poised to mobilise and to invade the six counties to take back what is rightly ours. And now what? Our women folk and our children suffer under the jack boot of the fucking British bastards. They are no different from Hitler's mob, so they are.'

Mac glared at him. 'That language has no place in my council, and I won't have it, do you understand?'

'I'm sorry, comrade, emotion got the better of me,' the young commander apologised, he knew better than to get on the wrong side of Mac for the wrong reason.

It was O'Conner who spoke next. 'So, what is it you want from us, Martin?'

'Better weapons, for a start, those Garands you sent to us are museum pieces. We want something that not only matches the SLR but is better than it.'

'Such as?'

'AKs or Armalites would give us the range and firepower we need to get us on the front foot.' The room was silent for a moment or two.

'OK, we will see what we can do on that score.'

Sensing a conciliatory air, the young man continued.

'We need more money, too, lots of it. We have set up our own intelligence services, we have over 100 dickers across Derry to watch all major junctions to report on what the Brits are up to and it's working well for us. Our capability goes from strength to strength. We come to learn when a troop rotation is on the cards, usually every four months. We slow things down in the middle of the tours and then just when the Squaddies are counting down the last few days to their exit, we hit them hard. They are the most vulnerable when their guard is down.'

'So, this intelligence group are working well you say, what else are they turning up then?'

It was the man from Belfast who spoke now. 'We stuck against the Proddy Scots this week; no doubt you will have heard how we topped those soldiers who'd been out on the piss? We also found out those Orange lot have a new ally in town.'

'How so?'

'Before the Jocks were executed, we had them singing like birds. It was them who told us all about a unit based in palace barracks. It's a newly formed Brit special operation team; they call themselves the MRF – mobile reaction force. They drive civvie cars, dress in civvies, grow their hair long and are covertly working with scumbag Loyalist groups. We've since found out that they have already met with the butcher Johnny Adair of the Ulster Freedom fighters and Lenny Murphy of the Ulster Volunteers force. It seems they are forging an alliance made in hell. They have new money, too, they are using it to try and turn our own people against us. For all we know, they may have succeeded with one or two, we have to be extra careful going forward.' It was MacStofain who broke the train of discussions.

'I took a call from Jack Lynch yesterday, he was extremely unhappy about the young Scottish soldiers; he believes this honey trap of yours will have far reaching consequences, including the deployment of more boots on the ground. The repercussions will be swift so best be guarded.'

'Already have been. A Battalion strength sweep of the Lower Falls took place last night, they turned the place over. They forced women and children out on the street in the middle of the night. The men folk had to stand idly by while the Soldiers threw whatever furniture that would fit out of the windows onto the street. It was mayhem. It did however serve some positive purpose; we had over 50 new volunteers this sign up to join us. Things are gathering momentum, that's why we need the extra firepower Mac.'

'Indeed, well you'll have it and this MRF, we will have to watch out for this Unit, it seems as if Westminster are taking the gloves off and if Hereford is behind these teams, we can expect no subtly or prisoners for that matter, that's for sure. As for the collusion with the UVF this is deeply troubling, while the Prods have been doing their own things across disparate groups, they have been largely ineffective. If they have a unifying force that's a whole new kettle of fish.'

'Oh, and there's one other thing, Mac, the soldiers mentioned that they had heard something big, very big was about to go down. They didn't tell us what it is, but we believe they genuinely didn't know themselves.'

'Something big? What am I supposed to do with that scrap of rubbish? Bring me real intelligence, not fish and chip shop gossip.' Sean stood up from his seat, clearly agitated by the last few minutes of conversation.

He was annoyed because he'd not been aware in advance of the plans to use the honeytrap.

It was O'Connor who brought the room back to order. 'Give us four weeks; we will get you the weapons by hook or by crook.' He nodded across to the bank manager who climbed out of his chair and handed over a brown paper parcel wrapped tightly with tape.

Without a word the bank manager returned to his chair.

'There is 100K in that bundle, all in used British notes. Keep it safe and use it well. It takes a lot of fundraising in America to raise that amount of cash.'

The man dropped the parcel into a small bait bag, the sort a fisherman would carry.

'I think we are finished here,' it was Mac speaking.

'There is just one thing…' It was the young man from Derry speaking up.

'Speak up,' Mac remonstrated, clearly annoyed with him.

'We hear tell you have a Brit Squaddie in your midst.'

'So, what if we do?' Mac responded aggressively.

'So, it's true then?'

'And?'

'Well, you can't trust the Brits, and sorry but aren't they our sworn fucking enemy? The man is likely to be a plant, a spy.'

Mac stared out the Derry man, furious, not least for his swearing again.

'Don't you dare preach to me about our mission, I have plans for our Brit which needs neither your approval nor blessing, young man, right?'

The room went silent, you could cut the tension with a knife. Tom moved his coat to one side to expose his pistol, he was the only one carrying, and all the rest had been searched before being allowed into the room.

Each man knew Mac had the power of life and death over all of them. The strains in the organisation had been increasing steadily for months with different factions expressing different ideas as to how the war should be prosecuted. Mac was in power but for how long, nobody knew. The IRA in the north were increasingly agitated by the lack of progress and the lack of support they could call on from the main council. There was even talk of a major split looming.

'As I said, we're done here gentlemen.'

As the men and Marie all got up to leave Mac spoke again. 'Not you, Tom, stay where you are.'

The room emptied quickly leaving only Mac, O'Connor and Tom.

'OK, Tom, let's have it, you can speak freely.'

'Mac, it's just that a stranger turns up out of the blue, an ex-soldier at that, and within ten days you have him taking one of our best men to Belfast. Isn't that playing with fire and asking to be burnt?'

Mac sat awhile before answering.

'A bit of a gamble, I'll give you that. He drove the lads up to Belfast without asking who they were; he cleared the check point without either of them having to show their false ID. By my book, that was slick, no fuss and it allowed us to get McGoldrick into position easily. I'd use him again tomorrow.'

'All you have said is true enough, so it is, but, well, just hear me out. What if he is a mole? He wouldn't be the first.'

'A mole, you say? I'd be more feared of my Irish countrymen than a self-confessed squaddie. Some mole, he was living rough on the streets with a mutt as his only companion and then takes a beating like the one he got from Andy Conner's crew. If he is a mole, I wish we had men of that stature; he's never tried to hide a single thing about his past, has he? Just think a while, we have someone who can come and go up north whenever he likes, no hassle. I've no intention of telling him the intent of his errands at all. He is just a deliveryman for the time being. He's an asset to us and he has an important role to play as this war plays out, I can feel it in my bones. I'm far more concerned about our own countrymen becoming turncoats.'

Tom knew it was an argument he wasn't going to win, so he changed tack slightly.

'What about the fact he's humping Ciara, doesn't that bother you?'

'Ciara's a big girl, she makes her own decisions in terms of the men she beds. And no, I don't condone it, I don't approve of relationships outside of wedlock. It's sinful, but she is not my daughter and she's returning to Boston in a couple of days anyway.'

'No, but she is our accountant, Mac.'

Mac raised his index finger in a silent gesture. The conversation was over.

Tom read the sign and turned to leave. As he did, he shot a glance over to O'Conner, who all the while had sat in observation.

After a few further moments of contemplative stillness, it was David O'Connor who spoke first.

'The lads are just a wee nervous about him, that's all, Sean. Tom's solid, a great man, as was his father, true patriots, the whole family.'

'Yes, I agree completely,' responded Mac, 'that's why I have heard him out.'

'So, now to matters in hand, how do we get our hands on Armalites and the Kalashnikovs?'

'We can get both,' replied O'Connor, 'the AKs can be purchased from the Russian sailors in the docks, there are not cheap though, they want 150 quid each for them. As for the AR15, we can get them in the States and arrange shipping. Realistically, we won't have them for six weeks. With ammo too, of course.'

'OK, get onto it.' Mac was in an authoritarian mood. 'I've a bit of good news for you, too,' volunteered Mac. 'One of the contractors down in Tipperary has just won a big project in Libya to work on the defence estates of the new leader, Qaddafi, I think he's called. The boss, Noel Quinn got friendly with some of the presidential guards over there and they are prepared to share some Semtex with us. The contractor is prepared to ship it back for us amongst his electrical panels. It will be good to have an alternative source other than the Czechs. Now let's go and wind down with a snifter, shall we?'

Miller picked up the newspaper to have a quick scan through it. As he turned the first pages, the black news jumped out and washed over him like a tidal wave of despair. Surely not, this cannot have happened, he stared disbelievingly at the print in front of him. The report was of an incident in Belfast, the reporter laid out the events in graphic detail. Three soldiers from the Royal Scottish Fusiliers had fallen victim to a classic honeytrap. The off-duty soldiers, minding their own business and relaxing in Mooney's bar had left with two local Irish girls.

Their bodies had been found later that evening by children playing in a remote location known as White Brae on Squires Hill, north-west of the city. The three unarmed soldiers had been executed callously in cold blood. The official IRA had already claimed responsibility. Two of the men were brothers, John and Joseph McCaig from Ayr and the third soldier was named as Dougald McCaughey from Glasgow. The brothers were only aged 17 and 18, only boys really, far too young to be serving in such a shit hole. They were all privates serving with the 1st Battalion, The Royal Highland Fusiliers, stationed at Girdwood barracks in Belfast.

There was no doubt in Miller's mind, these were the same three happy young men he had met in Mooney's. He reflected on how cheerful and invincible they had seemed to him. The girls who had befriended them in the pub had been part of a well-planned conspiracy and had enticed them to a gruesome execution. The news made him sick to the stomach. *Life was cruel, and Belfast was fucked up*, he thought. He took the newspaper up to his room to read over the article again and again.

He was incensed. This war had just become personal to him.

Chapter 17:
The Weapons Cache

Miller climbed out of his bed to turn off the small table lamp situated on the chest of draws, as he did so, he heard a single muffled bark, it was Pilgrim. A shadow across the window caught his eye. Carefully moving the curtain to one side, his room in total darkness he peered into the small garden of the house. He could just make out the silhouette of a man in the frame of the side door of the garage. Waiting quietly and patiently, the hairs on the back of his neck were raised. He felt extremely tense.

After only a few minutes, two other men appeared carrying a bundle under their arms, quite a heavy one and entered the garage from the side door. It was a full ten minutes before anyone exited.

After locking the door, Miller watched as the last man stooped down, presumably to replace the key to its hiding place. As silently as they had arrived on the scene, they were gone. What had he just witnessed? He pulled on his shorts and T-shirt deciding to go and investigate. Miller pressed his ear to Ciara's bedroom; she was fast asleep, gently snoring.

As luck would have it, he encountered Mr and Mrs Corcoran on the lower stairs. Had they been aware of the nocturnal visitors? Almost certainly not.

'Just off to look in on Pilgrim, he threw up earlier, he's a bit off it tonight.'

'Well, we're off to bed, lad, can you make sure you lock up properly? Can't be too careful these days, once upon a time we never had to lock anything.'

'Yes, of course, Sean, good night,' replied Miller.

Miller went into the kitchen and rummaged through the draws until he found what he was looking for, a black rubber torch. *Click*, it worked, *click*, off again.

Miller stepped into the chill damp night air, still in his black T-shirt and shorts. His feet were bare and the floor outside was both damp and cold. He walked down the side of the house to the front and looked down the street and listened at the same time. There was nothingness, all except quiet of the night, a little breeze and the florescent glow of the streetlamp.

Now on his hands and knees, he quickly found what he was looking for, a key to the outhouse.

Before he used it, he lifted the latch on the old coal house and gave a low whistle. No response.

He went to check. Pilgrim was lying in the cardboard box on top of the old covers fast asleep. Stupid dog.

Miller had been in the garage several times before and knew exactly where to look. Down the centre of the room was a disused vehicle inspection pit covered over with heavy, oil stained timber slats. Miller did not rush. Instead he studied the layout of the timbers carefully. Looking for signs of a tell-tale, an item or object which would have been placed to be a give-away if anyone had disturbed the covers. There was none. Slowly and carefully he removed each timber plank, placing them in a set sequence onto the floor of the garage. It didn't take him long.

Miller switched on the torch. The concrete stairs run down from the front of the pit, eight of them. At the bottom of the narrow pit lay a bundle wrapped in a tarpaulin. Miller crouched on his haunches and stared intensively into the dark pit. He could see nothing obvious, but there just had to be a tell-tale somewhere. The light caught what he was looking for. At either end of the bundle barely visible to the naked eye lay a piece of fishing line. It was the tell-tale. If disturbed, the lines would let the owner of the bundle know someone had tampered with the contents.

Carefully, he removed both and lay them on onto the floor with the timbers. He ran his hand over the top of the bundle just in case he'd missed something. Clean. He lifted the whole bundle onto a clear space on the garage floor and peeled back the covers.

He could have guessed what was inside. Rifles. American Garands, they looked quite old and well used. There was a square separate bundle too; he didn't need to open that, judging by its size shape and weight it contained the magazines for the weapons, fully loaded. Miller picked up a Garand, it had a long wooden stock, wooden front hand guard, open sights, semi-automatic, it was an old weapon but tried and tested and much loved by American troops. Miller had used it during exchange visits to the Ranger's Fort Bragg in the mid-60s. He set the piece down and set about slowly and carefully re-wrapping the weapons.

Placing them back into the same position in the pit, he was especially careful with the fishing line. To get it wrong would be catastrophic for him, fatal probably. The tension he felt caused him to break out into a cold sweat. Next the boards, each one replaced in the exact same position with similar precision.

Before he exited the garage, he stopped and listened to check his surroundings, all quiet. He replaced the key and stepped back into the warm home belonging to the Corcoran's. You could be certain they would have no idea that their house was being used as an illegal weapons cache for the IRA.

As he crept up the stairs as quiet as he could, he was suddenly startled to meet Ciara waiting on the top landing. Hands of her hips, she asked, 'and where might you have been?'

Without panic or hesitation, Miller responded, 'Your dad said he thought he'd heard Pilgrim whining so I've been out to check. He's out of sorts, must be something he's eaten. He's such a scavenger, that dog of mine.'

'You and that bloody dog,' she replied, grabbing four of his fingers with her own lily-white dainty hand, she led him to her bedroom. 'I'm cold and you can be my hot water bottle.'

Chapter 18:
Clearing Out the Cellar

The next morning, Miller was at the pub, Fagin's; he'd been called there to earn his keep.

'The skip will be here before nine. Catriona will supervise and tell you what we are keeping and what needs to be thrown out.'

Cullen's, the landlord, voice was monotone and expressed no feeling other than hostility. Miller never answered. passing through the pub the stale stench of ale mixed with cigarette smoke was pervading and unpleasant to the nostrils.

'I expect you'll be needing this,' Catriona thrust out her hand, offering Miller a large mug of strong sweet tea.

'Cheers, I'm told you are my boss for the day, shouldn't I be making you tea instead?'

'Yes, I'm your boss, so don't go setting your lip or I'll be on you like a ton of bricks.' Catriona laughed at her own humour.

'So, boss, do you have a plan?'

'Now don't get shirty, of course I have a plan. You lift all the furniture out of the cellar, bring it into the alley and I'll tell you which we are loading into the van and which is going for firewood.

'Now come on, let's get stuck in we haven't got all day!'

The two cellar rooms were stacked wall to wall with all kind of paraphernalia of pub life. Old juke boxes, pin ball machines, chairs, tables, lights and junk, lots of it too. For some reason, Catriona was in good spirits.

'How was your lunch with the ladies?' fished Miller as the two of them struggled to carry a heavy iron framed table up the stairs and into the alley.

'Fab, just fab actually, I bet your ears were burning?'

'No, not all, just that when Ciara got home, she seemed a little tipsy, that's all.'

'Well they should have been.'

Catriona beamed a broad smile. She was dressed in sportswear, tightly fitting tracksuit bottoms and a long-sleeved top with buttons. She clearly wasn't wearing any bra. At the neckline, three of the buttons were open which put her more than ample cleavage on show for all to see. She looked alluring. Catriona was a similar age to Ciara, perhaps a year or two younger. She wore her hair short and it was a lovely rich auburn colour and her eyes a warm shade of brown.

Miller certainly found her attractive.

They continued to make idle chitchat as they cleared the centre of the floors by carrying the tables out.

Pilgrim sat in the alleyway, looking on in a sort of supervisory role. After forty minutes or so, Catriona excused herself to pop to the bathroom after which she returned with another brew for both of them. Miller was perspiring a little from the manual work, whereas, Catriona, well, she was just glowing as ladies did.

'Slight change of plan, we need six of the large tables and 30 stools putting to one side. Seemingly, scrooge Cullen has managed to find a buyer for them, some friend of his up north, bloody fool, they are as old as the hills.'

Catriona pulled one of the chairs up and sat astride it backwards, cowboy style. She was no more than two feet away; her legs were splayed, and her elbows rested on the chair back.

'So, Mr Mysterious Miller, what are your plans, do tell?'

'Don't have any, if life on the street taught me one thing was that it was never good to plan, that way you can never be disappointed.'

'Could have fooled me,' replied Catriona, 'your feet are well under the table at my auntie's, including fringe benefits, I might add.' Miller stared without response.

'You do know Ciara's due to fly back to the States on Tuesday, don't you?' Miller never answered and just continued to look forward.

'I take that silence as a no, shall I?'

'Well, I'm not going anywhere this side of the century and guess what, I like a nice walk in the woods, too.' Catriona was enjoying teasing and flirting with him and he liked it too.

Miller blushed involuntarily, finished the last of his tea and stood up without further acknowledgement of their conversation. He set back to work, and Catriona smiled to herself.

The stools were light, and Catriona was able to manage two together on her own. She timed her run to perfection to ensure she would catch Miller on the stairs, forcing him to turn sideways to squeeze by her. At the same time, she puffed out her chest like a pea hen. She was baiting him.

After several runs, Miller's discipline broke. As Catriona descended the stairs, Miller raised the stool he was carrying and pinned her to the wall with its legs. She was a good foot smaller; he leaned in and kissed her full on the lips. She offered no resistance and closed her eyes to savour the moment. It was a massive turn on for her.

It was Pilgrim's bark that caused him to pull away. Miller looked up into the light to see the silhouette of Cullen.

'Not finished.' It was a statement rather than a question.

Catriona was the first to react.

'Are you kidding me? We've worked like blacks all morning and no; we are not finished.'

Cullen asked Miller to come up to his office. He did not engage in conversation, rather he barked out a series of orders.

'Mac wants you to deliver this furniture and fittings to Belfast tomorrow. Here is the address of the pub, reckon you will be able to find it. It's just off Crumlin Road, you need to get there before twelve.'

'In what, exactly?'

'O'Donnell, the lad you travelled with before, will meet you here in the morning with a van for you.'

'Don't suppose he's going to help, I suppose?'

'No. He's got another errand to run.'

Miller looked up at the big clock on the wall.

'I've to run me dog back to the vet at one today. I shouldn't be gone for more than an hour.'

'That mutt of yours is more trouble than it's worth,' answered Cullen.

Catriona was peeved and didn't try to hide it. She knew the moment was lost and now Miller was going missing, leaving her to finish clearing up the cellar on her own. *Ah*, she thought, *at least the ice is breaking between us and he's clearly interested in me*, she mused. *He is a real hunk, for sure, and those piercing, blue eyes would melt any lady's heart.* The kiss, albeit brief had been wet and passionate and dominating. She was certainly looking forward to some more intimate time with the mysterious Mr Miller.

Chapter 19:
Second Agent Contact

Miller was extra cautious this time. He had no appointment with the vet; he just took a seat in the waiting room for five minutes just in case any prying eyes were following him and then left for his pre-arranged rendezvous in the park. This time, he would need to throw caution to the wind. As he approached the path into the park, a recognisable figure approached him. It was the big ex Para he'd seen during training, Littlejohn. As they passed each other, the Para winked but otherwise didn't overtly acknowledge him. Rosie was already at the bench, presumably she had just finished with Littlejohn. She engaged Miller on arrival by looking down at his dog and asking its name, which of course she already knew. Head still bent down, she asked for a quick report, adding that he was now officially hot property. Miller recounted his trip to Belfast.

'Yes, you were made at the check point.'

'Made?' questioned Miller.

'Yes, the soldier who asked for your driver's licence was one of ours, too. We couldn't make out who your passengers were without spooking them, care to shed any light?'

'Both were quiet the whole trip, however I found out their names this morning, one is called Tom McGoldrick, the same one you mentioned during training, he stayed in Belfast, and the other man was called Rory O'Donnell. I'm returning to Belfast in a couple of days with him to deliver some chairs and tables to a pub just off Crumlin Road. Anyway, I think you will be more interested in something I have discovered at my digs. Three M1 Garrands in a cache in the pit of the garage, oh and a parcel of ammo too, probably about 100 rounds, I would guess.'

'Bloody hell, Miller, how do you find them, is it a set up?'

'No, of course not. I was careful.'

'Garand, you say, the one with the wooden stock?'

'Yes, what about it?'

Rosie fished into her large bag and placed a small disc on the bench, the size of a sixpence.

'And?' Miller challenged.

'It's a transmitter to you, we use them to follow vehicles or to track goods. I want you to get it into one of those rifles.'

'Eh?'

'Put the transmitter on one of the rifles. We know it works; we've used it before with the Garrand. No doubt these guns are to be moved up north; it could be that you are moving them in your van.'

'So, I take it you will stop me at the checkpoint and search me, is that it?'

'Of course not, don't be naïve, Miller, we are not interested in a few lumps of iron, they are of little value to us. No, we want them to be picked up by players and then they become terrorists with weapons, and we can deal with them our way. Enough, you've been here too long. Get that nark into one of the weapons and leave the rest to us. Also, we want you to prepare a written report with what you've got on Mac and his chums. Full profile, habits, routine, associates, nuisances, all the little detail's you can think of. Leave the info at the dead letter box drop we discussed and agreed during our last little chat.'

Rosie stood up, patted the dog for the last time, and as she was leaving, she added,

'Oh, you might want to stay clear of the city centre for the next few days.'

'Any reason?'

'Just sharing intelligence, that's all we have, word there might be something going down and I wouldn't want you mixed up in it, that's all. Be a good chap and do keep that to yourself, of course.'

With that she was gone, Miller stood up and walked briskly in the opposite direction with his faithful pet trotting by his side.

Chapter 20:
Ciara Leaves Dublin

'Fancy a walk, Miller? I thought we might take that mutt of yours for a bit of air.' Ciara had knocked politely at his door before sticking her head into his room.

'Don't see why not.' Miller carried his shoes downstairs; Mr and Mrs Corcoran were watching a quiz show on TV. The picture wasn't great quality and the screen flickered. Not only that, but the TV was on hire and needed feeding with coins every hour to keep it from turning off.

'We're off to stretch our legs, ma, be back in an hour.'

Ciara pulled on her coat which had been hanging on one of the several hooks by the front door.

'I'll meet you out front if you want to go and get Pilgrim?'

Clear of the street, Ciara linked his arm with hers and as she did, she planted a soft, wet kiss on his cheek.

'I hear you are playing removal man for Mac, taking some furniture up to Belfast?'

'Something like that,' Miller replied.

'I'm travelling tomorrow, too.'

'Yes, I know, you are on the 3:05 flight out of Dublin back to Boston.'

Ciara stopped in her tracks and turned to face him:

'Oh, and just who have you been talking to, bloody Catriona, no doubt. You ought to watch out for her, she wants to sink her claws into you, so she does.'

'Oh, and do I hear signs of a green eye monster coming out perhaps?'

'Well, I'm just saying, that's all.'

'Wouldn't touch her with a barge pole actually, she's not my type.'

The lie rolled easily off his tongue. Miller had already decided in his head to bed her at the first opportunity. Ciara had awaked his libido and he was hornier now than he had been for several years.

'Anyway, what do you care, you're off back to the bright lights of Boston and your life over there?'

'Yeah and my 7-days-a-week job,' Ciara let out a sigh.

She stopped once more and turned to face him for the second time:

'Will you come over and visit me? Please, I want you to.'

Miller looked directly into her eyes; she was deadly serious.

'Even if I wanted to, there a couple of little snags.'

'Such as?'

'Well, firstly I don't own a passport, never have and secondly and more importantly I don't have the price of a train ticket to Cork let alone pay for a flight to America. Thirdly, even if I had the money to go, what point would there be, you've just said you work all the time anyway.'

Ciara walked on a little further without speaking, she then interrupted the silence between them:

'Actually, I have a ticket for you already.'

'Ticket, really?'

'Well, yes and no. I bought it for ma and pa as a surprise only to have my hopes they would visit dashed. daddy would never leave his allotment and me mam would never leave him. So, I just deferred the date, I have promised Maria one, but you could use the other, it only needs a name change.'

'It's a pipedream, Ciara, I am a broken man, a bum, I live on the streets with my mutt, don't you remember?'

'That's in the past, things can change, you can change. That was then, this is now. It's all about choices, I believe in fate and for some reason God brought you into my life and I like it, I like you, Miller.'

She paused before adding;

'I have never met anyone like you before.'

Miller wasn't totally stupid, he could read the signs. Ciara had fallen for the man she thought he was, how wrong she was. If she had any inkling just why he was in Dublin in the first place she would despise him, of that, he knew for sure.

They continued in silence, as they turned the corner of the terrace street, Ciara turned to pull him in close and gave him a kiss. They shuffled into the entrance of an alley and snogged like two love struck teenagers. Miller slipped his hand into her coat to cup her breast with one of his large hands. The sensation sent shivers through Ciara's body.

'Let's get back to the house; its past my bedtime,' she offered.

He knew what she was suggesting. 'And what about your mum, may I ask?'

'mam likes you, a lot actually, she said you were a gentleman, not like the rest of the men in Dublin, she says you have an inner strength that other men just don't have.'

'Does she now? Well OK, let's go back, but I am definitely not sleeping over!'

'Deal!' replied Ciara, her face lit up with anticipation of the carnal pleasures which awaited her. She was already moist between her legs.

Miller was tense, it was over two hours since he had tip-toed out of Ciara's room after their lovemaking session and back to his own bedroom across the landing. Now he had to dress to go out of the house and get into the outbuilding to place the nark. If anyone was to see him, the consequences didn't bear thinking about; it wouldn't be a swift death, that he knew for certain.

The IRA could be ruthless and cruel adversities, he'd been taught that at Hyde. He worked carefully and diligently and in less than an hour later he lay on top of his own bed, the deed done. The cold sweat was still evident on his brow; he could still feel the tension ever present. None of this was easy and it wasn't set to get any easier he thought to himself. He was, as they say, "up to his neck in it".

Chapter 21:
Return to Belfast

Early next morning, he opened the door to Ciara's bedroom quietly, she was still in a deep sleep. He'd enjoyed their session last night; their lovemaking was passionate, and she certainly was no prude in the bedroom. She knew how to pleasure a man and talked to him gently, coaching him to move his tongue a little higher here and there, giving instructions to ensure a climax was achieved, which it was. He liked a lady in tune with her own body and Ciara certainly was. He liked the fact that even when he was inside her, she would drop her hand to gently massage her own clitoris at the same time; he found that a huge turn on. She looked so peaceful lying there and as tempted as he was, he left her, stooping only to place a soft gentle peck on her forehead and left the house to walk to Fagin's.

It was 7:30 and the man he now knew as O'Donnell reversed the large box van gingerly down the alley to the rear of the pub. Releasing the roller door noisily to the rear of the van revealed an empty cavernous space into which the two men started loading the bar furniture, starting with the largest tables. Forty uninterrupted minutes later, the van was full to the brim and even the bench seat to the front of the van had two stools on it.

'Someone will help unload at the other end; you know where you are going, right?'

'Mac told me to follow the M1 until it became the A12, skirt around the city up to the New Lodge area and deliver them to a pub called Hannigans on the corner of Henry Street and North Queen Street. That's as much as I know. Is this correct?'

'Yeah and here is a little map I've drawn of the area off the A12. It should be straight forward enough for you.'

As he handed over the folded paper, Miller looked at it and thought to himself the sketch was something an eight-year-old child could have done better.

'Yeah sure, this will be fine,' he responded.

Miller was no authority on Belfast, but he'd taken the trouble to study meticulously a street map he'd found at the Corcoran's house and he was, after all, an expert, trained navigator. He wasn't going to share that part of his personal history with O'Donnell though. The journey north up to the border was, as expected, uneventful. The traffic was queuing by the time they hit the check point marking the border between the two divided countries. This time the van attracted for more interest.

Miller was instructed to pull over into an inspection search area, step out of the vehicle and produce I.D. He did as he was told, and the soldier passed his I.D. to a runner who doubled across to the portacabin serving as a control room. Miller was asked to explain the purpose of his journey. The roller door to the rear of the van was opened and the corporal gave instructions for it all to be removed. Miller made no comment. There were now six soldiers around him and the van. The runner returned and spoke quietly to the corporal, who, with a look on his face of annoyance, strode immediately off to the control building. The soldiers continued to unload the cargo of tables and chairs. After a few minutes, the red-faced corporal returned and barked instructions to his men. 'Put all that junk back in the van, he's good to go.'

One of the older ranks, still only a lance corporal, challenged the decision, 'Heh Corp, he could be carrying anything in this van, even though he is a Brit, I don't trust him, something about this guy smells. We should tip it all out if you ask me.'

'Well I'm not asking you, I am giving you an order, put the fucking stuff back, get it?' he said in a threatening sort of way.

The men turned away muttering to themselves about the decision which they didn't agree with, but the Corporal could be a vindictive sod when he wanted to be. So, begrudgingly, they did as they were ordered. The Lance Corporal then walked up to Miller and stared him out.

'I don't like Geordies and I don't like you, big fella, you're trouble. I've got my eyes on you,' and then proceeded to punch him so hard and so unexpectedly in his stomach Miller was forced to double over and take several steps backwards as the soldier walked off.

Not at all pleased with the events at the VCP, Miller climbed into the cab, started the engine and drew slowly out of the search area and onto the main road again. As far as he knew, he had nothing to hide yet he still felt like a smuggler. Then again, perhaps he was?

In only a few minutes, he became aware that there was a car following him. It had two men in it about 40 years old. After about 20 minutes and several miles into Ulster Miller pulled the van to a stop at some lights, the trailing car pulled alongside with its window down. The man in its passenger seat indicated for Miller to wind down his side window too.

'Two miles ahead there is a turn off to an industrial estate on the left, just past the next village. Follow us, Miller.'

Miller had no idea who the men were, but their accents singled them out as being British and more significantly they knew his name.

The car, now in front, and leading, indicated well before the turn off to give Miller ample time to make the manoeuvre. After a couple of more turns on the trading estate the car pulled into a fenced area announcing, "Industrial Laundry: work clothes overalls all laundered here". The roller shutters to the unit opened as they approached, and the car drove immediately inside, Miller followed. As he did, the shutters started the slow journey to a closed position. As soon as they were within a few inches of the floor a dozen bodies appeared from nowhere.

Approaching Miller's van from the front was Rosie.

'Come and get a cuppa, Miller, whilst the guys are busy.'

As they both walked along a corridor Miller recognised the young officer he'd befriended during training: Nairn.

The officer looked pale, tired and somewhat drawn but smiled a welcome and raised his polystyrene cup to acknowledge Miller. On the table in front of him was the unmistakable Thompson sub-machine gun.

'So, what is it you think I am carrying?' Miller asked.

'We will know soon enough, that over keen patrol manning the check point nearly blew your cover, chucking the stuff out like that. Well, for a start, we know your Garand is among the cargo for sure, the nark told us that. We had no idea it would be moved so quickly, great work, Miller. If there are any more weapons, we've got narks for all of them here.'

A balding man, over 50 and overweight, came in and spoke softly and quietly to Rosie.

She turned to Miller as the man exited the room and with her face lit up said, 'Bingo! Nine weapons in total, your three and interestingly two new pieces we've never seen before. Russian AK 47's. The IRA has clearly found a new source for their armoury, upping the stakes they are. It's the first time we've had the AK in the north, we need to alert our friends in Customs at Dublin docks, there is no doubt that's where they are coming in from.'

'So are we all done, mission accomplished,' queried Miller.

'All done?' scoffed Rosie. 'Hell no. This play is just unfolding, we are only in act one. All the weapons are as they were left, back in your van, we will have you back on the road in a jiffy.'

'What do you mean, surely we want to confiscate the weapons or at least remove their firing pins to render them useless?'

'Miller, weren't you listening the other day? It's not the guns we are after; it's the people who are prepared to use them. We want to know when they will be used and by whom, so we can neutralise the threat, not just postpone it. Right, let's get you back on the move, the chances are you were followed by some of Mac's henchmen up to the border with the north, so if asked, stick to your story, you were stopped and searched, just not thoroughly. Got it?'

Miller got back on the road, more nervous than he had felt for a long time, his stomach was knotted, he didn't know what to expect when he made his delivery. He missed the turn off the A12 and had to circle back for a second run at it. As he slowed in front of the pub which was his destination, a chap leaning on the wall outside sprung up and came over to the van.

'That'll be the furniture, follow me around the back with your van.' The short scruffy man spoke in a harsh unfriendly and unmistakable Belfast brogue. The alley was narrow, but Miller reversed the van gingerly toward the open back door of the pub. Three young men, two of them only in their teens came out and opened the back up. Immediately after them, a short portly woman appeared and directed her comments to Miller.

'Come inside, big man, there's a bit of dinner and a pint for ye before you head back south, these lads can take care of this.'

Miller did as he was bid. It was obvious they wanted privacy whilst the henchmen unloaded the weapons and ammunition. He was joined at the table by the women, presumably the landlord's wife. She was only in her early 50s but looked older, a bit overweight but probably a looker in her younger days. Her eyes sparkled.

'An' what part of England will ye be from lad?'

'The north-east, Hartlepool, to be exact.'

'Does the wee doggie have a name then?'

'Yes, it's called Pilgrim, as in Pilgrim's Progress,' he lied. The dog was happily lapping up some cool water from a small bowl placed on the floor of the snug.

'An' what do you think of the situation up in these parts then?' she asked. 'Not like Dublin, is it, bloody soldiers on all the corners?'

'No,' Miller answered singularly not wishing to get drawn into a political debate.

'That Callaghan, your prime minister, now e'es a bit of a rum one now, promises one thing and does the bloody opposite.'

Miller responded with a shrug of his shoulders. 'I have never voted in my life.' That part was at least true.

'Really, you surprise me. Thought the north-east was a working class labour strong hold. Now you're a big lad, you look like a fella that can handle himself in a corner and I can see you have a few bruises, just 'ow tall are ye?'

'6'3"' answered Miller. 'My brother's even taller than me by two inches, he's in Melbourne.'

'Is he now, I have a cousin in Brisbane, have you been, what's it like down there?'

Miller paused, and chewed on his food, it was his first mistake. He'd told Mac he was an only child.

'Never been to Australia, never had any desire to go there, never owned a passport even. I just like my own company and me dog, of course.'

The landlady took the hint. 'I've a few things to do myself so I'll get on, the boys will let you know when they have finished unloading.'

Miller was finishing off the very tasty stew when she returned several minutes later.

'All done, lad, best be on your way, the way things are around here I'll be the talk of the town, so I will, feeding a Brit an all.'

Miller nodded his thanks for the food, let out a low whistle and with Pilgrim alongside walked towards the alley. He was nervous but was doing his best not to show any outwardly sign. He imagined that anytime now a bag would be thrown over his head and that would be it. 'Stop!' It was a man's voice.

Miller turned nervously, expecting the worst.

'Here, give this to me man, Tom.' It was an envelope full of fivers. 'For the chairs an all. Oh, and there's two quid for self, a tip for ye, I'm feeling generous.'

Miller nodded and muttered his thanks to the stranger, stuffed the money into his trouser pocket and climbed into the van. As he reversed out of the jaws of hell and the danger he was obviously in, he let out a large trump. His bowel had been churning the whole while and the gas had built up, the relief was bliss. Pilgrim turned and looked at him disapprovingly. The road back south had never been more inviting.

Chapter 22:
An Unwelcome Christmas
Surprise

The Dublin families were going about their early Christmas shopping. Mothers clutched their children's hands urging them to keep up as they rushed feverously around the shopping area's stressing about how best to spend their meagre savings. As joyous as Christmas was, it was also a stressful time for all the mothers. It was they who had the responsibility for just about everything in the season of advent. The streets were bedecked with decorations and seasonal messages of goodwill to all men. There was always a joie d'vivre across the city at this special time of the year and the churches all advertised their carol services and services to the masses. For many, it would be the only time of the year they would cross the threshold of these religious bastions.

Mrs Corcoran busied herself amongst the crowed city shops, she had need to buy gifts for her nieces and nephews, all sixteen of them. Money was tight, but Christmas was special, and she couldn't save herself from her own generosity. She would get Father Treahy a nice bottle of Port too, he would appreciate that. What was it about giving? She so enjoyed buying gifts. However token they might be, it made her smile warmly on the inside. Of course, she had lived in Dublin all her life so she would always bump into folk she knew and stop for a few moments to exchange pleasantries. She let them all know that her Ciara was back from Boston and how well she was doing over there. Like all mums, she was so proud of her daughter and didn't tire of telling others of her accomplishments. She didn't share that Ciara wasn't even staying for Christmas dinner and was about to leave to return to her life in the United States.

Just a short way across the city behind St Stephens green in Leinster House, the Irish parliament, Dail Eireann, were meeting to discuss internal security and the activities of the IRA and the unfolding drama was compelling viewing for Maria as she sat in the spectator's gallery. She was charged with reporting on the proceedings. The council knew that the British government had been lobbying the Irish Prime Minister very hard to crack down on their activities in the south.

The Brits couldn't be ignored, most of the country's exports found their way to the UK and the market was crucial. At lunchtime, the speaker announced a break in the proceedings, so Maria took her leave and went in search of some refreshments. If she could find a quieter café perhaps, she could start editing her notes she thought. No one in Irelands capital would have believed that their world was suddenly about to change forever.

At first, there was just a lot of raised voices and shouting. Then chaos kicked in, people were running in all directions in general panic. A few Garda officers vainly trying vainly to marshal people towards O'Connell's bridge and across the river Liffey in the direction of the Harp bar.

The shoppers were bewildered and in fright; they didn't know what to do, or, more importantly, where to run or why they even had to. That last question was answered for them a few minutes later.

In the maelstrom and now chaotic city, the first of bombs detonated.

The second explosion followed closely after. They were so thunderous they could be heard far into Dublin's leafy suburbs.

Maria stopped in her tracks and looked toward where the noise had come from. Twin plumes of black smoke rose into the still winter air like a belligerent genie signalling their menace to all who looked in.

The first bomb had detonated close to Lanigans pub near the river. The second on Sackville street close to the main GPO building, ironically, the former beleaguered headquarters of the IRA heroes of the 1916 Easter uprising.

Black ash and assorted debris rained down on the city like snowflakes from hell.

As the soot began to settle on the damp streets, the screaming and groaning from the injured made for a terrifying clamour. The air became even more deafening as the first of the police cars and ambulances arrived on the scene their sirens reverberating off the grey buildings. The city had been plunged into a chaos people had never experienced. Close to the detonating sites people stumbled in every direction, disorientated and dazed. A mother tried to hold all her three children to her bosom simultaneously trying to smother their crying.

Mrs Corcoran was inside the crowded Boyers department store and as the first explosion was heard, shoppers and store assistants alike dropped to their knees. Terrified, not knowing how many more explosions were to follow. No one had ever experienced anything like it before.

Dublin city had not experienced explosions of this kind for sixty years.

Close to where the bombs had detonated, screams for help could be heard from those victims who laid prostrate on the floor, so seriously injured they were unable to stand. And in their midst lay the still corpses of those closest to the blast who had drawn their last breath. They would Christmas shop no more.

Although their Catholic faith was being challenged, everywhere there was random acts of kindness. Strangers lifted babies out of prams to give help to the mothers by gently rocking a child in a hollow attempt to stop their crying.

The angels of evil and goodness were present at the same scene and at the same time.

Without anyone taking charge, bystanders started to load private cars and taxis with the many injured urging the drivers to speed to the local emergency rooms of close by hospitals.

Most of the more minor injuries had been caused by the stampede, people falling over, fainting and collapsing with pure shock. Madness had come to visit the city in a way no one had ever imagined. All around the children cried loudly as if in a chorus of fear.

Maria was confused as to what to do. What had just happened? People around her were similarly confused. She hesitated, did she go towards the river and where the smoke was rising, or did she head over to Fagin's? She concluded she needed to be around the council, these were bombings and were a challenge and an act of violence against them and needed a response. She felt angry but somewhat excited at the same time. It was time for MacStiofain to get off the pot.

In the Government buildings, the Irish Members of parliament were dumbfounded. The Troubles which until now had been fought only in the six counties in the north had suddenly and dramatically arrived on their doorstep.

Over a hundred good people were to pay a price that day either with their lives or by the scars they were saddled with by this terrifying act of terror. Two young men were killed outright; they had worked on the local buses and were selflessly helping to coax people to safety. They each left behind children, wives, mothers and large extended families. The effect of the premature death of men so young would be like a pebble which breaks the surface of a still lake and sends it ripples far and wide. The magnitude of the terror caused that day would not remain solely in Dublin. It would have reverberations around the world, in the cities of Washington, Boston, Chicago and London.

In the final judgement it was the caring, Catholic folk of this tolerant society which would have to bear the brunt of the scars of the trauma unfolding.

Mrs Corcoran like all the rest of the shoppers just wanted to get home and into the arms of her husband, Sean.

Miller was clear of the border check point and back into the Republic when the radio cut into the music to make the important announcement.

'Two bombs had gone off in Dublin city centre, details were scarce, emergency services were attending the scene, but the casualties were understood to be significant.'

The Troubles of the north had finally reached the south. Miller was in shock. As he drove his now empty van, he looked out for a telephone box near to the road. It wasn't long before he spotted one and soon found a place to pull over. He rang the Corcoran's house.

'Oh, dear God, it's a terrible, terrible thing,' Mrs Corcoran spoke emotionally down the phone.

'I'm OK, no, Ciara wasn't in Dublin with me, her flight had already taken off, she was better out of it. When will this madness end? There is a Mass tonight to pray for all the lost souls and those injured, she would go along and light some candles and pray for them. Who would do such a thing?'

Who indeed? thought Miller. Satisfied that Ciara was safe, he rang his emergency number.

No, Rosie wasn't available and there was no one else he could talk to. Whatever instructions he'd been given he was to stick too was the curt advice.

His mind was spinning as he drove back to Fagin's on automatic pilot, the roads had emptied save for commercial vehicles. Nobody wanted to be abroad.

Miller slowed the van to a stop directly outside the pub. As always there was two men on lookout pretending to smoke. On seeing him approach, one darted inside and a few seconds later it was O'Donnell who rushed out.

'I'll take the keys, best you are away home quickly, lad, insides not the place for a Brit tonight. You'll be strung up.' Miller nodded without speaking and set off to walk back to his digs. His head was still in spinning mode.

He'd been caught up in someone else's web, how deep he didn't know. Who was responsible for planting the bomb? It must have been the Prods from the north, or the British Government, surely not? Why had Rosie warned him to stay away from Dublin city centre, did she know about the bomb, what was Littlejohn doing in Dublin, was there a connection? Had the intelligence services sanctioned the attack to send a message to the Irish Government? Just what were they capable of? He really didn't know.

The Irish, after all, just wanted their island back. Seemed reasonable to Miller, it was such a small bit of the Earth, how could it be two separate countries, he mused. He could never understand why Britain just didn't give the six northern counties back to them and save all this trouble. As he entered the house it was eerily quiet, the door, as ever, was unlocked but there was no one at home. He felt forlorn, alone and depressed. He made himself some beans on toast and what beans he didn't finish he fed to Pilgrim. Under normal circumstances the dog wasn't allowed in the house, but this wasn't a normal evening. Miller went into the lounge and put on the news.

In the summary, the reporter announced that in the wake of the bombing, the Dial Eireann would introduce special emergency powers to begin to reign in and start to combat the IRA. It had taken this brutal act, costing several lives to wake them up to the reality of the terror which was facing ordinary people both sides of the Irish sea. Was this the intent all along of the perpetrators, was it all planned by some dark force? Miller didn't know for certain, but he certainly harboured suspicions.

Chapter 23:
Drifting Again

When Miller came downstairs the next morning, the Corcoran's were both sat at the breakfast table. Sean was devouring a plate of the best tripe. *An acquired taste*, Miller thought to himself.

The conversation had only one place to go and that was the shocking events of the previous day.

As usual, Mr Corcoran had been out for his morning newspaper, in his slippers of course. He was in a dark, sombre mood.

'Where will it all end, we are all meant to be Christians, Catholic and Protestant alike, such savagery, sometimes I think God has abandoned this island.'

'Now don't you go speaking like that, Sean, I won't have blasphemy under my roof, so I won't.'

'Yes, it was a black day, all those poor shoppers, what sort of Christmas are there families going to have now eh?' Miller felt he had to say something.

'Aye, lad, and we are sorry for those wee soldiers too, young boys they were.'

'Soldiers, not sure I understand you,' was Miller's response.

'Those three Scottish soldiers who were taken from that pub in Belfast, it says here that their bodies were found in a shallow grave up on Squire's hill north of Belfast. Well, at least the families can lay them to rest now.' Miller was hushed. Sean was talking about the three young lads, two of them brothers, the same ones he had chatted to in the Gem pub in Belfast on his last trip.

Miller swallowed. What he had to say wasn't going to come out easily for him. He stumbled through the speech he'd prepared in his head. How much he had enjoyed living with them these past weeks and how he felt so much better. Better in fact than he had felt for several years, living rough on the streets. He paused.

'I want to thank you both for letting me live under your roof, you are both very kind people. I can't explain but with all that going on I feel the need to move on, I am feeling a lot better and there is no reason for me to stay here now.'

'There's no need for that now,' Mrs Corcoran interjected. She sounded genuinely distressed. The lodge money from Mac was welcome and in truth, much needed.

'Where will you go, lad?' Sean was clearly resigned to losing their lodger. Secretly, he was not overly disappointed, one or two of his friends had already commented on him having a Brit under his roof.

'Wicklow,' answered Miller randomly.

After several more meaningless pleasantries, Miller stood up to leave. He shook Sean's hand first and then lent over to kiss Mrs Corcoran lightly on the forehead.

'I know someone else who is going to miss you and I think you do, too.'

'Leave it, go ma,' chirped in Sean.

Miller collected Pilgrim from the coal shed and set off down the road to walk the two miles to the central bus station. The closer he got, the busier the road became, and the traffic slowed alongside him.

One car seemed to take an interest in him; two scruffy men stared out of an open window brazenly at Miller and his dog. Without warning, it broke from the line of traffic and did a U turn back towards the north accelerating away in the opposite direction of the traffic.

At the bus station, Miller strode away from the counter with his single ticket to Wicklow and sat on a painted hardwood bench near to the stand. The next bus was due in just over 25 minutes, so best to be patient. A young couple in their early 20s sat on the next bench close by. Both clearly non-conformists adorned in a mixture of clothing that intentionally did not match and the boy was sporting piercings in both his ears. *An unusual pair*, thought Miller.

He sat browsing at a newspaper someone had left on the bench. It had several pages devoted to the bombing.

It saddened him, his mind drifted back to his time in the Radfan patrolling through a Yemen village which had been targeted by Hunter Jets from the RAF, supposedly because it harboured the enemy, something which was never proven. Bombs were indiscriminate, almost certain to kill innocent women and children, just like this one in Dublin. *When I killed*, he thought, *it was for survival, the enemy was armed*. They were men just like him and had chosen to take up arms.

The killing of combatants was totally justifiable but innocent civilians?

Two young men had arrived and sat across the bus station trying to act in a nonchalant manner but were clearly clocking him. They were both in their very early 20s, were scruffy, fidgety and somehow didn't look like they were waiting for a bus.

Miller became tense and his senses were on full alert now. A family of five drifted noisily down the station. Shortly after, at the far end of the bus depot, two very heavily built, aggressively looking characters appeared from nowhere. They were here for him. The hairs on the back of the neck told him as much.

Fight or flee, thought Miller. The odds were stacked against him and he had no idea who the men were, but it was clear he was very vulnerable and now found himself in a precarious situation.

He kept the pretence up of looking at the newspaper whist he looked for an escape route. His stomach was churning. Nothing.

He scanned the area again, this time looking for a weapon of some sort; the two big men were getting closer now. A driver stepped out of the wooden rest cabin to Miller's left, oblivious as to the scene unfolding and crossed the yard to a parked bus. Miller leant down, patted Pilgrim and at the same time released it from its lead. The dog stood up, clearing sensing the tension emanating from its master. Tucked in a corner next to the door of drivers rest room, Miller spotted what he was looking for; a weapon.

As Miller stood, the young couple continued to ignore him locked into their own lovey-dovey world. In a few short steps, he was at the door of the wooden cabin, he stooped and picked up two newly washed empty glass milk bottles. The two young men opposite stood up as Miller turned to head in the direction of the two heavyweights. The two bottles were held menacingly at his side. The older of the two bruisers was a step ahead of his wing man who reached into his coat to reveal a short truncheon. They meant business. *Must be pikeys*, thought Miller immediately, they will be out to collect the reward for him.

20 yards, 15 yards and closing Miller, smacked the two bottles together sending the shards of glass across the platform and bus depot. He then leant forward onto his toes and started sprinting the last few yards towards the men. At the very last moment, he jumped as high as he could into the air and as his body descended the first man was in range and with his right-hand Miller buried the neck of the bottle into the man's fleshy shoulder. The stranger dropped immediately to his knees and let out a bloody curdling scream. He was completely and utterly immobilised, the glass bottle buried deep into his shoulder with only the neck protruding.

Someone else screamed further down the depot. A split second later, the truncheon smacked Miller hard across his left hand, forcing him to drop the bottle he had held there. Miller reeled at the pain but still had the survival instinct to grab the man's jacket with his right hand pulling him forward and at the same time, he gave him a Hartlepool kiss, his forehead landing with precision on the bridge of the man's nose with full force. Miller's brought his knee up and into the startled man's groin, burying it deep into his stomach. His assailant bent double and in doing so exposed the back of his neck giving Miller the perfect target to drive down with his elbow into the nape.

Both assailants were now on the floor, neutralised. Now it was time to deal with the other two. He crossed the bus lanes with a wide stride his left-hand throbbing. The two young men, now standing, hesitated momentarily wondering what to do, and then took flight and ran off, they had seen enough.

The onlookers stared in incredulity at the scene they had just witnessed. Miller jogged slowly towards the entrance of the depot, tucking his own left hand into his jacket to give it at least some minimum support. As he exited the bus station, he turned left into the streets the first siren from the oncoming police car could be distinctly heard close by. It was approaching him head on. Miller turned to his right, turned the handle of the nearest door, of course it was open, he quickly entered and was aware of shouting but not much else as he made his way through to the kitchen opened the back door to step into the yard beyond. Washing was hung on the line as he unbolted the yard door and made his way into the alley. He jogged as best as he could, zigzagging his way down the maze of terraced streets, red faced, his arm was hurting like hell. As for Pilgrim, he had no idea as to where the dog had disappeared too; it would have to fend for itself. It was Darwin time, survival of the fittest. Hopefully the dog would find its own back to the Corcoran's house.

Miller's hand throbbed incessantly; it was in dire need of attention. He couldn't just walk into an A&E ward; the police would be on the look-out for him now. He decided the only course of action was to call the emergency number he'd been given. He would leave out the detail as to why he was sat in the bus station in the first place.

As promised, the line was monitored 24 hours a day and the person on the other end gave Miller instructions.

The time to the rendezvous passed slowly and not without eye wincing pain. At 4:30, the agreed time, the unmarked van slowed at the junction and the side door slid open.

'Climb in quickly,' Miller did as he was bid. A second man was also inside, and two men rode up front totalling four. Miller was asked for his hand; it was very badly discoloured and heavily swollen. The man reached into the medical pack and took out two small pills. 'Take these,' he prompted, 'they will help a little with the pain.'

It was uncomfortable sitting on the floor of the van, albeit it was on a rubber gym mat.

'You need that taken care of, it's certainly broken, there is a 24-hour A&E at Inchicore, St James's.'

'But,' interjected Miller, 'the police will have notified all the emergency hospitals, they will be looking out for me.'

'Trust me, they are not that good, they won't move that fast and we will have you out of there before they have even alerted the hospitals closest to the city centre. Just tell the staff you were helping out on a friend's farm and your hand was trapped under the blade of a digger. Give your name as Miller too; it's important you leave some trace. As for your address that can be false, make something up.'

'Then why use my own name?' Miller asked.

'That's so interested parties can at least check out part of your story, that's why. You leave the thinking to us, it's what we do for a living, don't forget. We'll standoff in a corner of the car park until you have been sorted.'

The doctor who examined him wasn't Irish; he was African, from Ghana or Nigeria, perhaps. He viewed the x-ray with great concentration.

'Your hands are made up of many, many small bones and at least four to five of these are clearly fractured. There may be more, it's difficult to tell because of the swelling. Your hand and wrist will need to be immobilised but right now it is far too swollen for a full plaster. You caught your hand under a mechanical shovel? These injuries are not consistent with crushing; they have been broken by a hard blow of some side.'

If the doctor was expecting a response or a comment from Miller, he was going to be disappointed. He scribbled on a form and peeled it of the clip board.

'Give this to the nurse in the dressing station,' he said brusquely.

After only a short wait, his name was called out and he entered the dressing station area. The nurse and the orderly wore clear plastic aprons over their uniforms. They were marked with white smears from the plaster of paris. The nurse quickly read his notes and without looking up, she informed Miller that they were only going to fit a half plaster because of the swelling.

'You need to keep this on for four days and then come back and we will put the full plaster on which you will need to wear for another six weeks.'

Miller nodded, only slightly, but didn't speak. The procedure was quick but uncomfortable as they pulled on his arm to get it into the correct position.

Now wearing his arm in a sling expertly made from a white triangular bandage, he strode across the dimly lit car park to where the van was parked. As he approached within a few steps the door was slid open and he climber back into the rear.

'All good now, what did they say?'

'Several bones are broken, and they have fitted this half plaster and told me to return in four days, which of course, I am not.'

'By the way, we have run the incident up the line. Are you sure the men attacked you were pikeys and not the IRA?'

'Are you for fucking real? I didn't ask them for a visiting card. I haven't got a bloody clue where they were from. They just looked like scruffy gypos, that's all.'

'So, do you think you have been compromised, that's what upstairs need to know?'

'Listen, I'm tired, my hand is throbbing, I am now wanted by the Irish police and you are asking me banal questions, what planet are you from? Take me back to Dublin, I want to look for me dog.'

Miller sat in silence, he didn't share that he had already left the Corcoran's and they weren't expecting him back. He had a reason to, of course, he could say he had lost Pilgrim and wanted to see if his dog had found its way back.

The backup team dropped him a few streets away and gave him the RV point to meet with Rosie in the morning at 11 am.

Miller knocked gently on the front door. It was Mae's voice who asked who it was through the closed door. It was locked which was unusual and she fumbled with it for a few seconds. When it eventually opened, Mr Corcoran stood in the frame with his wife to one side. There was clearly no question of him being welcomed in.

'No, we've not seen ye wee dog, we're sorry it's gone missing.' They asked no question about the fact he was stood in front of them with his arm in a sling.

'Mac left a word with us if you turned up, you've to go straight to the pub.' It was clear word was out about the incident and they had correctly guessed he would show up at the Corcoran's house too. Miller walked off into the damp, dark December evening.

The two dickers outside of Fagin's nodded their acknowledgement to Miller and stepped to one side to allow him to enter.

Catriona came straight over, genuinely concerned, and asked him how he was. The attack was clearly the talk of the pub. The clientele drinking in there to a man turned and stared at Miller. She ushered him into the snug where Mac was waiting. There was another man with him who stood up as Miller entered and left without speaking.

'Your man Conner's underestimated you once again Miller. He'll not do that again. Ye did for one of his main enforcers, Chaz Neaves, who was one of the hardest men in Dublin, very well-known so he is. A champion bare knuckle boxer, that is until you came along. He'll never be the same again; you severed a main tendon in his shoulder, so I hear. You are a very violent man, Miller, but you already know that, don't ye?'

An uncomfortable silence ensued.

It was Miller who spoke next.

'What was I supposed to do? I was cornered with no escape; it was them or me.'

'Yes, you did just that for sure, it's just that there are only a few men alive today that would have that aggression and the ruthlessness to carry it out. One man against four pikeys and you get away with just your arm in a sling.'

More silence, even more uncomfortable than last time.

'And just what were you doing at the bus station, lad? You left the Corcoran's place without a word, and may I remind you it was me paying your lodge. You didn't think to speak to me, tell me that you were leaving. I feel insulted after all I have done for you, lad. There are folk around here which think I have lost it; they have taken to calling me Santa Claus.'

'Wicklow, your own men told me to go away after the bombings, so I was taking their advice.'

'The bombings, ah yes, the Brits got their way, the Taoiseach are breathing down our necks and have even lifted several patriots. It is a sad time, all those poor folks, out buying their Christmas presents looking forward to celebrating the birth of Christ. Now they are faced with arranging funerals. Dublin has never seen the like since 1916. Your arm, Miller?'

'Nothing that won't heal in time, just a few broken bones that's all.'

'Who fixed it for you?'

'I just jumped on a bus and it took me out of the city, I think the hospital was called St James's.'

Mac scribbled on a note and nodded into the main room to fetch him a refill, when the barman returned Mac slipped him the note without trying to hide it from Miller.

'The Garda are looking for you, lad, the photo fit likeness is quite good, too.'

Miller, as was his usual demeanour, remained silent.

'I've a bit of news for ye lad, some good, some bad.'

He had Miller's attention now, his stomach was churning.

'And?'

With a wave of a hand, another strange face entered the snug.

'He's something to show you,' his tone was very conciliatory, and Miller didn't feel threatened, just anxious.

Miller followed the stranger into the yard out the back, who proceeded to walk over to an old carpet laid in the corner. The man flicked it open and at the same time said, 'sorry about this, mate, someone dropped it off out back an hour ago, that's all we know.'

Miller dropped to knees to examine Pilgrim's lifeless body, its throat had been cut and its eyes were rolled back into its head.

'Who did this to my dog?' His voice was shaking with rage.

'Presumably the same crowd that attacked you. If Andy Conner's mob didn't like you before, you can be sure you are top of their list to be topped now. This alley is about as close as they dare come to Fagin's. You are OK here, Mac hates them, petty fecking gangsters, the lot of 'em.' Miller was incandescent; a red mist covered his eyes as he marched back into the pub.

'Sit down, lad, calm yourself, they couldn't get to you, so they took it out on your wee doggie and cowards they are. Heh look, I am sorry, we all know how attached you were to it. They'd no right to do that to the poor wee thing.'

'This fucking one eye jack, Connor, where does he hang out, where can I find him? He's going to pay for this. You once said you could squash him then why don't you?'

'Calm down, Miller, and you know I don't hold with bad language, I won't have it. Revenge, as they say, is best served cold.'

Miller's breathing was heavy and erratic. He was out of control; his anger was in control of him.

'Listen, I know you are angry right now, a blind man could see that. I've another bit of news, better news for you. You've made a big impression on our Ciara, lad, that hand of yours needs a few weeks to heal before you can even pick your own nose.'

Mac slid an open envelope over to Miller.

It was an airline ticket to Boston.

'I think you should go, lad, that hand of yours needs a bit of time to heal and you need time to cool down.'

Miller was silent.

Mac stood. 'You can kip downstairs in the cellar so as not to bother the Corcoran's anymore, after all you're expert at sleeping on the floor, are you not?' Miller stood up to leave, as he turned, Mac spoke again.

'There is just one more thing, lad, I want you to look at this photo fit picture,' he slid a black and white picture of a man across the table. Miller recognised the person straight away; it was Littlejohn, the ex-Para.

'No, never seen him before, it is another bloody pikey?'

'No, lad, we think he's a Brit like you, thought you might have come across him in your past?'

'No, never,' Miller lied.

'The Garda have a warrant out for his arrest in connection with the bombing, we'd like to find him first, that's all. Take another good look: are you sure you've never come across him, only your face seemed to change when you looked at him?'

'I thought it was another pikey, that's all, they are all I can think of right now.'

'OK, get yourself off and get some rest, you'll be safe enough down in the cellar. We'll talk again in the morning.' Mac frowned, there was something in Miller's expression that he didn't like.

Forty minutes later, as Miller lay on some old curtains to insulate him from the concrete floor, he stared at the ceiling, and lights from the alley beyond allowed some light into the room and shadows moved as branches of the nearby tree rocked in the wind and the moonlight.

Pilgrim was lying outside in the alley, all alone with its throat cut. His loyal friend, they'd been through a lot together, companions through thick and thin.

Some bastard had cut its throat to get back at him and it had worked. There would be hell to pay, he'd see to that. The fucking pikeys would learn what enemies around the world already knew: "You don't mess with the SAS!"

Meanwhile upstairs, Mac was climbing into his over coat ready to leave.

'So, boss, what do you think of our Brit tramp now then? Still think it's a coincidence he turned up outside our pub? He's just taken down one of the hardest men in Dublin singlehandedly.'

'Do you think I am stook? Well there is a lesson here for us too, if our man, already past his prime, one might say, can do the damage he has, then what chance have we got of defeating the Brits military? None, I tell you! All we can hope for is to be a stone in their shoe to bring them to the table.'

'But boss, with all due respect, that's not we are here for, we want rid of the fecking Brits and we want our country back. And if necessary, we'll take it by force.'

'Brave words, lad, but foolish ones. We don't have a cat in hell's chance of removing the Brits from the north by force, sooner or later we will have to sit down at a table and compromise with them. In the meantime, we must be a sufficient nuisance to make them want to come to the table that's all. And as for your man in the cellar, let's just agree that I think there is more to our Mr Miller than meets the eye, granted. But for the time being, I have use for him. Let him go to Ciara and to Boston and cool off for a couple of weeks. Meanwhile, we'll do some more digging into his past. What did you find out from St James's?'

'Story check's out. He signed in as Algeron Miller, cause of injury: mechanical shovel on a farm.'

'OK that's interesting, who do we have in the north-east of England? Someone to ask a few discrete questions about our Mr Miller.'

'Plenty, especially in Hebburn, Newcastle area. I've a good man: p Paddy Martin is his name, one of three brothers. Handy he is, loyal too, works as a scaffolder in the local shipyard and he won't attract any attention. He can do some digging for us. But boss, if you have doubts, then why are you allowing him to go to Boston and get into the middle of our fundraising? Let's just err on the side of caution and I'll go downstairs and top him right now. We'll be rid of him once and for all that way.'

'Because I said so, that's why. He's not to be harmed, I tell you. Not without my express order, is that clear? Is that understood?' He repeated himself for effect.

'Now I'll be best on my way home.'

Chapter 24:
Farewell Faithful Friend

At best, Miller was only able to get a couple of hours' sleep. After weeks of sleeping in a nice bed at the Corcoran's, the cellar floor proved very uncomfortable. Well, that and the fact his arm hurt like hell and his mind was racing as he plotted the revenge, he would extract from the pikeys.

He needed to get busy tomorrow, he had to bury Pilgrim first and that had to be done before people were out and about. There was an old peat spade in one of the outhouses, he would use that. He also had a meeting scheduled with Rosie that might prove tricky, so he'd better be careful.

Mac had seemed a little less comfortable around him last night and yet it was clear he didn't want to lift him and showed no obvious signs of distrust, just an uncomfortable uneasiness, that's all.

It was drizzling with December rain when Miller left the cellar; it was almost hailstone but not quite. It was cold and damp, typical of Dublin at the time of the year. He closed the yard door to the alley and set off with Pilgrim slung over his shoulder and the spade in the other hand. He's slipped his arm out of the sling to keep it out of the way.

He didn't have to walk far down the canal before he spotted suitable place. He's passed a couple of men on their bikes using the tow path on their way to work; he must have looked quite a sight with a bundle over his shoulder and spade to hand.

It was difficult to dig. The topsoil was rock hard and semi-frozen and having only one good hand didn't help either. All soldiers were taught to dig during basic training. On exercise during his para training, Miller had been paired with Dick the pit, a former miner from the Durham coal field who could dig for England. His technique was effortless and swift. Miller wished his old chum was here now. The stand of spruce trees afforded him some cover; they were evergreen so could not be easily seen through.

He dug deep. At three foot he decided that would be enough, he didn't want Pilgrim being dug up by some foraging animal such as a Town fox.

He kept his treasured pet wrapped up in the carpet; he was far from squeamish but didn't want to look at it again, he preferred to hold in his memory the sassy little dog he shared his life with these past four years.

Once he replaced all the topsoil, Miller scooped up some wet broadleaves from about 20 yards away and spread them all about the dig site. They provided excellent camouflage to mask where Pilgrim lay.

All finished, Miller stood hands to the front and head bowed to say a few words of farewell to his loyal friend. Speaking out loud now for the entire world to witness, he made his promise: 'The man or men who did this to you, my friend, will pay with their lives. That is my solemn promise to you.'

Finally, he recited Flecker's Poem taken from the clock tower at the Barracks:

'We are the Pilgrims, master;
We shall go always a little further; it may be
Beyond that last blue mountain barred with snow
Across that angry or that glimmering sea.'

Chapter 25:
An Angry man

When he got back to Fagin's and slipped through the door from the alley into the backyard Catriona was stacking empty beer crates ready for collection by the brewery.

She looked at the spade and immediately realised where Miller had been.

'Sorry about your wee doggy, Miller, we all know how attached to it you were.' Miller nodded his thanks without speaking; he wasn't in any mood too.

'Let me fix you a bit of breakfast, how's that arm of yours today?'

'Sore actually, don't suppose the doctor would have approved of me using it to dig a grave would he now?'

Fifteen minutes later, Catriona returned to the back room with a large wooden tray and on it was a plate of full Irish breakfast accompanied by a large mug of steaming hot tea.

Miller tucked into it with gusto, he was hungry and always very partial to a fried breakfast.

'I hear Ciara's given you her pa's ticket to go and visit her, I'm still waiting for mine.' She paused.

'She's keen on you, isn't she?'

'Wouldn't know about that, perhaps she just feels sorry for me, that's all.'

'I've decided to take her up on the offer, Mac's suggestion, just have to get a passport first, that's all, I've never owned one.'

'Really? You do surprise me; I thought the Brit Army liked fighting all over the world?'

'That's as maybe, when we travelled all that was ever needed was Army ID, the RAF would do the rest.'

There was an awkward silence between them for a couple of minutes.

'1968.' Miller announced totally randomly.

'Sorry?'

'1968.'

'You said the Brits are mad for fighting, you are right we are, 1968 is the only year since 1939 we haven't lost troops in combat. Now we are losing them close to home, just up the road to be exact.'

'Miller, what's it like fighting someone else's war on the other side of the world?'

'Never give it much thought really, it's just what we do, and we do it well. He was being emboldened and reckless. Anyway, until 1920 those British forces which ruled our Empire would have been made up of tens of thousands of your countrymen, all volunteers to take the King's shilling. Until 1939, we'd never fought in a war that didn't have a large Irish contingent. You take Waterloo for instance; the iconic picture of the battle is of the Scots Grey's charging the French, but it was Irish troops who held the line in face of Bonaparte's canon's and charges. They never gave a yard despite their losses. Brave men, all of them. And now Irish forces are fighting against us, a battle we'll never let you win.'

Catriona was startled by Miller's words and frightened too, she never intended to trade politics with him, this conversation could get them both in serious trouble.

She walked across and picked up the tray, leant over and whispered to him:

'No more talk like that around here, somebody will take off your kneecaps, Miller, trust me.'

A little voice in Catriona head told her not to be so friendly anymore, this man was clearly trouble and once Mac had finished using him, he was destined for a shallow grave, alongside that dog of his.

Chapter 26:
Treading Water

'Where do think you are off to, lad?' Tom Cullen was keeping a close on Miller now.

'Post office for a form, that's all,' Miller replied.

'You'll not get a form for British passport in any Dublin post office, lad, you'll have to get someone to send you one over. Well I feel the need for a walk anyway.'

'Sorry, lad, you've a short memory, Mac told you the photo fit of you is a good likeness the Garda will be looking out for you. You've to stay here, Mac insisted on that.'

Miller knew there was no point in arguing, he would just have to miss the agent contact. If he forced the issue it would compromise him.

'Any books to read then?' Miller asked.

Cullen lifted a cardboard box of various books that had been left by customers over the years; pick your way through this. There should be something in there for you.

There was quite a new book in good condition that caught Miller's eye. *The Agony of Easter* by Thomas M. Coffey. The book's cover gave a précis: *Dublin, on Easter Monday, 1916, a half trained army led by poets launched an invasion of Dublin's General Post Office. Agony at Easter is not just another book about this foolish, yet somehow magnificent, rebellion.*

If nothing else, it would help pass the time and who knows he might even learn something about the failed revolt which awakened Ireland masses to seek independence from Britain which they eventually accomplished in 1922. He wasn't going to be able to get a message to his handlers about his no show but that couldn't be help. His arm still hurt so the rest would be good for it.

At the rendezvous, it wasn't Rosie waiting for Miller, she was in London. It was the officer Nairn. He'd seen the report come in of the attack and the recovery of Miller to the hospital by the intelligence team and volunteered to drive south for the meet. Of course, Miller didn't present himself at the prescribed time. Nairn was concerned about the no-show and decided to break protocol to see if Miller needed any help.

The pub began to fill near to lunch time as regulars drifted in. The noise level rose, and more than one group looked over at Miller and then muttered quietly in their groups about him. It was time to for him to look scarce. He picked up his book and headed down into the cellar. Just as he commenced to descend the stairs his ears pricked up as he could hear the familiar voice at the bar.

Nairn, the young British officer, had presented himself at the bar and ordered drinks in the only Irish accent he had, a plumby one, trying hard to sound south Dublin. He had, after all, spent three years studying at university there. He was not short of boldness; some would even say it was rashness on his behalf. He had brought one of the new female officers with him as cover and as they had entered Fagin's, heads had turned to watch the two strangers as they took up their corner seat.

'Not seen you in these parts before,' quizzed Cullen as he pulled the pint Guinness.

'No. I'm not from here that's why, I am a lecturer at UCD, and my girlfriend and I have just been to see a house nearby, so we thought we'd call in. Nice pub, by the way, if we end up buying it would make a nice local.'

Miller was aghast. If he returned upstairs, his cover could be completely blown but if he didn't God only knows what Nairn was capable of. He decided to retrace his steps back up to the main room.

'He reached behind the bar to drop the book back into the box, tried that book but it wasn't floating my boat, thanks anyway, Tom.'

He turned to look directly at Nairn and then disappeared back to the cellar. If Nairn was looking for proof, he was still alive, it had just confirmed that. It was all getting complicated and it was unnerving Miller.

The cellar had become an open prison for him. He couldn't just take off, he had no dog to take out for a walk, in fact he had no reason to go out of the pub at all.

An hour later, he plucked up the courage to return to the room. Nairn and the female had left assured that their man was still alive and still active. O'Donnell spotted him and beckoned him over to join him.

'I'm sorry about your wee doggy, Miller, only a savage would do that, it was a disgrace.'

'Thanks,' replied Miller, O'Donnell seemed genuine in his sympathy.

'I've a run to cork to do tomorrow, how would you like to join me, I could fix it for you with Mac.'

'Yeh that would be great, I am just down there stewing in my own juices, so that would be a distraction for me, and I've never been down there. How far is it?'

'That's the rub, it will take us four to five hours each way, but it would be a help if you came along and we could spell each other with the driving.'

'It's not like I have anything else to do, driving might be a bit tricky with this arm, but I'll manage.'

Catriona came over to the table and put down two more pints. She was distant with Miller now, either she knew something or was just jealous that Miller was planning a trip to Boston to see Ciara, or both.

Chapter 27:
Journey to Cork

The countryside from Dublin down to Cork was spectacular. It was green and just beautiful.

The road wasn't that busy, traffic seemed to be heading in the opposite direction, back up to Dublin. When they stopped for a cuppa and to stretch their legs, Miller asked O'Donnell for some coins as he wanted to ring a friend in England and get a passport form sent out to him. He would use the Corcoran's address.

The number he rang wasn't England but the emergency number to his handler's operations room. He quickly explained they wanted him to go to Boston and he needed a passport under his cover name. That would be arranged. For the time being he could not be seen to meet up and they need to come up with some other means of contacting him than turning up at Fagin's unannounced. Whoever was listening at the other end was unaware that Nairn had travelled down from the north to do just that. Miller had dropped him it, as they say, but how was he to know the visit to the pub was unauthorised?

'All sorted?' asked O'Donnell innocently.

'Yes, my aunt is going to post a form over to the Corcoran's. She's not my real aunt; she was just my mother's best friend for a lot of years.'

'We all have at least one of those,' agreed O'Donnell.

By the time they reached the outskirts of a town called Cashel, the silencer on the exhaust was fully blown and the noise was as loud as if they were driving a tractor.

'We'll need to get this fixed in Cork before we set off back, I'll call Dublin and let them know we've been delayed. In the meantime, we can get a bed for the night at a mate's house. If anyone asks anything, best you just say you work for Mac, don't let on you were once in the Brit army, they fecking hate the Brits with a vengeance down here, it is, after all known as the people's Republic of Cork!'

Chapter 28:
The Republic of Cork

Journey's end was Midleton.

Midleton wasn't in Cork at all. It was over 10 miles to the east on the N25 road which linked Cork with the ferry port of Rosslare. It was a one-horse town with a single main street with the chief employer at one end. Jameson Whisky distillery had been built in the 1860 and was still thriving and offered employment for the townsfolk. For recreation, as in most towns of Ireland, Gaelic football was the main sport.

O'Donnell pulled up the now very noisy car to the little lock up garage on the north side of town and as he manoeuvred to reverse into a gap between two others parked in the yard the two mechanics stopped working to watch but more importantly listen to the roar of the engine with its blown exhaust.

'I'm on an errand from Dublin and we need this fixing, can you do it boys and more importantly can you do it for me today?'

The two mechanics looked at each other and the older one shrugged his shoulders.

'Too busy, sorry, you'll have to wait your turn we have these to take care of first. Come back tomorrow and we'll take a look then.'

O'Donnell didn't answer.

He walked past the two mechanics and into a portacabin built inside the shed. Two minutes later, a balding older man, presumably the garage owner stepped out into the now failing winter's light.

'Pull the car onto the ramp and let's look at the damage.' He was talking to the older mechanic who didn't look the brightest tool in the box.

A few moments later with the car lifted into the air on the hydraulic ramps the Garage owner ducked underneath the chassis and returned as quickly as he'd gone.

'Totally shot, nothing to salvage there, you need a full exhaust system from front to back and it won't be cheap either, you've two boxes on this system.'

'Any idea how much?' asked O'Donnell.

'Hard to say, 25, maybe more, more importantly I don't have one, I'll have to ring round to see who's got one in stock for you and most places are closing now.'

'OK, can you do that, and I'll give you a ring later. We need to find digs, have you a car for us to use?'

'No. Unless that is you want to use that one over there.' The owner pointed to a battered old three-wheeler Reliant car. Miller chuckled; it was even worse that Ciara's old man's.

'If it's all you have, it will have to do boy.'

Miller climbed in, with a struggle and his bowed his head a little as all the available head room was used.

'We'll go across the town to Holy Rosary church; I've a cousin lives just behind who'll find us a bed for the night.'

After only five minutes of crossing Midleton, O'Donnell pulled up on Terrace Street with a pub at one end.

'You stay here, Miller; give me a few minutes to sort something out for us both.'

Twenty minutes later, Miller, in desperate need to relieve himself, climbed out of the small three-wheeler and turned into the cobbled alley to pee against the wall.

'Who are ye?' the young voice asked from an alley doorway. In the poor light he looked no older than twelve.

'I'm me and who are you, young feller?' responded Miller.

'I'm the man and this is my street. You talk funny, so you do.'

Two girls, about 14 years old having heard the conversation, stepped out of another back yard at the very end of the terrace to look on.

'We're ye from?'

'Dublin,' answered Miller. The response puzzled the young man ever further.

'Ye don't sound like you come from Dublin, anyway, what did you do to your arm?'

'I trapped in the shovel of a tractor,' lied Miller, amused by the young man's confident questioning.

'Where are ye really from, mister?' chimed in one of the girls who'd been silent until now.

'UK, England, Great Britain, you take your pick they are all correct answers.'

'You're a fecking Brit,' challenged the young man. 'When I'm older I'm going to get me a gun and kill you feckers.'

'Oh, are you now and why would that be, what have we ever done to you exactly?'

'Feckin all sorts, you knobhead,' the young boy's voice had become very hostile now. You starved us all, sent us in stinking prison ships to Van Damien's land and you've just bombed our capital city. Ye are all bastards. Me dad says we've to get you all out of Ireland and we will, just you wait and see.'

As the boy spoke, spittle ejected from his mouth, such was the venom he voiced. His whole face spoke of the hatred that had been instilled in him for the British. Miller shook his head, left the alley and returned to the van but instead of getting back in, he sat on the wing. It gave under his weight and the contours of the indent wrapped around the seat of his bum.

The boy and the two girls watched him from the end of the street, not wishing to chat to him any longer, just talking about him now. Miller imagined the young man impressing the girls by telling them how many fecking Brits he was going to kill to avenge his forefathers.

Such hatred for the British at such a young age, it didn't auger well for the future, he mused. The poor kid had been brainwashed. He'd never faced that sort of hostility in his time in Dublin. Just the opposite really.

O'Donnell had been gone for over 30 minutes now and it had turned dark and a December chill filled the night air. It was a cloudless evening; the sky was made darker by the smog which hung over it, no doubt caused by the peat or coal fires which afforded the townsfolk some respite from the cold. Miller had just climbed back into the passenger seat when he could see two men approaching the car from the front. It was O'Donnell. Miller climbed slowly back out and stood tall but didn't speak or engage the men in any form.

'Miller, this is me friend, Fergal; he's going to show us where we can put our head down for the night. I've rung Fagin's and let them know what's happened. It's OK; we just need to get back by two in the afternoon tomorrow.'

In the still night air, Miller could easily smell the beer fumes emanating from O'Donnell as he spoke. No wonder he'd been gone so long, he been boozing.

The three men left the little van where it was parked; walked down the street and past the corner shop, which like many others in Cork was owned by a quiet hardworking Asian family. Two doors down, the stranger turned and opened the unlocked door to step into a terraced house. It was a two-up-two-down property and there were sliding glass doors separating the front room from a small dining room. In the corner there was a bar. Three bottles of spirits hung from the optics and a glass drinks fridge was half stocked with lager and beer. To Miller, the décor was totally tasteless, to O'Donnell's friend Fergus; it was the height of sophistication. The stranger passed Miller a can of locally brewed Murphy's stout and for the first time acknowledged him.

'So, you're a Brit then? Rory here says you got into a fight with four pikeys and saw them off, you must be handy, eh? He says you are a Geordie from England an' all. Spent some time in Birmingham myself and I've a cousin in Liverpool. Now there is a great town, Ireland's second capital it's called, after Cork of course!'

'Don't know it myself except I passed through it once. I used to hang around Manchester.' Miller felt the need to respond.

'Do you follow the footy then? We're all either United fans or Liverpool fans down here, how about you?'

'Never been to a game in my life.'

'Really? And you lived in Manchester?'

'Aye,' Rory cut in, 'Lived on the streets he did until he got into a fight and then he came over to Dublin.'

'Seems to me you've a problem, fighting all the time, as big as ye are, there is always someone bigger. Better remember that.'

As the three men stood in the corner at the homemade bar chatting, a cold blast of air caused them to turn quickly.

In front of them, appearing out of nowhere, stood three ominously masked men, their heads covered in black Balaclavas. They all wore olive green combat jackets. Two of them had pistols out, ready for use if needed.

Miller stiffened, had they come to lift him?

'So, what the feck's going down here, Fergal, what are you doing drinking with a fecking Brit in your house?'

'It's not like that,' Fergal's voice trailed off.

'I'm just doing a favour for my cousin, Rory, here.'

'You, with your arm in a sling, turn around and stand facing the wall over there.' Miller had no option but to do as he was bid.

One of the strangers searched him from top to bottom, very thoroughly.

'Clean boss,' came the voice with a thick Cork accent.

It was O'Donnell who spoke next.

'Of course, he's clean, he's with me and I am from Dublin. I work for Sean MacStiofain and so does he. And, just in case you don't believe me, ring him.'

'Keep him there, and keep your eye on him, if he makes a wrong move, whack him. I'll take this one outside to find out what's really going on.'

O'Donnell and the stranger left the room; Miller could see their shadows track against the woodchip wallpaper of the house. He was now at the mercy of the extreme IRA and things couldn't have been worse. Who could have known he would be here in this random house? Miller leant forward cognizant that in the centre of his back was a pistol of some sort. He could only support his own weight with one hand as the other was in the sling of course. He didn't rate his chances of fighting his way out of this one so decided to wait for events to unfold. The cold air entered the room again and without any further voices Miller was cognizant of movement and then O'Donnell's voice broke the eerie silence.

'It's OK, they've gone now.'

Fergus spoke next, 'Jesus. When I said I'd put you up and didn't know I was about to cross the Ahern brothers, mad bastards, the both of them.'

'It's OK,' O'Donnell reassured him, 'Once I explained they were OK, it's not a problem, either to you or to us, really.'

'Are you sure? They are not known for taking orders from Dublin, you know that.'

'Everything is OK, trust me.'

'Well listen, if it's all the same, I'll leave you two here on your own, I'll go over to stay with my girlfriend. I don't fancy being around if they change their mind.'

'Suit yourself, Fergal; we'll be gone as soon as the garage opens in the morning.'

When they were alone, Miller turned to O'Donnell, 'Maybe he's got a point, I'd rather drive somewhere and sleep in that crappy freewheeler than be wondering if the boys are coming back. I like my kneecaps just as they are.'

'No, we are OK here, if they wanted you dead, then you would be already, trust me. No, they are just small-time players, they would dare cross Mac. Might have been different if we'd been staying down in the Glen or the like in the centre of Cork.'

'How did they know we were here?' asked Miller.

'Because you told them, that's why. I thought I said stay in the car, not go and chat to one of the IRA's daughters.'

Miller realised it was his fault, engaging the young lad and more importantly the two girls, one of whom was clearly the daughter of an active IRA member called Colin Ahern. He would be sure to include the name in his next report.

'Well on that happy bedtime story, I'm off to find somewhere to kip.' Before he did so, Miller went into the front room and picked up the poker, concealed it and set off up the narrow staircase to find a bed for the night. He quietly lifted the single bed so one end was against the door, preventing it from being opened in a hurry. Next, he went to the window and released its latch and closed it again without locking it. If he needed to, it could be swung open in a jiff, and it offered at least some chance of an escape route if one was needed. He wasn't expecting to enjoy a deep sleep and it lived up to his expectation; there was too much going on in his head to relax and sleep well.

The time dragged and when it was five o'clock, Miller gave up completely and went downstairs to the kitchen. The poker he kept with him. The kettle boiled on the gas hob in no time and he was able to make a cup of tea, albeit black, as there was no fridge or any sign of a milk bottle. He sweetened it with a generous spoonful of white sugar.

Quietly, he set about going through the cupboards and drawers looking for what, he didn't know.

There was nothing of interest or anything that you wouldn't find in any house in any part of Ireland. He slipped off his shoe and sock. Taking an envelope, he tore out the name and address and placed inside the sock before re-dressing. *The name may be of use*, he thought, and if nothing else it identified where the Ahern brother lived within a couple of doors anyway. He patiently ran down the clock by browsing through newspapers which were over two weeks old and contained nothing of interest anyway.

O'Donnell appeared a little after eight and Miller re-lit the gas hob and brewed up for both of them.

'Didn't sleep well, I take it,' he suggested.

'Do you blame me?' Miller responded. 'What is it with you Irish, are you born to hate Brits or is it something you work at?'

'Ye've a lot to answer for, boy, caused us trouble for hundreds of years, aye ye've a lot to answer for,' he repeated.

'I've told you my opinion, if it was up to me, I would hand the six counties back to you in a flash, they are nothing but trouble and God only knows what it costs us to have 10,000 troops up there. I don't hold with soldiering against my own kind either.'

'Aye, fair dooze an' all, trouble is, that's not how your politicians see it now. That man Callaghan, he couldn't lie straight in bed. No, if we are to be united, we'll have to do it by force, I'm convinced about that.'

'Well good luck with that,' Miller weighed in with the debate, 'Maths would be against you, of course. The British Army has about 130,000 regulars and another 35,000 reserves to call on. I'm not taking sides, but those odds seem a bit steep, if you ask me. If you want your six counties back, I suggest you walk up to Downing Street and negotiate. A military victory is a bit of a long shot, and you know how we Brits like a scrap.'

O'Donnell responded, 'I shouldn't be talking like this to you, I know, truth is you're right of course, most of us know we can't defeat the might of the feckin British army with all its resources, even Mac thinks along those lines. We just need to be a big enough stone in your shoe to warrant a conversation, that's all.' He was quoting Mac verbatim. It registered with Miller.

'Look, it's nearly eight, let's go and see if that garage is open. We might even find a greasy spoon café open for a butty on the way over.'

'OK, sounds like a plan.' Miller stood up from the kitchen chair, carried the poker in open view back to the fireplace and walked to the door.

The waiting around wasn't over yet, it was after 11 by the time the car was fixed, and they set off up the road back to Dublin.

Miller didn't ask any questions, he knew better than that, he'd been with O'Donnell all the time, well, all except for the 40 minutes or so he'd disappeared into the pub. Now they were driving back up north.

So, what had been the purpose of the journey in the first place? What errand had they'd been on? They hadn't met anyone other than the garage owner and the Ahern brothers and neither of those meetings had been planned. Had they dropped something off, picked something up, if so, how when? Miller was rightly puzzled. It was strange, and he just couldn't figure it out. He wasn't going to ask O'Donnell outright though, after all he was only asked along for a bit of company and to spell his new-found friend with the driving. They had been driving just over an hour when

O'Donnell pulled the car off the main road and turned into a side road leading to a town called Clonmel. It was a small town with a castellated arch way which led into the town centre.

O'Donnell reversed the car into a small alley. Now this time stay put, don't get out of the car. I will be no more than five minutes maximum.

It was less. The boot of the car was opened which prevented Miller from seeing what was loaded in, whatever it was it was reasonably heavy, as the springs of the car shook slightly just before the boot lid was slammed shut. From his wing mirror, Miller could see two young men, office workers perhaps, wearing ties walked off.

'Picked something up?' asked Miller quizzically.

'No, not at all, what made you think that?' was O'Donnell's response whilst at the same time he gunned the engine and began to exit the town. Miller was about to probe more but then thought it probably wasn't wise to do so.

The trip wasn't going to be a total waste of time, as they sat together in the car cruising through the plush green countryside Miller mused about O'Donnell's comments about the IRA's realisation that they were in a war they couldn't win militarily. *That intelligence alone must be worth something*, he thought. Add that to the IRA players he'd identified, the Ahern brothers, the address he had for them, the mysterious package picked up in Clonmel and the trip had been very worthwhile after all.

The ten days had passed reasonably quickly since his trip to Cork, one several occasions he had sat chatting to MacStiofain long into the night debating the merits of the Anglo-Irish animosities and shared history over the years. Mac seemed genuinely interested in Miller's opinion, even when it wasn't the same as his own. Miller was careful of course and diluted things to ensure he wasn't wrong footed or tricked into admitting something which would incriminate him. He was, after all, still a paid servant of the Crown. He had managed to slip away, unnoticed too, on the pretence of visiting the library, which he'd done but not before he'd dropped off his report to the DLB (dead letter box). When Miller got the message that an envelope had arrived for him at the Corcoran's house, his spirit lifted. It could only mean one thing: Rosie had come good and his official passport had duly arrived in the name of a Mr Algernon Miller.

Chapter 29:
USA-The Boston Scene

Miller had flown long distances before, only not quite in the same comfort as this airplane. The RAF was not exactly noted for their glamorous cabin crew.

He was somehow mysteriously drawn to Ciara, of course he was, and that manifest itself even to the extent of accepting her offer of the use of the ticket she had purchased originally for her parents. He knew her father, Sean, had no intention of ever stepping foot out of the Dublin area, let alone travel across the world to visit his daughter in Boston.

It was a day of firsts; he had never owned a passport until recently and certainly had never thought that when he did, it would be under a false name. Rosie had handled that part herself, all he had to do was to collect the application from the post office and then send it off to the Liverpool passport office. Ten days later, a pristine official UK passport had arrived back at the Corcoran's address.

The bright shiny passport embossed with the Crown of England on the front cover hadn't escaped the attention of the folk in Fagin's, especially MacStiofain. As far as the Chief of Staff was concerned, it was further proof that Miller was just who he said he was. The background check into Miller in his hometown of Hartlepool had drawn a blank. It was a common name and it was also common for Millers to serve in the British Army. Paddy Martin had tried his best; he even arranged to meet up with an ex-soldier he knew reasonably well, Frankie Miller was his name. This Miller was from up the road in Sunderland and paddy asked to meet on the pretence he was looking for an old chum. Frank had never heard of an Algernon Miller, but heh who would make a name up like that, they concluded. So, Paddy was left with no choice other than to report back that their Miller was probably kosher.

How wrong they all were.

Miller stared out of the small window of the jet. It would be nice to see Ciara again and Boston would be a welcome break from the damp streets of Dublin, especially after the bombings, the fight and the loss of Pilgrim. In his mind, he played out the revenge he would extract on Andy Conner's. If it was the last thing he did on earth, he would revenge Pilgrim. That was a certainty.

The flight landed early evening and after collecting his grip from the luggage belt, the bus into the centre of town was, just as Ciara had described to him, straight through the double doors of the luggage hall. Boston was impressive and the view from the high seats in the bus afforded Miller a good vantage point to look out into the Massachusetts landscape. The airport shuttle bus terminated at Boston south station where he then followed Ciara's advice and took a cab up Washington Street to the English school and there opposite on the corner of Williams Street was one of Boston's finest Irish pubs, established as far back as 1882 and as popular now as it was back then: Doyle's café.

It was busy in the main room, but he hadn't stepped in more than a few feet when in front of him appeared Ciara, a smile from ear to ear. She learned in and kissed him on his cheek and grabbing his arm, ushered him through the bar to a set of stairs. The four young barmen, all in their mid-twenties looked on and smiled to each other.

'Come on, I will show you where to put your bag and then you can come back down to enjoys some of Boston's finest fare and the best craic of course.' Her voice was singing, her joy at seeing Miller unmistakable.

She stepped through the bar into a small private lounge sparsely decorated; in the corner was a pair of doors leading off into the street and with a staircase which led up to the floors above.

Ciara pointed out, 'When you come and go, use this door, means you don't have to traipse through the pub, it's my private entrance up to my apartment.'

The apartment over the bar was huge. Miller stood in the doorway for a minute taking it all in.

There was a double bed in the corner, in the centre of the room, two sofas and a large roll top desk in the lounge area. A semi-open area, one end of the room served as a walk-in wardrobe for Ciara's personal belongings and clothes. At the other there was a small self-contained kitchenette. *All a single lady could possibly need*, thought Miller. It was certainly spacious and roomy. On the floor, there was both a fitted carpet and a large rug, Persian or similar.

'I'm impressed; you have a lovely place here, Ciara. Bathroom?'

Ciara smiled, pleased he liked her home and then pointed to the dark wooden door at the end of the walk-in wardrobe area.

Ciara pounced on him as he exited the loo and flung her arms around his shoulder and pulled him in for a huge kiss.

'I am so pleased you've come; I can't tell you how happy it makes me, really. My Christmas has come early, for sure it has.'

'Well I've always wanted to come to America and your offer was too good to refuse,' Miller answered.

'And you know I am really sorry about your dog, really I am, I know the poor wee thing was your best friend.'

'Thanks, that was weeks ago, it's in the past. I've moved on now,' he lied.

Now the preliminary niceties were done, Ciara wasted no time and pulled off her cashmere sweater revealing a red bra and started to unzip her trousers. She meant business.

'Whoa,' countered Miller. 'I thought you were working?'

'I'm the boss, aren't I? And I've just given myself a break to welcome my boyfriend, that's all.' It was the word "boyfriend" that stopped Miller in his tracks; he hadn't thought that far ahead.

Ciara was having none of his hesitation and taking hold of his hand, led him to the large bed with more cushions and pillows than Miller had ever seen in his life.

The libido didn't take more than a few seconds to kick in and he could already feel his own erection inside his trousers. Ciara was in charge and Miller liked the fact that she was. She sat on the edge of the bed, now wearing only her bra and panties and started to undo the belt to his cords and then helped him step out of them before pulling down his pants to reveal his already erect penis. She took hold of it and immediately swallowed it deep into her wet mouth. She closed her eyes and relaxed, allowing his cock to sink deeper into her throat. His hands were tugging on her hair now pulling it into a bunch. She looked up into his eyes and could see he was enjoying the moment too. He took his cue and pushed her right shoulder forcing her back on the bed. She bounced straight up surprising him.

'No, you don't, this is my town and I'm running the show,' she laughed.

She stood up and directed him to lie on the bed. Stepping across to the dimmer switch, she culled the lights until there was only a faint glow. Reaching for a bottle on the table, she oiled her hands.

Now on her knees next to the bed, she used one hand to raise his penis and with the other she massaged between the anus and the tip of his manhood. Moving her hands sensitively and slowly, she was clearly pleasing him as his back arched off the bed in response. She dropped her head onto him again and started pulsating with her lips. There was nothing spontaneous about this; each tiny detail of their reunion had been planned by Ciara these past few weeks.

She felt his free right hand take hold of her waist and in one movement he picked her clean up from her knees and onto the bed next to him. He was so strong, so masculine, so totally dominating, she loved that about him.

He turned her onto her back and mounted her. Her quim was already wet. She braced as his penis entered. *There is no sensation like the entry*, she thought to herself. He pulsed and rocked slowly at first, one hand supporting his body the other on her left breast. His penis was engaging her G-spot and it felt amazing.

Rolling off to change positions, he urged her to her feet, all control was now given over to him.

With her two hands on the bed, he coaxed his penis into her from behind and rode her hard.

She screamed out loud as he slapped her bared checks hard, it tingled, she wasn't expecting him to do that, but she wasn't complaining either, it turned her on.

Slowly, he dropped his body onto hers to allow him to reach under her body with his right hand to massage her clitoris whilst at the same time he thrust slowly and deeply into her.

The sensation was exquisite, and as good as Ciara had envisaged this past few days as she had masturbated in the shower in anticipation of his arrival. Both bodies were sweating now, and Miller could feel the climax coming.

He pulled out and rolled her onto her side and thrust his cock into her mouth once again, so she could finish him off.

The semen when it arrived came in floods. He ejaculated over her breasts and neck; some of the salty sperm settled onto her ruby lips. She licked them clean and swallowed.

He lent down and gave her a passionate wet kiss and then rolled over to lay entwined with her on the bed.

'Welcome to Boston,' she laughed, 'I trust sir likes his lodgings?'

'You betcha, especially the landlady,' he replied. 'If I am allowed to say, you are one horny bitch.'

'Yes, you are allowed to say and yes, you'd better believe it. I am a horny bitch and I demand lots of attention to make up for these past few weeks, got it?'

After a few minutes of savouring the intimacy, Ciara rolled off the bed and into the bathroom to freshen up and re-fix her makeup.

'Suppose I should head back down, it is crazy down there tonight, Christmas is almost on us and we are expecting a couple of office parties in tonight. Why don't you freshen up and I'll get chef fix you something to eat?'

'Sounds like a plan – no fish though, you know I don't like seafood, remember?'

'Don't worry, Mr Miller, I remember that. Your supper will be ready in twenty minutes, sir.'

'Oh, and what's the story between us, for your staff I mean?' he asked.

'That's easy, it's just how it is, your living over in Dublin, work for Mac and you and I are an item, the mention of Mac will settle people's curiosity, of that you can be certain. It will stop some of the tongues wagging anyway. I am always turning down advances to the extent I am sure they think I am a lesbian!' She laughed out loud. 'It's nice to prove them wrong!'

With that, Ciara exited the room and Miller was left with his own thoughts. Boyfriend, item, he was certainly in deep, too deep perhaps?

That might please Rosie, but it was perplexing him. Where would it all lead, only time would tell, of course. He was walking a tightrope and at any minute he could fall off and the world could come crashing in on him. However, until that happened, he had a job to do and he would do it to the best of his ability. He was in personal conflict. On the one hand he liked Ciara, a lot, but she was the enemy, a paymaster for the IRA, sending money back to Ireland to buy explosives and weapons so that they could engage in terrorist operations against his own kind, soldiers of the Queen. He was uncomfortable. All he could do was his duty, that's all. It wasn't personal; they were just two star crossed lovers serving in opposite armies.

Chapter 30:
A New Friend in Boston

It was the second night the big American with the loud flowery pattern shirts had sat at the end of the long bar. He was in insurance, he shared. The type of insurance contractors bought during construction and business he said was good. The travel could be demanding at times, he often had to go out of town to visit clients around the north east, but it paid a decent wage and the bonus was good. Just like most folk in the bar, he was, of course, a Red Sox fan. Several TVs were showing the ball game, college basketball or football. That was American football, of course.

The exception was the TV here in this far corner. This one ran the business news 24/7 with live feed from the big board. Miller was learning a lot and quickly. The big board was the colloquial name given to the New York stock exchange. He marvelled at the fascination middle class Americans had with stocks and investments, it was a total new phenomenon to him. It was yet another first; he'd never met anyone who had owned stocks in a company before. Unlike the UK, there was only a limited state pension provision in America, it was up to folk to save and invest for their retirement. The stranger explained that the 401k tax law made provision that it could be used to create a simple, tax-advantaged way to save extra for retirement. That was why so many Americans took an interest in the markets. It was a vital lifeline for them.

Miller, with over 18 years' service in the Army, just four short of the maximum to warrant a full pension, was entitled to draw his pension once he was 55 years old. Ten years ahead of all other normal men in the UK. That seemed to him a long way off right at this moment; the life he was leading could end at any moment so there was not much point in over thinking or planning anything.

The American was very friendly and offered Miller some tips on what stock he should look at. He eventually offered a hand to shake and introduced himself as Chuck Donnelly. Miller was forthright as was his demeanour and responded that he had just about enough for a cup of coffee and the bus back to the airport when it was time to leave. Donnelly laughed, clearly impressed with Miller's obvious integrity. The Irish lads serving behind the bar were warm and friendly towards Miller too, it was a relaxed environment. It seemed once out of their own country; the Irish were only too pleased to mix with all nationalities including the English. They kept true to their heritage at the same time, two of the barmen played in the local GAA team, the area boasted no less than 20 separate clubs all vying for the season's trophies.

One of the bar men, Cathal, had offered Miller the use of his bicycle which he never used. He accepted graciously, it may be a bit sore on account of his arm, but he never shied away from exercise and it would be a great way of exploring Boston, despite the often-sub-zero temperature. It was winter after all. As the bar emptied towards the end of the evening, Chuck called Miller over to show him something in the evening paper in the sports section. Having got his attention, his voice dropped to a whisper, and to Miller's complete surprise, he opened with, 'I'm a good friend of your Rosie from Dublin, we go back a long way, we are in the same line of business so to speak.'

Miller's jaw dropped, and his cheeks flushed, it was completely out of the blue and the remarks had caught him off-guard. He turned quickly to see if anyone was watching or more importantly was listening in.

'Don't worry, I checked first, your girlfriend is upstairs and two of the barmen are out back, having a smoke, no doubt.'

'So, exactly who are you?' asked Miller curiously.

'That's a tale for another day, you and I need some private time together. Do you fish? Have you ever been out into the bay perhaps?' From the vacant expression on Miller's face, Chuck neither needed nor waited for an answer.

'Let's take my boat out and do some fishing, its moored close by in south Boston at the Columbia yacht club. What do you say I pick you up at 7 am on Saturday? Sort it with your girlfriend.'

It was more of an order or instruction than an invitation.

Miller nodded, still in a state of shock, he hadn't been expecting it. Not at all.

Chuck picked up his daily newspaper and walked on down the bar to pay his tab at the till then left.

Miller was in bed after first taking a shower. Ciara was still busily working on something at the roll top desk.

She didn't think it odd at all when Miller told her that a total stranger had offered to take him out fishing. That would never happen in Hartlepool, he offered, more likely they would fill you in and steal your wallet, he suggested in a mocking and a comical way.

Ciara was very encouraging.

'It sounds like a great opportunity to me, that's one of Boston's oldest yacht clubs by the way. Check out his boat and if it is any good, get me an invite next time.' She was upbeat about the whole deal.

'It's quite normal over here for them to offer you things; they fall in love with your accent, English or Irish. They have a sense of yearning to be connected to the old country.'

'If you're sure you are OK with it, I'll go along, I've never been sea fishing so as this is a holiday of firsts, why not?'

'That's the spirit,' smiled Ciara, secretly pleased Miller wouldn't be constantly under her feet. As much as she enjoyed having him and she certainly did, there were still lots of things for her to do, most of which he couldn't know anything about either. That made him being around all the time quite tricky for her.

She was planning an important meeting in New York next week, with the Libyan go-between, Tariq. He claimed to be a cousin of Qaddafi or some such thing. Tariq came over to the US to study at Harvard several years ago and had chosen to stay. He owned a store on 5th Avenue, specialising in hand woven rugs from Persia. He'd built up quite a following amongst Manhattan's elite. His natural charm and confidence were his gateway to each gallery opening and social occasion; all the money people liked the idea of a friend who was an Arab and it sort of gave them a sense of being a citizen of the world. What they were not aware of was that the store also served as a front for Libyan intelligence in the city, in size and strength second only to the one in Washington. Strategically, it was an important city, for it was in New York where all the banking and investors were based.

The Libyans and Qaddafi personally had long been supporters of the Irish cause. Not just in words but in action. Weapons, explosives and most importantly, the oil rich Libyans were to act as hosts for IRA foot soldiers to go over to train in the desert camps and hone their military skills both on weapons and explosives.

Qaddafi would have liked nothing better than an old colonial power being knocked from their lofty perch.

They were in many ways a perfect partner. There were many dissident Arabs living in New York and the Libyan intelligence had no shortage of recruits. The diaspora from Lebanon, Palestine as well as Libya were only too happy to help where they could particularly if there was money involved, which of course, there was. To the diaspora, it seemed like it was their duty to help the Arab cause. The Americans were so overtly biased to Israel, which would have been wiped of the map, many years ago had it not been for the billions of dollars of US military aid which propped the Zionist government up. Tensions were very high in that area and relations between the Arab league and the Jewish invaders were at an all-time low. If that was possible. There had never been a high. The now American-Arabs, secure in their new status as citizens, portrayed their love for their new adopted country and all things "Uncle Sam", whereas they never forgot their true loyalty was always to Mohammed, son of the true prophet and the symbol of their Muslim beliefs. These beliefs could never be compromised or diluted, no matter which country was their home. They were willing agents, keen to do their bit, no matter how small to help their Muslim brothers, especially when it came to act against the Zionist aggressors.

Ciara had finished her work put on her creams, she pulled back the duvet cover and as she did, a cold blast of air wafted over Miller.

'Hey you, I just got this bed warm,' he chuckled.

'Well now you can get me warm, can't you?' Her legs straddled his body and she began to kiss him intensely on the lips. She was horny and needed servicing and Miller was not about to abdicate his manly duties. In fact, he was more than happy to indulge, he loved pleasuring her.

Chapter 31:
The Columbia Yacht Club, Boston

Saturday came around quickly. Miller was definitely a very organised morning person. He had laid out the clothes he was to wear for his trip the night before. He showered quickly to wash off last night's love making, he was careful to soap all his pubic area particularly well. He climbed into the beige chino pants and pulled on a white sleeveless vest before adding a polo neck jumper. The coat was a black duffle. Ciara was still asleep. Not surprising really, the girl worked bloody hard. Mac certainly got more than he would have got from just employing a manager.

With Ciara what Mac got was a committed, loyal servant and as honest as the day is long too, Miller thought. A very rare quality in the pub trade, no matter which country you were talking about. It would never have ever crossed Ciara's mind to skim anything off as would have been the case with anybody else. Mac knew all this, that's why he allowed her so much latitude and never sought to micromanage what she did or how she did it. The results spoke for themselves. Fundraising in Boston had always been good and now they had added Chicago and New York.

He leant over the bed and kissed her on the forehead gently so as not to disturb her, he then descended the steep stairs and made himself a black coffee in the kitchen. The cleaner, a black African-American lady smiled at him as she said good morning. Another first, he's always been a tea drinker as that was the only thing on offer in the Army, strong and stewed NATO standard as it was known. Now he'd crossed into the dark side and was enjoying the aromatic black coffee.

Outside, it was still mostly dark, and the Boston streets were quiet, it was a Saturday after all.

The toot of a car horn alerted him and set off to cross the street to Chuck waiting in his car.

Foolishly he walked straight to the driver's door and made to get in.

'I'll drive,' chuckled Donnelly at Miller's expense. Miller sheepishly walked around the car to the passenger seat, forgetting for a moment that over here they drove on the wrong side of the road.

'It's not far at all, we will be there in 15,' offered Donnelly.

'Rosie shared your "P" file with me, hope you don't mind?'

'Suppose so, anyway a bit late to mind now, isn't it? Never even seen it myself.'

'Did you ever work with US Special Forces Miller?' Donnelly asked.

'Nope, not in theatre, they were too busy in Vietnam and Cambodia,' he responded.

'If I wasn't on a tour myself; we used to come over to Fort Bragg annually, Exercise Honey Gift, it was called. Seven days on the camp and then 4-5 days on exercise out into the ulu somewhere. Florida swamps usually, although once we did get over onto the west coast around Lake Tahoe in California, enjoyed that trip. Just love those big Redwoods, nothing like them in England, climb to the sky they do, I like trees. Guess it's because I've lived in and amongst them all my adult life.'

'What was it like in the Radfan?'

'Hot and tough actually. I enjoyed the scenery there too. Big mountains, craggy, but tough work humping our Bergan's around in that heat. A ball ache, really. And they could fight too, don't let anyone tell you any different. They were used to the terrain, we weren't. If it wasn't for the fact, we had tanks and jets they probably would have won, but we did, and they didn't. The Russians were providing them equipment, like the AK-47 assault rifles, just like they provided the antiaircraft missiles against you in Vietnam. Always meddling those Ruskies. As for the Reg, we more than held our own, never lost a fire fight though several of us were shot up a bit, trouble was you never truly knew who the enemy was until they started firing at you. In truth, I was never sure what we were there to do, prop up the Sultan of Oman, I guess and stop it becoming like Yemen, a puppet state of the Soviets.'

'What else is in my file?'

'You were disciplined over an attack on a village I believe. It just say's you were cautioned that's all.'

'Ah, then it does mention it then. I wondered about that.'

'Care to elaborate?'

'Not much to tell, two of our guys went missing, taken by the ragheads, a Captain called Edwards and a mukker of mine, Jonny Warburton. We searched hard to recover them for three days, bribing the village elders for information but without success. They both turned up of course. Only they'd been decapitated, and their heads were placed on spikes in the capital Sana'a.

'The thing was, their poor wives had been told they were on exercise on Salisbury plain. The first news they got was when they recognised their men folk from the picture in the Sun newspaper. Shortly after that we mounted a full-blown Squadron raid on their secure mountain top base.

'They dominated all the main approaches to the mountain, so you couldn't have snook a mouse by them. The raid was awesome, they didn't expect us to climb the rocky cliffs for 10,000 feet with all our kit, the rag heads thought their base was impregnable. We proved otherwise.

'Once we were into position, we hit them with 20 minutes of mortars to cover two our sections who infiltrated up close. We started house to house clearance wasting them all. As you would expect in the fog of war there was a certain amount of collateral damage, a few women and children unfortunately came a cropper, not intentional of course, shit happens. My Troop commander berated me for being over aggressive and for not checking for civvies. Easily said than done when you are house clearing, trust me. But I guess my dander was up and I wasted one or two more than I needed to. I was threatened with court martial. In the end, it was all hushed up just as long as I resigned and didn't go to the press or write any books. That was then, and this is now. Here we are again, still playing our dirty wars.'

'Well for what it's worth, I really admire you. A lot. You guys are something else. I can't even begin to tell you the respect we have for your regiment over here. I'm a proud loyal American but I know we just don't breed many that can hold a candle to the famous SAS. I really mean that. You are awesome.'

Miller as was his usual demeanour choose not to respond.

On the inside, Donnelly's praise did make him feel proud all the same, not a feeling he'd experienced much these past few years. It felt good.

'Well, you did a good job of getting me to bare all, how about you, what's your story? You haven't even told me the agency you work for or shown me any official ID, come to think of it that's pretty naïve of me to spill the beans before I know who I am even talking to.'

'Ah, well there is a difference, what you told me was historical, all about your former life as a soldier; I am on active service still and subject to the full weight of judicial processes.'

'Ah, if you say so, so who is it you work for and what is your interest in the IRA? After all you bloody Americans, especially here in Boston can't get enough of the Irish, if you ask me.'

'I'll tell you as much as I can. For a start, I don't have anything to do with domestic intelligence or counterintelligence, I was, I am, a field agent in the Central Intelligence Agency.

'Our interest, my interest, is in tracking the disparate terrorist groups around the world, many of whom are interconnected. There are almost too many to mention: Baader-Meinhof, Red Brigade, PLO, ETA, IRA take your pick, the world is troubled in just about every country. That's apart from the Russian Bear who takes up most of uncle Sam's dollars. Yes, it's true, we love the Irish, but we don't support terrorist organisations living in our own backyard. And we don't hold with funding them especially. Your new Irish chums have Boston in their pocket. Can't help you with that, it runs too deep, but we're happy to stem the floods of greenbacks to them. 'So, at the risk of offending you, how does someone of your obvious talent end up living on the street, I'm curious?'

'Truth is, I've no idea. I signed up as a boy soldier, so I've lived away from home since I was 16, when I came out, it was under a cloud and I just found it hard to readjust into civvie street. I had no trade or skill to speak of. I was angry inside. Staying away from folk, being on my own and begging on the street, it just sort of happened. I did have my dog Pilgrim.' Miller's voice trailed.

'Did?'

'Yes, that's another story, some fucking pikeys from Dublin who had a grudge with me, took it and slit its throat to get me mad. They did that all right.'

'Pikeys?'

'Yes, gypsies if you like, travellers, Ireland is full of them, especially Dublin, beggars, thieves and crooks the lot of them. That was when MacStiofain encouraged me over here to cool off. That I'm doing just that, but it's not forgotten, I'll return and when I do, it will be payback time, big style, of that you can be sure.'

'Well reading your record, you are clearly not a man to be messed with; I am just glad it's not me you are going after.'

They arrived at the club and parked in the small tarmac area out front. A cold salt air sea breeze welcomed them as they climbed out of the car. Donnelly made a mental note to report back to Rosie about the conversation the two men had just finished.

It wasn't at all how Miller imagined. The club house was no more than a large two storey house sandwiched in-between other houses. It was all very earthy and modest in its aspiration.

They walked between two buildings onto the harbour front. On one side, there was a crude homemade structural frame for lifting the boats out of the water and a couple of gas pumps for fuelling the boats.

A long gang plank led down onto a well-worn square jetty. Some of the decking was in dire need of repair and several gaps were plain to see.

On each post of the pontoon, a flagpole climbed high into the air, proudly displaying the star-spangled banner of the United States. *You just wouldn't see that in the UK*, thought Miller. Americans were so loyal to their country and proud of their national identity.

Chuck raised his hand up in the air and greeted a couple of fella's working to pull a small inflatable out of the water. An old chap, with a dark leather face clearly the wrong side of 70 smiled a toothless grin as we reached the end of the deck.

'Hi there, Charlie, can we hitch a ride out to the Lady?'

'Sure, Chuck, hop aboard,' he grinned.

There were no fixed berths for the yachts; they were just laid at anchor around the jetty. There was about 25 may be less, maybe more.

'I can see you're a bit taken aback, Miller, not quite what you expected, perhaps? Well this is the Columbia Yacht club, been around Boston since 1896, not the biggest nor the richest but it's the one closest to town and there is a ten-year waiting list to join. My papa was a member here, and I have been too since I was six years old. Folk stay here forever, we're a family. Tight knit one too, you'll understand that, I'm sure.'

The boat boasted two large outboard motors which Chuck kicked into life. 'Slip the mooring,' he called out to Miller, 'And we'll take off.'

The cold winters air began to bite immediately, Miller's fingers were numb almost as soon as they left the harbour and he wasn't wearing any gloves. He loved it though.

The exhilaration was exciting as the boat coursed over the Massachusetts Bay waters.

Chuck fixed up both rods with live bait and cast them over into the dark waters.

'What can we expect to catch?' Miller enquired.

'Plenty, just you wait and see. Lots of cod out here, bluefish for certain; they'll strike at anything, Bass, flounder and mackerel. If we are lucky, we might even snag a tuna,' he added with an expectant air. 'The fishing out here in the best in the US, trust me.'

Over the next three hours, they chatted about the IRA and the bombing in Dublin, the abduction of the three Scottish soldiers, the trouble he'd got into with the pikeys and the comments O'Donnell had shared about wanting a negotiated peace.

That wasn't all they did though, the sea conditions were just perfect, and they began to fill the large white cooler box at the stern of the boat. Large Atlantic Cod mostly with an odd mackerel here and there, once or twice Chuck threw the smaller one's back in. All in all, they had hit a purple patch and for a first timer at fishing Miller could not have been more pleased with himself. They were enjoying a great day's fishing.

In between all the working, they managed to hatch out a plan to discover more about the activities of the IRA in Boston. Miller felt it was surreal, to be on the water, fishing and at the same time to be hatching a plot.

He helped Chuck manhandle the now very heavy cool box out onto the old jetty. It was full of the catch of the day. He watched as his friend spent the next 30 minutes diligently spraying all the above water areas with fresh water, washing off all the debris of the day.

'Why don't you grab us both a beer while I pop in here?'

Chuck lifted four of the largest cod out of the box and disappeared into the kitchens of the clubhouse. Miller sauntered up to the almost deserted bar, there was an elderly couple at one end and a solitary guy reading the paper at one of the low tables. The barmaid came over, she looked fit, was probably 50 but she clearly exercised. She was wearing bib and brace dungarees, a white blouse, with the first few buttons open allowing the generous cleavage to show through. Her waist was slim and when she turned her bum was both petite and pert.

'What can I do you for?'

'What's on draft, something local perhaps?'

'Nothing brewed local sir, we run mostly stuff from Frankenmuth brewery from Michigan, America's oldest brewer, goes way back to last century. But that's probably not even old to you, you're Scottish, yes?'

'Not bad, quite close, same island I guess, I'm English.'

'Really? You surprise me; don't talk like other English folk who visit here.'

'Probably not, I'm from the north, maybe 100 miles south of Scottish border, we have a strong accept so I'm told.'

'Hi, I'm Cindy,' the barmaid offered a small dainty hand.

Miller shook it, gently; he'd been told his handshake was too strong on many occasions.

'I'm Miller.'

'First time in the club, I take it?'

'Yup, I'm with Chuck, he's ducked into the kitchens with some fish we caught today.'

'Chuck Donnelly, nice man, he's part of the furniture 'round here. How do you know Chuck, you work with him?'

'Nope, not really, he comes into a bar I'm staying at in town, Doyle's Café, Irish Bar and he offered to take me out on his boat, that's all.'

'Doyle's nice place, been open longer that this beer has been brewed. Never employs locals though, only Irish can get a job in there.'

'Well, I don't know anything about that; I'm visiting a friend for a couple of weeks, that's all.'

'Hope you don't mind me, but you look a tough guy, craggy, manly, keep yourself fit too, I can see that.'

'Not particularly, just doing a bit of cycling at the moment, that's all.'

'No way, you're fooling with me.'

'Why would I do that?'

'I'm into my bike big style; try to do over 100 miles a week. I live across town so it's an 18-mile round trip just to come here.'

'Well done, you look fit too and at the risk of getting a slap, you've a nice rack.'

Cindy smiled a broad smile; her weather-beaten face clearly didn't take offence at his flirtatious remark.

'Never heard them called that,' she laughed. She cupped her breasts with both hands, 'Guess you could say you're not the first man to compliment me on these, had them since I was fourteen, meant I was never short of attention at school.'

Miller smiled, he liked Cindy and he found her openness and honesty refreshing.

'What sort of bike you ride?' she asked.

'No idea, a silver one if that helps,' Miller smiled.

'No, not really, got myself a lightweight aluminium racer, I can move on that bad baby, trust me. Got to watch out for the idiots on the road over here, they pass within an inch of you; when one does and if I catch them up at the lights, I bang their hood, that usually pisses them off.'

'That's the same the world over, bikes and cars don't mix, I guess.' Chuck stepped out of the kitchens and joined them.

'Just paying my dues, chef was ecstatic, cod steaks on the menu tonight, see you've met our Cindy, cheers.' Chuck raised his beer and touched it against Miller's raised glass.

'We were discussing our common interest, cycling, this lady is hard core and she cycles over here.'

'Yup, we all know that, nobody messes with our Cindy, she runs a tight ship here.'

The two men chatted about their successful day, finished their beer and just as they were about to leave Cindy walked down the bar and pushed a folded piece of paper across to Miller, 'That's my number, I'm off work Monday and if you fancy a bike tour of Boston, I'd be happy to take you.'

'Really? Thanks, I'll check what I've got on and might just give you a call.'

Their eyes met and there was an instant mutual attraction, Miller could sense it.

Chuck finished his beer and made to leave. As the two men climbed into the car, he opened, 'You're all charm, Miller, I've never seen Cindy pass anyone her number before and she's worked at the club over five years.'

'Must be the accent,' laughed Miller, flattered by the attention he'd been paid and secretly thinking to himself he was attracted to her too.

'Are you going to ring her? Might get a bit tricky for you; just remember you're here on a mission, Miller.'

Miller made no comment. Miller reflected on that as the car navigated its way through the early evening Boston traffic.

As they pulled up outside Doyle's pub the winters light was fading already.

'So, we are all good then, you'll call this number to confirm your Irish lady has left for New York on Monday, yes?'

Miller confirmed, 'Sure thing.'

'And don't forget when you ring, we need the make and serial number of that safe.'

'Roger.'

'Here, take your catch to the chef, they will be amazed at what you've brought back, trust me they will, this lot would cost them a few hundred dollars at the fish market for certain.' Miller waved as his new friend pulled away into the Boston traffic.

The road was busy; there had been some event on over the road at the English school. *Perhaps Christmas fare*, thought Miller and now the cars were exiting the car park to join the traffic flow.

It had been a good day with the man from the CIA and he'd enjoyed himself. They had hit it off and the two men were comfortable around each other.

Chuck was 100% correct; the chef nearly had an orgasm when Miller emptied the large bag of fresh fish onto the work tops.

'Amazing, beautiful fish, so big too, we will have to get them on the specials board tonight, thank you, thank you.'

Cindy was wrong about the staff all being Irish. *Wherever the chef was from, he wasn't Irish*, he thought.

Two of the barmen came through to see what the fuss was about.

'Wow, some fish you've caught here, you're a jammy bugger, I've been here three years, and no one has ever invited me out anywhere!'

His mate looked in and responded, 'Are you surprised? You are a fecking boring twat, that's why.' They both laughed, it was all part of the craic.

Chapter 32:
A Busy Night In Doyle's Café Boston

Ciara was sat at her desk when Miller entered the bedroom. She stood up and kissed him full on the lips.

'Hello Mr Fisherman, survived your first trip into the bay I see. You look weather beaten and you have a nice healthy glow to your face. So how was it?' She asked.

'Actually, I wasn't too sure what to expect but I really enjoyed it and we got lucky, we must have caught more than 20 big fish between us, I brought my haul back and gave it to your cook, nearly had an orgasm he did.'

'That's so nice, I am pleased you've had a nice day, how was your host, Chuck isn't it?'

'Yeh, nice bloke, down to earth, I like him, we got on great actually. Likes this place, says he'd not tried it until recently. He asked about you,' Miller was lying. 'I think he only comes into Doyle's because you are here.'

'Get away with ye man.' Ciara was obviously flattered by the compliment Miller was paying her.

'He's probably married anyway.'

'Was, not now. He's divorced, quite messy by all accounts, has a son who is 18 and about to go to college.'

'Not been made to join the Army and go over to fight in Vietnam then?'

'We chatted about that, he's registered for the draft lottery, it's mandatory at 18 but I guess he's name hasn't been pulled out of the hat, he's off to college in Penn State.'

'Is he now, must be bright. What's your man do?'

'Construction insurance, for buildings and the like, don't say I fully understood it. His still pays for his missus and the kid of course, costs him a pretty penny he shared, that's why he plays with the stock markets. No girlfriend on the scene right now, say's his travel makes it difficult for him to keep one.' Ciara responded.

'Yeh, university over here is bloody expensive, out of the reach of just about all ordinary folk so he must be doing alright for himself. As for the girlfriend bit, he needs to shed a few pounds and lose those awful shirts, the man's got no taste in wardrobe, no wonder he's divorced and single.' She paused.

'I've a big favour to ask you,' her voice was hesitant.

'Oh, what's that? Shoot.'

'It's a bit tricky. Well,' she hesitated again.

117

'Next Saturday, that is a week for now, there is the annual winter ball in the Fairmont, I'm expected to attend and for the last three years I've gone on my own, unaccompanied. For once, just once, it would be nice to have a hunk on my arm, that's where you come in. What do you think?'

'A ball, me, are you joking with me? I'm from bloody Hartlepool. I've never done a posh job in my life; I would just let you down. Also, I'm not the best mixer, sorry, no way.'

Ciara sat back at her desk, forlorn and totally silent, it was the answer she expected but not the one she hoped for. She never made any further comment and stared at the ledger in front of her but could make any numbers out, her eyes were wet, and the tear drops were rolling out of her. Miller never noticed them from where he was sat but could sense the situation was tense.

He walked across the room to the desk and took hold of her hand. She remained starring at the desk.

'Heh, what's this Ciara? Please don't cry, I don't like to see you like this.'

Silence.

'Ciara, all this normality, it's taking a bit for me to adjust, that's all. You know my past, I've spent the last three years staring up from a cold wet pavement hoping they would chuck a couple of coins my way, now you want me to dress up and go to a ball. I just don't know if I've got it in me.'

'Yes, I know your past, Algernon.' She never used his first name, ever.

'But it is your past, this is now. You've never been on a boat before today, but it was clear you enjoyed it, you were positively buzzing when you got back. It's your choice; do you want to stay stuck in the past or move on and live a normal life?'

Miller walked back to the bed and lay on it, staring at the ceiling.

Ciara's comments had struck a chord. He was completely messed up. His mind was spinning. He was here in Boston on a spying mission as much as anything circumstance had thrown his way.

He'd spent the day with another spy, and he was about to commit a crime by allowing the CIA into her bedroom when she buggered off to New York on Monday. It was all way too complicated for him and messed with his mind.

Ciara left the desk and went into the bathroom to tidy her-self up, reappearing after several minutes, her eye's still puffy.

'I'm off downstairs; we've a busy night ahead, several groups are expected in for their Christmas bash. Come down when you want to eat.'

Her tone was, as you would expect, the tone of a jilted, scorned lady: frosty, harsh, and unwelcoming.

Miller reflected further. He felt something for her, she'd been good to him, no, and she'd been good for him. She had made him feel normal again. He owed her. Big style.

After flicking through the scores of channels on the TV in the corner for half an hour with nothing at all worth watching, Miller got up and went to shower.

Even that he was taking for granted. His home in Hartlepool was similar to most other household's in the north-east and only had a bath to soak in. For most folks that would be once, perhaps twice a week.

He shaved and as he did so and looked in the mirror, he reflected on his reflection; Ciara was right. He did have a healthy glow to his face.

Chapter 33:
Folk Band Night in The Doyle's

The noise from the big room below met him halfway as he descended the stairs; it was clearly very busy and raucous in the bar. Ciara was behind the bar, pitching in with the lads, they were working flat out. Over their heads, at the back of the bar, there was a silver tin wine bucket. Whenever they got a tip, they rang the bell next to it to alert the customers a tip was going in the hope they would get the message and add to it. They were quite a sight to watch. They could serve three or four customers each simultaneously, set the pump to flow whilst taking the next order. Poetry in motion, there was clearly a knack to be a barman in a busy pub. These young fellas were certainly experts.

Miller made himself busy. He went around the room along with the two young college girls hired just for the Christmas season and collected all the spent glasses and cleared the finished plates of food from the tables. It was chaos, but he was glad of something to do. The group in the corner, young crowd, looked affluent were a little too raucous.

Ciara called over to Sean one of the barmen, 'We checked all their IDs, didn't we? One or two of them look as if they could be only 20. I don't want us getting into trouble for serving minors.'

Sean walked across to the group, he was of a similar age, perhaps two years older that's all.

With a really pleasant smile, he opened; 'Heh folks, all having a great time here are we? Listen, I don't want to sound like a pleb but the boss just got word that we might be getting a visit by Boston's finest tonight and we don't want to lose our licence on account of serving underage drinkers. Perhaps we can just do a quick check of your IDs please, it would be a big help.' Miller listened in.

Not only was he a great barman but his disposition of getting on their wavelength was exceptional. The entire group reached into their personal belongings and coats to fish out a small state ID.

All except the young Asian man, probably Korean, he looked at the others with guilty written all over the place.

'Do we have a problem, sir?' Sean asked him politely.

'I haven't brought mine with me tonight; perhaps I can show it next time?'

Sean reached down and picked up the half drank beer from in front of the man.

'Sorry, sir, I don't make the rules, you are welcome to stay, have something to eat and stick with the soft drinks, that OK with you?'

'I suppose so,' he answered awkwardly.

That was that.

17 was the age they could volunteer for the Armed services and go to fight and die in Vietnam, but 21 was the legal age to drink, no exceptions.

Back in Hartlepool, most young men were regulars in their local by 15, 16 at the latest.

Miller walked across to the bar where Sean had returned and was pulling more beers.

'Heh Sean, nicely handled, I was impressed, no angst or challenge there, you have a real professional way with you, well done.'

'Thanks, Miller, I appreciate that coming from you, it's all in a day's work. Do you think you can come into the cellar and watch me change the barrel, then next time you will be able to do it yourself? There is a bit of a knack to it.'

'Happy to.'

At 9:30, the serving of food was finished. In the corner, three musicians were setting up their gear. It didn't take them long and soon melodious music was livening up the already busy bar.

The girl was magic on the flute, so talented and a beauty to boot. Of the two men, one played a guitar and the other sang and drummed with his Bodhran, a traditional Irish instrument favoured by the folk bands of the day. The place was soon rocking; it was easy to see why Irish pubs the world over were so popular. The Bostonians played there part too, they cheered and applauded to show their appreciation of the band.

After the second set, the musical troupe stood down and an open mike was offered to the punters.

There was no shortage of takers, first one of the young men from the group who showed their ID got up and obviously could sing and set about to impress the girls in his group. An older man, clearly a country and western devotee, bashed out a reasonable rendition of Dylan's blowing in the wind, slightly changing the mood before one of the barmen jumped up and totally nailed Fields of Athenry, one of the songs Miller had practiced at the training camp on the English coast.

Miller couldn't believe the time; the clock had already passed 1 am and the bar was as full as it had been at 9 pm. Ciara came across and slipped her arm around his waist.

'Listen, I'm sorry about being a bitch earlier, I can be a handful at times, it's OK about the ball, I've been on my own for the past three years, what the heck, another one won't make any difference. I am just pleased you're here, now, with me.'

'Well, thing is, I've been thinking about it too. I am a selfish pig; I've been on my own too long. I can see it's important to you and after all I'm only here because you bought me the flight. So, yes, I will go; in fact, I'd love to!'

Ciara looked in at him, she never answered with any words, she just pulled on his arm and led him to the back room and then the stairs, 'Can't talk here, let's find somewhere private.'

They climbed the stairs and on reaching the apartment, she pushed open the door, turned and placed her arms around his neck before jumping up so her legs were wrapped around his waist.

She gave him the biggest, wettest kiss, full on his lips.

Miller fell slightly forward, off balanced by Ciara hanging off his neck and they both tipped forwards towards the bed laughing. She was pulling his crew neck sweater over his arms, undressing him.

Standing up, she quickly pulled off her dress over her head in one move and pushed him backwards.

Now wearing only bra and knickers, she sat on his lap and kissed him full on.

Miller picked her up, keeping her in the same position wrapped around his waist and waddled across to the captain's chair near the desk.

Putting her down, he ordered her to kneel, facing away from him, with her hands placed on the back of the swivel chair.

After several seconds of fumbling and some giggling from her, she felt him enter from behind, she was still wearing the panties; he had just pushed the gusset to one side and forced his cock into her. The bra was still in place too, he just pushed the cups on top of her breasts.

She remained in the kneeling position, facing the desk and the big mirror above it whilst he pounded her from behind. She watched her own facial expressions change as the pleasure coursed through her body. The mirror added to the decadence of their coupling.

It was raunchy, raw sex, lustful rutting, just like the cave man he was. She was loving it!

He held her by the breasts pulling and twisting her nipples whilst all the time his rhythmic thrusts pleasured her deeply.

He paused, lifted her off the chair and lowered her onto the floor, whilst she crouched on her hands and knees on the carpet, he remounted her doggy style.

His penis penetrated even deeper. After a few minutes of thrusting, he reached under her and grabbed one of her arms, so she had no option but to drop her head onto the carpet.

Lifting her hands behind her back and holding them there as if they were bound by a rope, the only support was her cheek which lay sideways onto the floor to prop up her head.

He was pinning her arms behind her as he continued to pound away and then release. He ejaculated with a large growl. Rough sex, the man was pure Neanderthal, but it was just amazing.

The sex was narcotic, the more he gave her the more she wanted.

Ciara rolled over onto her back, 'Where did that come from? Have you just come back from six months in a monastery, Miller? That's was totally awesome.'

'It's all your fault, you turn me on, you are a very sexy woman.'

'I'm glad about that and more importantly I can't tell you how much it means to me that you've changed you mind about the ball, really, I'm so thrilled, I can't wait to show you off, you handsome brute!'

'What am I supposed to wear? The wardrobe of a street tramp is very limited, you know.'

'That's the easiest bit,' replied Ciara. 'All the men will be wearing the same, black tie, and before you say anything, we will just hire one for the night. Most folks do that anyway, no point in buying a suit to wear once a year,' she lied.

'OK, let's go back downstairs, no doubt the tongues will be wagging as to where we are.'

'Let them wag,' replied Miller. He genuinely didn't care what others thought about him, in that respect he was a totally free man.

The singing continued until 3 am. It was a totally brilliant night. Miller couldn't remember the last time he'd had so much fun.

He even astounded himself, he got up and sang the only songs he knew most of the words for, "The Boxer" by Simon and Garfunkel and his favourite, Neil Diamond's "Sweet Caroline". The best bit was all the guests sang along too.

They left Sean to throw the last guests out and retired to bed, this time to crash out. It had been a long and eventful night. As she slipped into a deep drunken sleep, Ciara turned to him and murmured, 'Good night, I love you, Mr Miller.'

Chapter 34:
Visit by the Plumbers

Sunday had been a very quiet sort of day; the Dutch proverb rang true: 'tis many a good day spoilt by a good night. It didn't matter that they were lazing about all day, they had enjoyed the previous night and it had been memorable for many reasons.

Monday came around all too quickly, they both rose together, Ciara was booked on the 8:05 am train out of South Boston to New York, she was going away on business for two nights. Miller was planning a ride around the sights of Boston; Ciara thought it was a great idea. She wouldn't have if she had any inkling that he was to be joined by the tour leader: Cindy.

But that was not until the afternoon, there was more pressing skulduggery which needed his attention before he could contemplate a bike ride.

That's when she dropped the bombshell that shook Miller to the core.

'Oh, one last thing before I go, I had a long chat with Mac last night, he sends his regards, I told him you were making yourself useful around the place and earning your keep. He asked me to ask you which cemetery your mum and dad are buried in, a bit of an odd request I know, he wants to send someone around to the grave as you haven't been around for many years and don't have any brothers and sisters. Unusual I know, but he is such a strong Christian it's the sort of thing he thinks is important. You can tell me when I get back on late on Thursday and I'll pass it on. Don't forget, if you need to get hold of me, the name and number of my hotel in Manhattan is written on the note paper by the side of the bed.'

Ciara was fussing all the way up to the taxi arriving to take her to the station.

'I don't think you should go bike riding; you look very pale actually, perhaps you should get some rest, do a bit of reading perhaps? Here is the taxi, give us a hug, oh, I wish you were coming but I've got lots of meetings with accountants going over lines and lines of numbers, all very boring,' she lied.

Miller leant down and pecked her on the lips and tapped her rump, 'Have a great time, I will be OK here, don't worry that you've abandoned me completely.'

'Oh, don't say that.'

'I'm only kidding, go on, get on your way.'

The tyres of the Boston taxi screeched as the driver accelerated into the early morning traffic. Miller pulled the number out of his pocket and rang as per the instructions he'd been given.

The pub was very quiet, it was Sean's day off and, in the lounge, the only people present were the two lady cleaners. He was alone, but not for long.

The plumber's van pulled up within five minutes, they must have been stood off waiting for the green light.

The side door opened directly opposite the private side entrance to Ciara's apartment.

Donnelly must have travelled independently as he turned from the corner of the street to greet Miller with a brusque handshake.

Four men all in coveralls and wearing plastic gloves on their hands and covers over their shoes spilled out of the van, marched into the building and climbed the stairs.

Once in the main room, Miller took Chuck across to the dressing room alcove, their below all the dresses hung on hangers was a tall safe.

'Miller, this is the MOE (Methods of Entry expert). Stand to one side and let him work his magic.'

'AMSEC gun safe,' the expert stated. 'As we thought, it's an old obsolete model, stopped making these in the 50s, must have bought it second hand.'

In under a minute, the door to the safe was swung open.

'That quick, you have got to be kidding me,' Miller was gobsmacked.

Next up was the camera man with a large polaroid. He took several pictures of the inside of the door onto which was hung a short sawn-off shot gun and a machine pistol. Diligently he took pictures of each of the shelves to ensure once removed they could be returned in the exact same place.

The contents of each shelf were removed and placed diligently on the fold away table the specialist had carried up the stairs with them.

Folders upon folders of detailed accounts.

The plumbers set to work with their cameras. They carefully and expertly took shots of each page on the legers.

Lists of address were next.

Several were for overseas.

Miller turned as Chuck spoke, 'What's in the desk?' Without waiting for an answer, he nodded to the MOE man who shuffled his lock pick into the tiny keyhole in the desktop. Seconds later he rolled up the desk. It was completely empty save for a couple of bits of stationery.

'Nothing, boss.'

On the base of the desk was a base blotting sheet.

'What about this? Take a good look,' Chuck ordered.

Another of the plumbers sprinkled a white power across the surface and then shone a bright light.

'Bingo, it's a name and some numbers.'

'Tariq Maka**ah 17th, time is six. Can't make out all the letters of the surname, it's definitely Arabic though.'

'Obviously. Is it pm or am?'

'Assume pm sir.'

'That's this Tuesday, tomorrow, when is she due back, Miller?'

'Wednesday evening, late, about 10:30.'

'We can run the name through our database and see how many matches for Arabs resident in New York, probably thousands but we'll try anyway.'

The last shelf had contained a black moleskin package.

A plumber opened it up carefully like an expectant child at Christmas; it was quite heavy and only semi-solid. It revealed a rectangle of money. All in $100 bills.

'How much?'

'I'm guessing between $250–300K, sir.'

'Phew, that's quite a nest egg your girlfriend is sat on, a cool quarter of a million at least, secured in a safe that a 12-year-old kid could open. These guys are amateurs.'

'Shall we check anywhere else, sir?'

'What do you think, Miller, any secret hideaways or any other safes around here?'

'No idea, none I've seen.'

'Let's take a look, there is no personal jewellery in here, maybe there is another safe.'

Chuck was right with his hunch. On the top shelf of the wardrobe, there was a small strong box. One of the plumbers placed it on the desk and opened it with his pick again.

Another jackpot. Seven passports, two with Ciara's picture, one under a false name, the rest were of men aged between 25 and 55.

'More money, smaller bills this time, perhaps another $12K, boss, the rest junk: earrings, rings, bracelets, two watches, personal effects. There was one nice necklace, three strands of pearl with a black pearl drop pendant. Family heirloom, most likes.'

'OK, get busy; I want pics of them all.'

Less than seven minutes later, the team were collapsing the kit and packing it away.

From the time they arrived in the apartment to the time they left, 12 minutes, 15 tops. They were slick, very slick, they were clearly professional and well experienced at such interventions.

'Your little princess is up to her neck here, Miller, based on what we have seen today, we could send her down for a 15-20 stretch, more if we link it to funding terrorist organisation, life maybe.'

Miller nodded his acknowledgment.

'Give me a ring later this afternoon, better still, lets meet over at the yacht club at six, we can chat then.'

Miller nodded.

The room emptied as the plumbers and their van pulled off down the street.

No one in the pub was any wiser as to what had just transpired. Ciara's trip had provided the perfect timing. Miller's stomach was churning. Life imprisonment for Ciara, what the hell had he done to her.

He walked down to the kitchenette and made himself a drink. When in doubt, brew up was the British Army's maxim. *It usually worked, shouldn't think it will this time*, thought Miller.

Then his mind cleared, and he remembered he'd forgotten to mention his other major problem as of today to Chuck. What the hell was he expected to tell Mac about his parent's gravestone?

They were both alive and well and still living in Hartlepool, more comfortable than they had been for several years due to the beneficiaries of Miller's monthly allowance. Ill-gotten gains from his spy work, which included shopping the only person who'd made him happy since he was a child. Just what had he done?

One thing was for certain, he would have to unarranged his little cycling trip with Cindy today. He felt like shit, he was in the middle of a swamp full of alligators with only himself to blame.

He was not in any mood to engage anyone until he could see some sort of path forward, both for himself and his lover.

It was time to get his thinking cap on.

Chapter 35:
Cork Target Recce

It had been a ball ache of a drive down from Belfast. Stop, start, rain sleet, wind, the elements had thrown the lot at them to prevent them from reaching the very south of the Ireland, Cork. Nairn had chosen a van to go south. It was an Austin A35, with 1100CC engine. This specific model was only about five years old and had been overhauled by the RCT (Royal Core of Transport) so the engine was well tuned and could be relied upon. The fleet of cars owned by the British Army numbered in their hundreds and they were used extensively for clandestine reasons across the six counties.

One the side of the van, the previous owners livery could still be seen although only faintly. That was deliberate too. It was meant to look like someone had bought an ex-trade van at an auction, that way it was hoped it would blend in and not draw attention.

Of course, none of that troubled Nairn. He liked to sail close to the edge of legitimacy. He was not going to be using the car for reconnaissance in the north, more emboldened than most; he was driving south, all the way to Cork to be exact.

They stopped at Mitchelstown, some hour short of their destination to fill up with petrol and to relieve themselves.

For this Mission, Nairn had chosen a new member to the team. He was a Corporal seconded in from the Royal Irish Regiment. Fergus McMenemy was a staunch patriot. His Belfast brogue was as thick as a plate of cold porridge. Nairn liked that.

His father had fought for the British in the 2nd World War and his grandfather both in the Boer War and the Great War of 1914. He was a practicing Christian too. Almost to a man in the RIR they were of the Protestant faith. Many had strong links, brothers, friends with the outlawed paramilitary organisations active in Ulster such as Ulster Volunteer Force (UVF) and the Ulster Freedom Fighters (UFF) The line between loyalty to the Crown and loyalty to one's family and friends was very blurred at times and it was inevitable this led to numerous security breaches. Many documents naming suspected IRA operatives found their way into these rival paramilitary groups.

Nairn sent the young Corporal in to pay for the fuel and to buy them both a snack.

In just over an hour later, they were cruising around the centre of Cork in their van in the area of St Finn Barre's Cathedral looking for digs. They needed a place to stay; Nairn spotted what he was looking for, an artisan's bed and breakfast lodging. On the pretence he wanted to check something out, he again sent Fergus to sort things out. The corporal, keen to make a good impression, did as he was bid. A few minutes later, he returned to the van to tell his officer that he'd been successful and that he'd acted on his own initiative to book them both into the last available room, a shared twin bedroom and hoped this was acceptable. When Nairn never confirmed his agreement immediately, he sheepishly added, the rate included a cooked breakfast.

'Splendid!' was the officer's response.

The two soldiers lifted their own respective bags out of the car taking car to lock it up. Nairn slung the sailors kit bag over one shoulder and ordered Fergus to lead the way.

When they got to their room, Fergus brewed them a cup of tea with the kettle provided.

Nairn lifted his pistol, the Beretta out of the kitbag and onto the bed.

'Don't know why you brought that other antique down here, it's only a quick recce, the Browning is just fine. Where did you get it from anyway, it's not standard issue?'

The corporal was carrying a concealed 9mm standard issue Browning pistol as he'd been ordered too, whereas his superior officer was carrying both the standard issue Browning and the illegal, non-issue Beretta pistol. Oh, and two spare magazines of ammunition for each of them. As far as Fergus was concerned had they been stopped at any time once they had crossed the border into the Republic of Ireland they would have been arrested and sent down for a long time.

Nairn was so well tooled up he could have taken on a full section of the Garda.

Nairn switched on the TV, BBC of course was showing, the Irish have always enjoyed the privilege of being able to tune into the BBC channels when folk on mainland in Britain had to pay a license fee. For people in the Republic it was free, an Ariel's transmitting electronic waves cannot just stop at a sovereign border! Nairn wasn't interested at all in the TV, the noise it emitted was useful to drown out the sound he made whilst he meticulously cleaned both of his pistols.

'Heh Fergus, I noticed a chippie at the end of the road, how about you go and buy us both some supper?'

'OK, my Lord,' he said sarcastically. 'What would you like?'

'Fish and chips laced with vinegar but not too much salt please,' he smiled.

Fergus pulled on his coat, a short bomber jacket, and left to do the chippie run. Nairn went back to this cleaning. Once he was sure that each micro speck of dust was removed, and all the working parts were lightly oiled, he reassembled his weapons and placed them under his bed.

Fergus was soon back with their supper and it smelt delicious.

'Nothing better than fish and chips from old newspapers eh Fergus, beats all your fancy west end restaurants, trust me.'

'I wouldn't know, I've only ever been to London once.'

The two men ate in silence clearly hungry after their long journey. There was no connection between them, Fergus was conscious that he was a lowly corporal and his roommate was from the privileged officer elite. There could never be true rapport.

'Let's get some rest, we've a long day ahead of us tomorrow.' He then leant over the side of the bed and switched off the TV and the main lights.

Both men slept soundly, and Fergus was first to wander down the corridor to use the only communal shower. When he returned Nairn was sat on the bed dressed and waiting for him to breakfast.

'No shower for you, sir? Sorry, I mean Bob.'

Nairn was clearly annoyed. 'What the fuck? Don't ever do that again.'

'I'm sorry, it just slipped out. I'm very sorry, it won't happen again. Bob.'

At the breakfast table, Nairn kept his head buried in last night's newspaper they had purchased from the garage and let Fergus order them both a cooked breakfast.

'Not from these parts, just visiting, are we?' asked the inquisitive landlady.

'No, that's true, we're down to look at a house a client has recently bought over in Midleton, needs a lot of work seemingly, asked us to take a quick look to price the work, that's all.'

'Oh really? I can help you out there, I know all the best builders for 100 miles, anything you need doing just let me know.'

'Great, that's a stroke of luck, we haven't seen it yet, but we'll take your card and give you a ring when we've worked out just what needs doing to it.'

'Where's the house exactly?'

'Oh, again we've not been just yet, we have a sketch in the van, it's about 3 miles outside of Midleton, you take the Rosslare Road and then turn off left somewhere, I'll expect we'll not have too much trouble finding it, and if we get stuck, we can always ask eh.'

'OK, well you be sure to give me a ring, now won't you? There are plenty of cowboys out there, folk who tell you they are a plumber and they don't know their arse from their elbow, trust me, I've employed them in the past but no more. I've a regular odd job man, Noel, nothing he can't turn his hand to, for sure.'

'Thanks, we'll be off now, we have a long day ahead and want to drive back before its dark. We only have short days now.'

'Yes love, you carry on, it was nice to meet you both, if you are back down any time give me a call and I will be happy to put you up again. Most of my guests are regulars, you know.' Nairn smiled at her and nodded an acknowledgement but still never spoke.

Slamming the driver's door shut, Fergas gave out a loud trump.

'Jesus, that was like the Spanish Inquisition, I thought she was going to offer to come over to Midleton with us at one stage. I told you we should have put our doss bags in and just kipped out somewhere quiet, we'd have not drawn as much attention if we'd done that.'

'Just drive,' ordered Nairn as he wound down the window to let the nauseating smell out.

As they drove the 20 minutes or so across to Midleton, Nairn buried his head in the map studying the local features and various routes around their person of interest target.

'OK, this is the pub Miller mentioned in his report. Find somewhere to pull over. Drop me off, give me ten minutes and I'll meet you back here and don't go anywhere.'

Without waiting for any response, Nairn climbed out of the van and set off down the road to the house which Miller had lodged in overnight.

He counted down the numbers, all odd on this side of the street. *Just as Miller had noted, he is very good*, thought Nairn. Number 31, bingo, this is it. Now to the end of the street to the alley, yes, then he said the girls lived on the end terrace on the opposite side of the alley. Now for the front, first house.

'Oops, sorry.' Just as he passed the front door of the targets house, the door opened, and a teenage girl nearly knocked him over as she rushed out of the house. Presumably she was late for a bus. Seconds later the door slammed again, and Nairn turned to see another girl rush out too, this time she was even more in a hurry. Great, house confirmed, target confirmed.

Nairn walked down to the end of the street, turned and retraced his steps.

It was his lucky day, as he approached the target house, who should walk out and towards him? None other than Colin Ahern, IRA Brigade Commander of Cork and the person of interest, reason they were in Cork in the first place. He was unshaven and scruffy; no coat, just a V-neck woollen jumper with no shirt underneath which exposed his neck and the hairs on his upper chest.

Clearly, he wasn't going far.

The two men's eyes met. Ahern was switched on; he'd never seen the man approaching him before and that made him uneasy. It was not a street used to strangers, he knew everybody in this area and more importantly they knew him and what he was capable of, he was a respected and even feared man. He suddenly felt vulnerable.

He was right to be unnerved. As they closed, Nairn offered a boyish charming smile as they drew within ten meters of each other. Ahern scowled; he wasn't about to get friendly with a stranger. He was too wrapped up in his own feelings to react to the movement.

Nairn, still smiling, reached inside his jacket revealing the Beretta. Ahern was taken completely unaware and checked his stride. The street reverberated as the pistol was brought to bear, Nairn fired off two rounds in quick succession. Double tap, centre of seen mass, just as he'd been taught and had practiced, literally hundreds of time before. Ahern's legs buckled, his arms came up to his chest as the blood started to appear immediately from the entry wounds and he collapsed in a heap to the floor. He was dead.

Coolly, Nairn stood over him and as Ahern lay there his final facial expression was one of pain, he fired a third round into the centre of his forehead at close range, just to make extra sure.

He broke out immediately into a jog, still carrying the pistol in his right hand and turned the corner, crossed the mouth of the alley and continued to jog down the street. The van was parked 100 meters away, but Fergus alerted by the gun fire had started the engines was already panicking and wondering what action to take. He now gunned the vehicle forward, meeting his partner halfway down the road. Nairn slipped nimbly into the passenger seat and bellowed for him to move quickly. Several people, women and children with maybe one or two men were already on their doorsteps as the van sped past. It was clear the van would be made, and the registration numbered.

'What happened?' screamed Fergus.

'I was just doing a walk by the house, first time was OK, as I turned to walk back and meet you out stepped Ahern with a weapon raised, he missed, but I didn't. That was it, nothing more to tell,' he lied.

'Don't worry, I have a plan B prepared just in case we ran into trouble.'

The officer fished into his bag. 'The next train to Dublin from Cork station is in 45 minutes.

We'll catch that.'

'And the motor?'

'We'll burn it, it was made.'

Nairn turned back to the map.

'Pull left up ahead, it's a minor road leading to Cork town. Put your foot down, overtake this bus.'

As they accelerated to pass the bus Nairn looked behind him,

'It's heading to Cork, keep the pedal to the metal.'

The speeding van swerved down the country lane passing an odd row of houses and an isolated farm. After two miles, they were on the outskirts of the conurbation. Nairn spotted what he was looking for, a bus stop.

'Stop, turn in here quickly lad.'

He jumped out of the car and opened a five-bar gate into a farmer's field. In it was a large empty barn.

'Pull the car in here, get our grab bags out and be quick about it.'

Whilst the young corporal was emptying the boot of the two overnight bags and a spare coat Nairn was making a long rag by ripping a cloth used for demisting the windows.

'Quick, take the bags over to the bus stop and when it approaches flag it down; I'll be over in a jiff.'

Fergus was in a cold sweat. The adrenaline was on full flow now. As the bus approached, he stuck out his arm signalling for it to stop. The bus slowed to a stop, as it did, Nairn sauntered confidently over it, took his bag from Fergus and stepped by the driver, leaving the corporal to pay for the two fares into Cork. He walked to the back of the bus on the lower deck; there were only two other elderly people and a young mother struggling with a small boy. He took up a position on the back seat. The bus accelerated away. As it did so, Fergus made his way down the bus to join his partner. From the rear-view window, the smoke was already rising above the barn, the car was well and truly alight.

Nairn was the first to speak in a soft voice to ensure the words only reached the intended ears.

'Don't you just love this job, you never know what is around the corner, do you?' he was smiling broadly.

'I can't believe you,' was the retort.

The journey was short, only several minutes, the bus made only two more stops before reaching the city centre, the two men alighted to set to walk to find the railway station.

Of course, by now the pattern was set. It was Fergus who had to queue to buy the two tickets to Dublin. They sat in different carriages; Nairn joined a father and two sons going up to Dublin to watch a big football game. Fergus sat by himself, but he could see down the carriage that his boss was enjoying the journey much better than he was. Out of his bag, Nairn had pulled out a pack of cards and was entertaining the two boys who were maybe 10 and 12 with his tricks, they clearly enjoyed his company and were smiling happily.

How can that be? thought Fergus. The man's just blown away another human being, they were probably being hunted right now, stuck on a train for at least three hours and he is laughing and entertaining two children. It was a surreal moment.

Dublin couldn't have come quick enough; Fergus had counted down each station they stopped at, each time fully expecting the train to be invaded by armed police and for them to be arrested.

He'd even moved his bag down three seats to distance himself from it. It contained his Browning pistol. Nairn was still carrying his on his person.

Once on the station concourse, Nairn assumed control again. He went to the nearest phone box and made a short call. They both went out onto the station entrance and in under ten minutes, a white soft top Morris minor pulled up with an attractive young lady, about 25, driving.

Nairn pulled back the passenger seat and encouraged the Ulsterman into the backseat with both bags. Still smiling Nairn leaned over and kissed the woman on her cheek before she engaged the gear lever and pulled away. In only a few minutes, they pulled into a large Victorian house with a long drive, wet and covered with decaying sycamore leaves.

'Be a good man, bring in the bags; we are staying over here tonight.'

Fergus sat in the back seat, alone, gathering his thoughts, his two companions walked off arm in arm to the house. He'd never felt more like a spare part than he did right now. No one had made any introductions, he felt like a black servant running after his colonial master. He couldn't believe Nairn's disposition; he was still on a high.

After he'd been shown to where he would be sleeping the introductions had finally been made. The young woman it turned out was a classmate from his time at university in Dublin and was called Rosie.

'Nice big house you have here.'

Fergus was on a fishing expedition, trying to understand more about his host.

'Don't be silly it's not mine its daddies. He is over in Riyadh working.'

'Saudi you say? What is it he does?'

'He is a gynaecologist.'

'He is a Catholic gynaecologist to Muslim ladies in Saudi Arabia?'

'Yes, apparently, he's quite good, they all like him, mummy and daddy have been there five years now. They abandoned me as soon as I graduated.'

Mummy and daddy? Who called their parents that at 26 years of age? Her accent was that of a plumby English female, yet she was born in Dublin and had never lived anywhere else. There wasn't a trace of any Irishness. She worked for a magazine and had her own column. Fergus had never experienced the Dublin aristocracy before, he was bewildered. It was another world; he'd left Belfast only yesterday, the city where you took your life in your hands just to go into the city. The threat of bombs or assassinations was a constant and ever-present daily risk.

'I have phoned a brief report in Fergus, I'll file a full one tomorrow when we get back to Palace Barracks. Don't fret, it's all OK they are sending a driver down to pick us up at 10 am.'

'Your call, Bob,' he almost said "boss" but remembered not to.

'Good, well that's all settled. Rosie and I are going out for drinks, will you be OK here? There is a nice library, a TV, or snooker room if that's your bag?'

'I'll be fine, Bob. You and the young lady can go out and enjoy yourselves.'

When they left, Fergus wandered the several reception rooms which formed the ground floor. It was simply the largest home he'd ever stayed in and the young lady was living here all alone. At the rear of the house was a drawing room with floor to ceiling French windows and heavy drapes. He turned the door handle, it was open. *How careless*, he thought. Stepping out onto a veranda, the cold air rushed passed him into the room, he peered into the darkness, not only was the house not over looked it enjoyed a huge empty grass field of several acres, here in the centre of Dublin, who were these people, he felt like an alien. He picked up a magazine which was lying on the floor next to a chaise lounge, Horse and Hound. *What else could it have been?* he thought to himself. The TV was a bit of a challenge, but he eventually figured out how to turn it on. The news report when it came on caused him to jump out of seat and stand upright two foot away from the set.

'A sectarian killing took place in Midleton, Cork today,' the reporter was standing on a rain-soaked payment in front of a crime scene. Two Ulster Freedom fighters had callously cut down a local innocent man in his prime, husband and father to three children as he walked to the corner shop for a newspaper. Their getaway van was found burning in a nearby farmer's field. A nationwide hunt for the men was being mounted as the violence of Northern Ireland had now been exported to this peaceful and law-abiding neighbourhood. The dead man did not have any connection what's so ever with any para military organisation and it was believed it was nothing more than a revenge attack for recent assassinations allegedly carried out by the IRA against members of the Protestant communities in North Ireland. It was a sorry day for the whole of Ireland. It was the first time the Troubles had found their way down to this peaceful town and it marked an escalation of the senseless sectarian violence. The bishop of Cork had condemned the cold-blooded murder and would be offering a mass for the poor lost soul tomorrow evening. It was a time for the community to pull together and help this family in their hour of need.

Innocent man, my arse, thought Fergus, they were working on first grade intelligence that this poor family man was, until yesterday, a violent aggressor of the Catholic scum, the IRA. It would be only a matter of time before the owner of the Lodgings came forward with descriptions; they needed to get out of south and quickly but where was his commanding officer? Out enjoying himself somewhere in Dublin bars, that's where.

Of course, it was not likely him they would be looking for, it was him who had done all the talking wherever they met. What next? Even if they made it back to Belfast, they would face court-martial for sure. They had crossed illegally into a foreign independent country, with weapons, and had killed an innocent man when all they were meant to do was to gather intelligence? It was an almighty cock up and Fergus felt physically sick. He was going to jail, either in Ireland or in Northern Ireland, but jail it was for him.

Chapter 36:
US Marine Corps HQ

Miller was lying on the bed when he heard a voice shout up the stairs for him. As he descended, one of the barmen shouted to him that the American guy was on the phone for him.

Miller listened in before answering.

'Yes sure, happy to, can be over there in about an hour.'

'OK?' Questioned the barman.

'Yes, sure, it was just Chuck, he is over at the yacht club and he is there with one of his cousins who wants to meet me, seemingly he is booking a holiday to England and wants to pick my brain. Not sure I'm the best travel agent there is but I guess I owe him a favour after Saturday. It's not as if I am doing anything.'

'Tell him not to waste his time, it's Ireland he should be visiting, castles and queens and the best countryside the world can offer!'

'I'll be sure to tell him that,' laughed Miller.

Miller walked to the junction at the end of the street and waited a few minutes before hailing a taxi.

'Where to buddy?'

'495 Summer Street please, driver.'

The building was, as Chuck had advised, a recruiting centre for the American Marine Corps. Miller paid the taxi driver for the short ride and walked up to the security window.

'I'm expected.'

'Full name, sir.'

'Miller, sorry I mean Algeron Miller.'

'ID?'

'Sorry?'

'ID, sir.'

'What, you mean like my passport? Sorry, I didn't bring any.'

'Sir, this America, it is mandatory to carry ID on your person at all times. Perhaps sir can return to his place of residence and return when you have proof of your identification?'

'Sorry, young man, I have been forgetful, I apologise. Could I ask a favour perhaps?' Miller decided it needed a charm offensive.

'I was asked over here on an urgent basis, can you please call my host and explain I need to return and collect my passport and can return later this afternoon.' The young Marine Corp soldier at the desk hesitated.

'Do you have a contact name sir?'

'Yes, it's Chuck Donnelly, or perhaps Charles? He is a government employee, I believe.' The Marine checked his clipboard of daily orders and right at the top underlined was the note to expect an English visitor called Miller. He suddenly felt very foolish.

'Sorry, you are expected sir, I will ring Mr Donnelly immediately.' Chuck waived as he soon as he saw Miller in the small anteroom.

He used his ID card to swipe the lock and the door opened outwards and leant his head out.

'Nice to see you again, Miller, come on through.'

'Sir,' the Marine intervened. 'The gentleman is not signed in and had no identification on his person.'

'That won't be necessary.' He blanked the Marine from any possible further protest by staring at him. The young Marine's cheeks flushed; he didn't like the fact they shared the building with so many spooks. Miller followed his host down a white stark corridor and through three sets of double doors. They climbed up a single flight of stairs and then passed through one more doorway. The office was huge, open plan; it was populated with dozens of non-descript individual cubicles manned by both male and female workers. Several looked up to see who was entering but offered neither a greeting nor even a nod to acknowledge him. Miller guessed there were upwards of forty people working there.

The operations room opened in front of them, along three walls were notes and pictures and all manner of documents. Several he recognised. Miller also recognised two of the plumbers who had searched the apartment yesterday.

'Folks, listen up, this here is Mr Miller. He is with our cousins in London and is here to help us on this case.'

Several of the team raised their hand and said, 'Hi.'

'Take a seat and I will bring you up to speed. You remember Charlie over there; well he's worked on your stuff all night since we got back from your apartment.'

'It's big, much bigger than we thought, and we now have two branches working on your case.'

'How so?' asked Miller.

'We have been in touch with New York department. Our office down there has quickly scrambled a team. We've added a tail to your girlfriend and bugged her hotel room.'

'You've lost me, I'm afraid I don't know why Ciara's trip to view the accounts of other pubs would create all this fuss?'

'Do you remember the name "Tariq" we picked up off the blotter? Well, we came up bingo almost straight away. He runs an intelligence cell for the Libyans out of a carpet shop on 5th Avenue. He has been on our watch list for two years. Seems he's just got very active. Our President, Richard Nixon that is, takes a strong personal interest in all things Libyan.'

'Still not getting it,' replied Miller honestly.

'OK, Miller, take a seat, let me give you a quick potted history of why Libya was so strategically important to us and why Nixon takes a keen interest. First of all, there is the money. In 1968, the balance of payments with Libya showed $800 million in our favour. That's a lot of greenbacks for uncle Sam's coffers. All stopped now. American oil companies Esso and Occidental were big players in the discovery and exploitation of the Libyan oil fields. Your BP were out there too though not as big as Esso. Our interests weren't just about oil. They were strong military reasons we were in Libya too. The Wheelus airbase was the US largest Military operational facility outside of America. At its peak we had over 15,000 people stationed there. That's big, Miller, very big.'

Miller had no prior knowledge of the base; he'd never even heard of it.

'Even without mid-air refuelling Wheelus airbase brought our B50 Super fortress Bombers well within range of all of the Soviet Union's strategic oil refineries and reserves along the Black Sea, the Caucasus and the Urals. Take out their Oil and what are they going to put in their Tanks if they want to invade Europe, fresh air? We learned that from Hitler's mistake he failed to close those fields down in '42. Those oil facilities are a priority one target for our strategic bomber command. We also often used the bombing range at El Hotia deep in the country to train our fighter pilots as well as the big bombers. Most of our bomber pilots cut their teeth on missions in Libya. All that ended in 1969, we, that is, the CIA fell asleep at the wheel so to speak. Congress has never let us forget it. That was the year Nixon visited CIA headquarters, the first President to do so whilst still in office. King Idris, the tame, pro' US ruler was overthrown in a coup by a certain Muammar Qaddafi.

'Qaddafi, a Bedouin, was literally born in a tent. He joined the military, rose to the meagre rank of colonel and yet managed by his charisma and charm rallied other younger offices of the Signals Regiment to stage a coup to seize control of Libya in 1969. Unbelievable that could happen, but it did. We didn't see it coming and no one had ever heard of Qaddafi until it was too late. So, he went from tent dweller to Billionaire just about over night! Ever since he gained power, he has been hell bent of funding terrorism, starting with the PLO and now it seems the IRA.

'As I said, Nixon loathes him with a vengeance and would love to overthrow him, trust me.

'Nixon's war chest of election campaign funds were beneficiaries of many big dollars both from Esso and Occidental. They all lost out when this relatively junior officer gave the country his own makeover and nationalised all the refineries and oilfields. He would still be in his tent riding on camels if it hadn't been for good old American ingenuity in discovering the oil in the first place. His wealth was paid for by the sweat from American brows.

'It doesn't end there. The man is a big problem to us and especially so to our close allies, the Israelis. He is funding the organisations who've swore their lives away to destroy the State of Israel and knock it off the map. The Arabs are all still smarting from having their backsides well and truly kicked in '67 and so now they've turned to acts of terrorism to get back at the Jews.

'I am sure I don't need to tell you how much Capitol Hill is influenced by the Jewish Diaspora, they just about run Washington, unseen and some would say unchecked.'

In truth Miller had no idea of the influence of anyone or anything American, he chose not to comment.

Chuck continued:

'It doesn't surprise us they are dealing with your IRA. However, they are and now your lady is of great interest to us. I started off just looking you up as personal favour to Rosie, it's way past that stage now.

'The case file has been shared with the FBI too; all that money is undeclared tax dollars and is probably the tip of an iceberg. I'm no longer running the case either, it's been handed over to one of my superior's in New York, he's running the show down there for the next few days. He then he wants to meet you in person. Not sure whether that's a good thing or a bad thing, but it's not for debate.

'First thing I must ask you for is for your passport, now I know you don't have it with you today, but I need it first thing in the morning, insurance if you like. Don't worry, you're not under any suspicion, it is standard operating procedures in these cases, trust me. We need to know where you are and who you are with from now on. I'm not going to ask you personally, but I am warning you, the FBI will want to wire trap both you and that apartment. They will need to start building up their evidence for any future court case.'

Miller's head was reeling; he seemed to be caught in a web of intrigue which snarled him deeper and deeper. passport, wiretap, under surveillance, it was all very new territory for him.

It was Miller's turn and he suddenly remembered.

'Oh, another thing, I forgot to mention I might have a big problem myself.'

'Oh really, what's that?'

'After my trouble in the bus station, Mac began to look at me in a different light. His lieutenants were whisperings things in his ear about me, I guess. I know he ran a check on me right from the off and that seem to work out OK. Now he sent a message via Ciara that he wants to tidy up my parents' graves, as I haven't been up there these past four years. The problem is, Miller is not a real name, he doesn't have any deceased parents and as for me, mine are alive and well living in the same council house these past thirty years. Once he discovers that, my cover will be blown. After that, I'm destined for a short walk and a shallow grave. Perhaps it's time I called it quits.'

'That's all? That's easily solved, trust me. Why don't you tell Rosie herself, we have a call scheduled with her in 20 minutes?'

Miller didn't think he would get off lightly; but he would press Rosie and ask to be taken out of the field. After all, it was his life at on the line, not hers.

Miller ran through as much as he knew about the pubs under Ciara's responsibility.

Whilst he floundered because his knowledge was only slight, Chuck called one of the team over and asked for the list to be rattled off: 11 in New York, 7 in Chicago and of course the original five in Boston that made 23 in total. That wasn't a small operation it was a bloody Corporation!

No wonder Ciara worked seven days a week, thought Miller. All the details were there in the legers they had meticulously photographed.

After a coffee break in the kitchen where the conversation had focused on their huge haul of cod and other fish, Miller followed Chuck into a small room with a frosty looking elderly lady with a headset on her head. She was sat at a small table with three spare chairs, Chuck gestured for Miller to take one.

'Hello, this is London,' the call came down the line crystal clear, almost if the person was sitting in the room themselves.

'Good evening, Rosie,' opened Chuck, 'A long day for you?'

'Business as usual,' came the brief reply from a lady's voice.

'I have your man here with me.'

'Hello, Miller, how are you, how is that wrist of yours? I heard about the incident at the bus station in Dublin, but then again so did the whole of Ireland. Trouble seems to find you in all kinds of places, doesn't it? Your photo fit ID is posted on all of Dublin's police stations. The family who witnessed your assault was traumatised, but not as much as the victim, of course. I believe he lost the use of his arm completely.' Her Ulster brogue was harsh and unfriendly.

'Col Gilbert sends his regards, said something about you start remembering to play the grey man and less of a Hereford hooligan. Now down to business, you have hit a mother lode, Miller, we never thought for one minute you would be able to provide this level of intelligence, it is simply outstanding work, a breakthrough, even our new Prime Minister is delighted. We want you to cooperate fully with Chuck and his team. It is of vital importance to both the Americans and Her Majesty's security forces. Vital, I say.'

Chuck intervened, 'Miller has a minor problem he needs your help with, I will let him explain.'

'Hello Rosie, I think Mac and more importantly his henchmen are starting to doubt my cover story, ever since the bus station incident.'

'How so?'

'He has asked Ciara to get the details of my parents' graves in Hartlepool and as we both know they are alive and well.'

'Is that all? Miller, our graveyards are full of bogus deceased, I can get on it straightaway. Where would you like them to be buried?' Miller was silent, he was taken aback.

'I know there's at least two in town but the main one is at Stanton Grange, it's on the outskirts of Hartlepool.'

'OK, we will get onto it immediately, give us 2–3 days to get a headstone out up, any special requests?'

'No,' Miller gave in a hesitative response.

Donnelly gave out a chuckle.

'Didn't think that would be a problem for you, Rosie.'

'I'll ask Miller to step out now and you and I can go over the Libyan angle in more detail.' Miller took the hint and stood up to leave. As he did so, Rosie interjected.

'How are you managing for money, Miller?'

'I just have what Mac paid for me for the job, that's all.'

'OK, Chuck can advance you some, a modest amount so as not to draw to much attention.'

'And how do I explain that?'

'Miller, we checked, you have a Bradford and Bingley building society account with over 3,000 pounds in it, presumably saved whilst you were still in active service. You can say you have drawn on that. It's perfectly plausible; many street beggars leave money in their accounts. It's a fact of life.'

Street beggar, she was insulting him now and he didn't like it in front of Chuck. She was right about the money, of course, it was so long-ago Miller had put it to the back of his mind, begging made him believe he didn't have any money, how strange. He sat in the coffee room and chatted about nothing to the occasional folk who stopped by. Over an hour had passed when a secretary came looking for him.

'Mr Miller, I'm afraid folk are still engaged, so Mr Donnelly has suggested you might want to go home now. He will be in touch tomorrow morning. Please follow me.' As polite as she was it was still an assertive instruction for him to leave immediately. One strange day seemed to follow another; life now was complicated, very complicated. He wished he was back in Manchester sat on Deansgate on a damp piece of cardboard with Pilgrim by his side.

Chapter 37:
New York – Iroquois Hotel

Ciara had stayed at the hotel several times before, it felt like a second home whenever she was in Manhattan and the staff acknowledged her. The Iroquois was conveniently situated too. Sandwiched between 5th and 6th Avenue on west 44th street it was a short journey up from Grand central station and close by to Times Square. Whenever she clawed a few hours to herself, she liked to walk the two blocks to Bryant square and sit there watching the comings and goings of New York's diverse inhabitants. It was a long way from Dublin, that's for sure. In her apartment in Boston, one of the pictures hung on the wall was a framed photograph of the iconic James Dean. He had lived in the Iroquois for over two years the manager had shared with here on one previous visit. She felt somehow connected to him.

It was strange that even though he had died in 1955 he was still so well-known and well liked.

Ciara had arranged to meet Mac's right-hand man, David O'Connell in the hotel bar. O'Connell was more hardcore than Mac. Testament to this was his preference to use his Gaelic name: Diathi O'Conaill. This was the passport he travelled on to meet Ciara. He was a few years younger than her, but he didn't act that way. He was old in his way of thinking and chauvinistic. He didn't like the fact Ciara enjoyed so much influence in the movement; armed struggles were a man's work, according to Dia. The bar was quiet, save for an odd guest or two, there was a balding man reading his paper intently over a large coffee, that was about it.

Dia dispensed with any niceties, he didn't even shake Ciara's hand.

'Have you brought the money?'

'Yes, $500,000 all of it, it was quite heavy I can tell you to lump down here on my own.'

'Good, I can follow you back to your room when we finish and take it from you. How is Boston?'

'All good, no issues, a couple of the pubs are down, a couple are up, no drama anywhere, nothing to report.'

'Mac allowed that fecking Brit to come over, where is he, what's he up to? We must be fecking stupid to have him around, why can't you find yourself a nice Irish feller. Jesus known's there is plenty of them.'

'Miller keeps himself to himself, he's a loner, he never asks anything of me. He has absolutely no idea about NORAID. Even if he did, he probably wouldn't care. He's proved he is reliable. Mac trusts him, why can't you, Dia?'

'Mac's a bloody fool, he is taking us down a road to sue for peace, I can feel it in my bones. He's getting soft. If it was left up to me, Ciara, your man would be slotted. He's a bloody liability, trust me.'

Ciara got up to leave.

'And where do you think you're going, girl? Sit down,' he demanded.

Ciara hesitated for a few seconds and then did as she was bid.

'That's my boyfriend you are talking about killing and I don't like it and I won't have it. You can come and get the money off me now and take the meetings with the Arabs yourself. I'm here to run pubs, not to do arms deals.'

'Heh, keep your voice down girl or you'll be in trouble yourself,' Ciara was livid at the threat.

'Trouble, you say? Well let me tell you, I work my fingers to the bone over here but if you can find someone else to do it, then you're bloody welcome to it. Can I remind you it's my head on the block, not yours?'

The waiter walked towards them; it was a welcome respite from the altercation they were having.

'Two of your special house cocktails, please,' Ciara requested, her head turned slightly away from the waiter so that he couldn't see that her eyes were moist.

'Not for me, I'll have a pint of bitter; I'm not one for fancy drinks with umbrellas sticking out.'

'Yes sir,' the waiter left promptly sensing the couple was not having a good day.

'OK, let's start again. We, I, appreciate what you do over here, I mean that. You run a tight ship and have collected more money these past three years than we did in the previous 15. I thank you for that. Just keep your business away from that Brit, that's all I'm saying. He's as much a risk to you as he is to the movement. Now, can we get down to business? Who exactly are we meeting tomorrow, what time and where? I want to go over all the details, we will be carrying a lot of money with us and I don't want to be double crossed.'

The balding man across the room stood up and the movement caused Dia to look across, it was OK, he'd been joined by a lady of a similar age, he must have been waiting for her.

'We've got a lot on. First up is Tariq, we are going to his shop just after it closes at 6 pm tonight. We've no choice but to take the money with us, he's expecting that.'

'You've brought me a piece, I hope?'

'Yes, a pistol and two magazines as you asked for.'

'Good, I have the shopping list.'

'Secondly, what about the Italians, when are we meeting this new Godfather?'

'Tomorrow, in a café in Little Italy, they chose it. He's called Gambino, he powerful and now runs the five families of New York. It doesn't stop there; his interests are in Cuba and all the way across to California. After Nixon, he's probably the most influential man in America today. He is different too. He believes in all the old traditions, respect honour, trust, all that Sicilian stuff.

'He's taken the Commission into construction, garbage collection, the Unions, especially the teamsters. His tentacles are widespread. police, Judges, Senators. Like I said, he is very important.'

'What's our angle?'

We keep out of his business, we share all we know, we'll also share those Politicians we are close too. Lastly we will seek his permission and pay our dues when we want to open another bar.'

'Dues?'

'Yes, a paltry amount, it's not the money, its loose change to him; it's the status he craves, the mighty IRA bowing to him.'

'Are we OK with that?'

'We'd better be, if he chooses to, he could wipe us out in a night.'

'What about the Winter Hill Mob, where do they fit in?'

They are now run by Howie Winter after their previous leader Buddy McLean was gunned down. They stick to Boston and don't come any further south; they know better than that. No, we need Gambino's blessings for our operations in New York and Chicago that's all. Howie is OK with us, likes helping the old country, I will be seeing him next Saturday, it's the Winter Ball, I have invited him onto the table I am hosting.'

'OK, let's go and get my weapon and more importantly the money.'

Dia left a $20 bill, enough for the drinks and something for the waiter.

The lift opened and they both stepped in. Just as it was about to close a hand was pushed in between the doors to make them open again and in stepped Sean, the barman.

'What the fuck?' Dia was taken by surprise.

'This is Sean; he's with me, watching my back so to speak. Mac thought it was a good idea. The money is in his room and I suggest it stays there until we are ready to move it. You can come and get the pistol; he has that too.'

Sean smiled and put out his hand. Dia was more accommodating this time and shook it.

'Nice to meet you, Sean, seems I underestimated our girl here, I thought it was all too low key.'

Back on the ground floor the manager, an Austrian was still having palpitations. The man from the CIA who had appropriated his office was standing in front of him.

William Joseph Casey, Bill, as he was known, was upwardly mobile. He done his time in Vietnam and served his country's spy agency with distinction. His promotion to section head necessitated a move back to the US, it had taken some adjustment, but he was very happy to be leading on this case. It had so many moving parts and was now a joint operation with the FBI, with him in overall charge. That all augured well for his future promotion prospects. International terrorists, IRA, the Italian Mafia, Boston gangsters, Libyans, multiple agency involvement it had the lot and he was determined to hoover them all up.

'My office, sir, when can I expect it back?' The hotel manager asked expectantly, at the same time he was prepared for the unfavourable answer.

'No time soon, just as long as these Irish folks are staying here it is of supreme national importance.'

'Wednesday morning, they are due to check out but that is too long sir, I have many pressing things to attend to. Perhaps you can arrest these bad people now, quietly of course, I have my hotel's reputation to think of.'

Bill never made any attempt at an answer, he barked out orders to his team and ushered the bewildered manager out into the private staff corridor.

The hotel had no cameras covering the corridors or public areas, listening devices had been planted in all the public rooms and the three guest bedrooms occupied by the Irish team. They had deliberately been put all on the same floor and two other rooms were occupied by even more agents. They had captured their conversations on tape. They had amassed plenty of solid evidence, enough to help convince a jury that these folks were not innocent Irish tourists, far from it.

Chapter 38:
Persian Rug Anyone?

The evening air in Manhattan was icy-cold. Sean sat in the hire car. Just half a block up was the Persian rug store owned by Tariq, the Libyan go-between. Ciara and Dia had been inside for over forty minutes, it seemed a lot longer. Time had dragged for him, perhaps it was the impatience of youth. The incessant stream of car headlights shone in his rear-view mirror as New Yorkers made their way slowly down 5th Avenue.

Suddenly, there was movement, it was Dia and he was waving the newspaper, the signal for him to bring the suitcase. Sean moved to the back of the car and lifted the case out of the trunk, it was very manoeuvrable. He pulled it down towards the shop and then lifted in over the threshold and straight through the display room adorned with colourful rugs into the back of the premises. In the back room, apart from his colleagues, there were also two Arabs, he presumed Tariq was one of them but didn't make any move to introduce himself or ask for any either. He tilted the case over onto its side and proceeded to unzip the cover to reveal two black tarpaulin packages neatly packed in the bottom.

'Care to count it?'

'No, why would I do that, my friend? Our business is built on trust that is why it is successful.

'No, let's leave this here and take another coffee, yes?'

'If you don't mind, I will give that a miss, I'm not used to it and I'll never get to sleep, I am still jet lagged.'

'As you wish, my friend.'

Dia and Ciara stood up and offered out their hands to make to leave. Ciara immediately dropped hers again, she'd already forgotten her earlier lesson, he wasn't about to shake hands with a woman, he was too much of a fundamental Arab.

The three Irish compatriots stepped out into the now sub-zero air of a Manhattan's December's evening. They didn't speak until they all were safely in the car and it had pulled away into the stream of traffic.

'I am very happy with that deal, Ciara, well done for setting the meeting up. I know a lot of folk who will be delighted with it too. Semtex, modern weapons, advanced remote detonators, I didn't think it couldn't have got better until he put the offer of stepping up the numbers through the training camps. Jackpot, it deserves a celebratory drink, we have just progressed the cause enormously, and you both can be very proud. I've even forgiven you for surprising me with young Sean here, wasn't expecting that one for sure. Well done, lad, I like you,' he added. 'It's all going to be quick too, he is going to arrange the shipment in the next few weeks. They are very organised. I'm impressed and I've no doubt they will keep their side of the bargain, this Qaddafi feller, he doesn't like the Brits either by all accounts. That's good for us.'

Ciara looked out of the window staring into the black night. What had she got herself into? She had never dreamed that she would be reeled in to support the cause in the way she was now.

She was OK with running the books of the pubs and even OK with skimming all the profit to contribute to the cause. She never signed up to smuggle guns and as for Semtex, never. She'd spoken to her mother the evening she had landed back in Boston when the bombs had gone off in her own city Dublin. So many lives ruined. Now she was an integral part of all that. She wouldn't be able ever to watch the news in the same way again. The next time a bomb went off in Derry or Belfast, it would be as if she had detonated it. How could she live with herself when innocent people were killed? It troubled her deeply it was totally against her Catholic upbringing.

She wanted out, she wanted no more to do with the IRA, she wanted to run off and marry Miller and live out their lives peacefully. She was cheating on him, pretending to be something she wasn't. If he knew she was part of the machine that was responsible for killing British soldiers, soldiers just like he'd been once, he would despise her. She would feign a migraine; she was in no mood to celebrate with the monster sat in the front seat. She was not like him, nor did she want to be like him.

They were all so pleased with themselves, they failed to notice the black sedan trailing them all the way back to the underground parking lot of the hotel.

Chapter 39:
Little Italy

The restaurant was small and understated like so many of the Italian restaurants in this district of New York. It wasn't planned for Sean to accompany them; he was due back in Boston but Dia had taken a shining to him and insisted he came along.

They were shown into a private back room. The introductions were warm and friendly, that is once they had all been thoroughly searched for concealed weapons. *It was like being part of some B listing movie*, thought Ciara. She had met the Godfather before and knew the protocol was to kiss his ring, like you would for a Catholic bishop, a manifestation of his status as the head of the five families and leader of the Commission.

The food was plain and simple, and the conversation was strictly limited to small talk. Gambino was flanked by his consigliere and behind him two-foot soldiers stood sentry like watching on. Again, this was purely symbolic; no-one could have accessed the room as there were several armed men already in the main room.

Mopping his lips to ensure no sauce was left on his lips, Gambino enquired of Ciara how the business in Chicago and New York were fairing and was she experiencing any problems.

That was easy to answer, the takings were good, and they were no issues. There were not likely to have any as they enjoyed his protection, she added.

It was the man to Gambino right who spoke next. He explained that one of the Boston families had been to him with complaints about the Irish mob up there ran by Howie Winter. He would like to see him to iron things out. Ciara explained that she was hosting him next Saturday at the Winter Ball, perhaps the Godfather would like to come along too as her guest, and he could discuss the matter in person.

He was clearly flattered by the invitation but declined. The consigliere whispered something, the Godfather nodded in acceptance and conversation was paused whist one of the sentries went off on an errand.

He came back with a young man, perhaps no older than Sean, he wore a wedding ring suggesting that despite his tender years, he was already married.

'This is my nephew, Alfredo.'

The nephew walked around the table politely shaking hands with each of the three Irish guests.

'If your kind invitation is still open, I would like Alfredo here and his beautiful wife to be your guest. It will be good for him to meet the good Bishop of Boston; he can also meet Mr Winter and discuss things on my behalf.'

Ciara looked in at Dia to encourage him to respond.

'Ciara will be delighted to host the young couple, I will not be there myself as I am due back, but I am sure Alfredo will enjoy the ball. We will ensure he has a good time; you have my word on that.'

'Good that's all settled,' the Godfather stood up as the signal that the meeting had run its course. Just as the group was exiting the private room the consigliere called Dia back for a few moments private chat. Ciara and Sean waited outside on the pavement, but it wasn't long before they were re-joined by Dia. He didn't share what had just transpired and they didn't ask.

Chapter 40:
Ambush in Armagh

It was to be the new Troop Commanders first live Operation. His squadron commander and the sergeant major were sat at the back waiting to hear him deliver to his orders. His voice sounded confident and the operational orders were comprehensive. His excellent training was evident. He had recently passed selection into special forces from his parent Regiment, the Royal Hampshire's. The young officer, only 24, was from Manchester, himself the son of a former SAS senior officer. He was, as you would expect, extremely fit and had Captained the boxing team during his time at Sandhurst Military Academy.

The veterans of the Squadron were not known to like the officer class per se. many believed there was no place for them in their Regiment. They were wrong and arrogant to even think so, but they did anyway. They seemed to respect the Senior officers but had scant regard for the juniors. They didn't seem to understand to get to be an experience senior meant spending time as a junior troop commander. The situation was unique in the British Army.

Firstly, no one could join the Regiment direct. Everyone regardless of rank had to first spend time in another unit. The parachute Regiment and the guards made up the vast constituency of the other ranks of this famous group of warrior elite. Officers had to pass the same selection as any of the other ranks with no deviation or short cuts. Those chosen few who were physically and mentally tough enough then had to subject themselves to officer week. It was a week that lasted ten days. Even that part was arranged to cause confusion.

Each day the young hopeful would take physical training (PT) of the troops before breakfast. That had to be planned to make it interesting and challenging at the same time. Then the rest of the day was full on, studying orders, preparing orders, delivering orders.

The pressure was relentless. It would be unusual for the officer to finish his duties before 1 am and then he had to be ready to start the next day's PT at 6 am sharp. With only 4–5 hours fitful sleep each day, it was both physically and psychologically draining. It was purposely designed to be that way.

It culminated with the big day. Presenting orders to the great and good at Hereford.

Generals, Colonels, grizzly Regimental Sergeant Majors and a host of senior's ranks usually amounting to an audience of over 30, were assembled to listen to the officer's orders for an operation.

Whatever solution to the challenge in hand the young officer had devised the audience was coached to be hostile and challenging. It was literally a baptism of fire.

If by some chance the officer managed to navigate through all these hurdles and minefields, he was in. A badged, Special Air Service officer. Many were called, few were chosen.

The operation due to take place was in the notorious Bandit country of south Armagh adjoining the border with southern Ireland. All locals were hostile period; all locals regularly could be relied upon by the IRA to report troop movements. It was a county in Northern Ireland but at its heart it was part of Eire, the real island of Ireland.

The orders were flawless and had clearly been well thought through. It pleased the two seniors at the back. He had given much thought to the actions on that is he had considered what could go wrong with the execution and had offered logical plans in the event. Excellent. The only question threw back at this was regarding the accuracy of the intelligence they were acting upon. Before he could respond, the lady who had stood quietly listening to the brief cut in.

'Gentlemen, I know we have experienced indifferent intelligence at times. All that has changed, we have reinvented how we do things within our group and I can confirm the accuracy of this event. I can even go further, though I might be stepping out of line. Tonight's planned ambush is down to intelligence provided by one of your own. He is a former Pilgrim, now working for me.'

That silenced the troop, it finished the brief on a high and the team were ready to draw blood, it what they were built to do.

The SAS team spent the next two hours preparing their equipment ready for deployment to the tactical theatre and the ambush.

It was now 5 am and the teams had been in place since 7 pm the previous evening. It was bloody cold and ten hours of lying on the damp ground had made their bodies stiff. The cackle came through on all their headsets, 'Targets approaching, watch and shoot.'

Four figures appeared along the hedge line and started to climb the small hillock. There were dressed in combats and their heads were covered in black balaclavas. It was difficult in the poor early morning half-light to see what the weapons they were carrying but they were certainly tooled up. Down in the far corner of the field several Friesen cows lifted their heads sensing the movement of the four men also.

The still of the Armagh air was suddenly shattered as the General-Purpose Machine gun opened, signally the ambush had gone loud. There was no challenge or warning, they were not about to give the element of surprise away; surprise, shock action and overwhelming firepower was their maxim. All the pairs of troops who could see the targets opened with their own personal weapons. For three minutes it was chaos, no shots were returned from the terrorist cell.

Tom was first on his feet, as the smoke cleared, he started to leg it over to where the bodies lay. Sharp movement to his left alerted him. It was one of the Terrorists, miraculously, he had escaped the fusillade, he had scrambled over the fence and was running for his life down the hill, it was incredible that he'd been unscathed.

Tom raised his M16 and steadied his breathing, concentrating as hard as he could. Squeezing the trigger slowly, applying just the required pressure of 4.5 lbs, released a single shot, the running man fell face down, taken clean in the centre of the back from 150 yards in poor light. Some shot. Tom raced over to where the man lay on the ground and kicked away the Garrand rifle the IRA man was still holding. Using his boot, he lifted the man over until he was facing up to the sky and then sent a second bullet into his forehead. He was dead now if he wasn't before he muttered to himself.

'On me, on me,' it was the young officer, Henry, calling.

The troop regrouped, held a quick head count and he led them off to the saddle of a hill close by.

Within minutes the first helicopter could be heard. It was a Sea King. It was followed by two more. This time they were Chinooks.

The troop sergeant knelt and one by one he urged his comrades on board. Meanwhile, the other two Heli's had landed and disgorged over 40 troops to search and secure the ambush area. The SAS troop sat in the fuselage smiling to each other. Clockwork, there was no other word for it.

All four terrorists had been neutralised.

The young troop commander, Henry had cut his teeth and Tommy K, the amateur deerstalker from Tyneside, had felled a running man, in poor light at over 150 meters, he would dine on that story for the rest of his life.

The ambush area would now be made secure with the resident Battalion responsible for this district and scene of crimes officers would start their investigations to enable a full report to be recorded. There would be no in-depth investigation; they were just simply following standard operating procedures.

The ambush party was debriefed immediately on arriving back at the Barracks by the operational support team and the senior RUC officers on duty. One of the terrorist cells had already been identified, a certain Tom McGoldrick, he had been on the security forces most wanted list for a long time and now his name could be struck off.

Clockwork, the operational combat orders had been executed to the letter. The intelligence on the IRA cell had proven completely accurate. Miller had already made a significant difference even if he was unaware of it. McGoldrick was one the passengers he had ferried in the car to Belfast, it was one less player for the security forces to concern themselves with.

The tide had turned. It was to be the first of many similar encounters where the winner was never going to be in doubt. This set back would send reverberations around the leadership council of the IRA. No longer could they cross the border un-checked, collect their weapons from safe houses or a cache and go about their even deeds with impunity. An unknown, yet unseen force was now engaging them. They were under attack on their home front in Dublin and now by a feared enemy in the tactical theatre of the six counties which made up Ulster.

Chapter 41:
Boston Winter Ball

Miller was playing it cool but secretly he was looking forward to accompanying Ciara to the Winter Ball. It was for him yet another first, a double first actually. It was the first time he'd ever worn a formal dinner suit and secondly it was his first black tie ball. He was a little apprehensive about the table they were hosting, he would have to make small talk and he wasn't good at that.

Ciara had run through the group which would make up their table of ten. A local Irish American businessman and his wife, called Howie Winter, the Bishop of Boston and his housekeeper, a young New Yorker, Italian American, Alfredo Gambolino and his new wife. Ciara had saved two places for her Irish colleague Dia but as he was already enroute back to Dublin, she had offered the two spare seats over to Howie. He would bring along one of his lieutenants and a lady. No name had been forthcoming so Ciara couldn't prepare the name place for the replacement guests.

The Winter Ball was the highlight of the year for the glitterati of Boston society. Having the Bishop accept her invitation was also a coup for Ciara. He was one of the most influential men in the City and the fact he chose to be on her table would not go unnoticed.

Ciara had spent the afternoon at her favourite salon, pampering herself to look her very best for the evening ahead. She never looked forward to the waxing, but it was for the best, she liked for her private areas to be as special as her smile. The shape she opted for today was "the landing strip", encouraged by the young Vietnamese beautician who attended to her. All the pubic hair was removed expertly, save for a neat rectangular piece leading direct from her quim to halfway up her tummy.

'Your man will like this, velly much, you sexy woman have lots of bang-bang tonight.'

Ciara giggled at the young girl's accent and comments, she certainly hoped so. The Vietnamese lady had no problem talking about sex and the importance of pleasing your man. Ciara was always amazed how openly they would talk about their favourite positions and their ways of keeping their man pleasured. As modern and open as her friends in Ireland were, they would never be as explicit as these girls in this salon!

Three hours later, Miller lay on the bed, watching Ciara get dressed for their evening out.

He found it very sexy. A turn on, it was a striptease in reverse.

Ciara was pushing the boat out tonight. She started to assemble her outfit. First, she fit the half cup black bra which lifted her breasts up and gave her an alluring cleavage. Next the black waist belt for the suspenders. She raised one foot at a time onto the lounge chair as she pulled on her black stocking with the heavy seam and connected it to the waist belt with the clips.

She turned and looked at Miller, she stood broadside on wearing only the bra and the suspenders waist belt.

'Does sir approve so far?' she asked mischievously.

'Sir does, very much so, but haven't you forgot something?'

Miller was staring at the bare naval of this sexy woman, the neat landing strip was on open view.

'Not wearing any tonight if its knickers you are referring to,' she was positively beaming. Miller brought out the full decadent woman in her; she found him such a turn on.

'Hmm, are you sure? I don't think the bishop will approve when I tell him,' he joked.

'Speaking of which, how can a man sworn to a life of celibacy bring along his housekeeper to such an event, it beats me.'

'She is just a platonic companion, that's all. Don't you besmirch our bishop; the man is a living saint, so he is.'

'If you say so, that wouldn't be my experience of men of the cloth, I'm afraid.'

Whilst Ciara diligently applied her makeup he jumped into the shower, purposely leaving the bathroom door ajar to ensure Ciara could see him from her mirror washing himself down. He shaved too, not something he was accustomed to.

Miller exited the shower wearing only a towel around his lower half. He was a hunk. Ciara reached up and with her hands around his neck pulled him forwards and down to plant a kiss on his lips.

'You scrub up very well, Mr Miller, and those eyes. I've never seen anyone with as piercing blue eyes as those. I could eat you.'

'Then why don't we skip the ball and settle in here for the night, you look ravishing too, that backless little black number you're wearing is very sexy, oh and I love those pearls, they are a family heirloom, are they not?' As soon as the words left his mouth, he flushed.

'And how did you guess that? These pearls were my grandma's, but I've never worn them with you.'

'Oh, they just look antique in a classy sort of way.' Miller tried his best to cover up his mistake; he had of course seen them when he had allowed Chuck to search their room.

'They really suit you though,' he fumbled the words. He turned to hide his red cheeks and pulled on his clothes. 45 minutes later, they were in the ballroom and seated.

Ciara was right. There was a constant procession over to their table as folk came to pay their respect to God's representative resident here in Boston. The guests all looked in again at their table as the bishop stood up, head bowed to give the mandatory blessing for the food they were about to eat.

Only when the starters had arrived did their final two guests arrive at the table.

The lady, well girl, to be more precise, was no more than 21 and the man dressed not in the conventional black tie but a pale lemon white dinner jacket with matching pants. Ideal for a Florida summer party no doubt, but completely out of place at the Boston winter ball.

Miller was never one to sit on a fence for long and by the time the man had walked around shaking hands, Miller disliked him. He was a jerk. Not particularly speaking, quietly he asked Ciara who the clown was who had joined them. For the next 30 minutes the table engaged in meaningless small talk.

Between the starter and main course there was a short interval and the organisers gave a short presentation on the charitable works that had been undertaken by the organising committee during the previous twelve months with the funds raised at this very dinner. It was designed to make the folk present feel good about themselves in order they might be even more generous this year.

Directly after the main had been eaten, lamb shank served on a bed of sweet potatoes and covered with a red currant juice, the bishop offered his thanks for the invitation and offered his apologies for leaving so early on account that he had several masses to preside over the next day.

That left a conspicuous gap on their table. Howie Winter, Boston's own gangster was deep in conversation with Alfredo and their respective wives stared forwards into space dutifully. The two men seemed earnest in their intent to build a genuine relationship.

As for the two strangers, Miller never heard their names, nor was he interested in learning them. They were, by now inebriated, not with the wine on the table but with whatever they had consumed prior to turning up late. By way of sport, the man patted Miller on the back firmly and passed him a champagne bottle to take a swig from, Miller smiled his decline.

'Come on, don't be such a broody git, let your hair down for once, you Limeys are so fucking uptight you don't know how to have a good time.' His boss Howie smiled, not sure whether to approve of the comment or not. Alfredo looked on impassively.

Sensing the immediate tension in her beau and knowing just what he was capable of, Ciara grabbed Miller's arm and pulled him up to diffuse the situation.

'Don't think you are getting away with sitting here all night, a girl likes to dance, you know.' The band was playing a Beatles number which at least Miller could identify with. Once they were together on the dance floor, Ciara leaned in to apologise for the man's behaviour and attitude to Miller.

'No problem at all, the man's a prat, he can't help that.' He was lying again of course; the gangster had clearly rattled his cage.

From the edge of the dance area Miller could see that the American had stood, excused himself and presumably taken off to go to the bathroom. Miller stopped dancing.

'I need to pee, Ciara; can we sit this one out?'

'Yes, sure, but be quick, I am in the mood for dancing,' she sang melodiously.

Miller's luck was in. The mysterious guest wasn't at any of the urinals, he'd taken a cubicle.

Miller found him, third stall down. Two or three men who were peeing looked over their shoulders puzzled why a man would be looking under the 12" gap at the bottom of the doors of the stalls.

Miller knelt quietly and reached under the door and with both hands and as quick as a flash pulled on the two crumpled trouser legs which were around the man's ankles.

The man sat on the pot was taken completely unaware and started shouting at the top of his voice as he was pulled forcibly from the pot towards the door. Miller persevered and with much tugging finally freed the trousers from the man's grip, stood up and walked out of the rest room. The other men present there taking a leak cheered, laughed and clapped at the great sport they had just witnessed.

Walking back towards the direction of the ball room Miller flung the trousers up high until they settled on a cross beam support, which was holding up the roof, some 15 feet from the carpet where they now stood. On reaching the table he encouraged Ciara to take to the floor once again.

Alfredo and his now happy wife were already there.

The lemon coloured trousers were eventually recovered but it was only after the staff had found step ladders to climb up to them. They had done so whilst a growing crowd of over 30 people, men and women stood looking in cheering and clapping, it had been the highlight of the evening for some! To add insult to injury, one of those enjoying the fun of seeing the trousers hanging from the rafters was the young girlfriend of the victim himself!

By the time they had finished dancing and returned to the table, there was only the four of them left. Miller shared with Alfredo his prank and both he and his young wife laughed voraciously.

They clearly hadn't enjoyed the man's company either.

It was after 2 am when they decanted themselves out of the taxi outside of the pub and using the private side entrance they adjourned immediately to bed. Any earlier plans of a steamy session had gone out of the window, Ciara collapsed face down on the bed, still wearing all her clothing, including her coat.

Not so carefully, Miller stripped her off, first her coat and then her dress and unbuckled her shoes, the rest would have to wait until morning. He stripped off his hired suit and climbed under the blankets to join Ciara in the land of nod.

Chapter 42:
Return to Whitehall (SIS Meeting to Review Progress)

Rosie was shown into the main briefing room. It was deceptively large, around the table sat a large group, perhaps over 20 people, and others were sat against the walls. It was a more than a little intimidating. As she moved to the empty chair clearly meant for her a friendly face stood up and shook her hand, it was Lt Colonel Gilbert who was the military liaison who was also working on the Monkey case. She returned his smile somewhat nervously.

She didn't know the assembled gathering, and no one was about to make introduction. She recognised the important people in room, sir John Rennie the head of the Intelligence services and across from him was Henry Tuzo, the General officer Commanding all the British forces in Northern Ireland.

It was an Army intelligence officer, wearing the rank of a Lt Colonel who opened the meeting.

'Now we all know why we are here. SIS has been invited to update us on their activity in the south and we are keen to fully understand the immediate fall out of the bombings in Dublin. The Irish parliament has of course brought in emergency powers to detain arrest and charge members of the IRA. They have been brought to their senses and finally they realise it is in both of our interests to: firstly, to control this open civil war and secondly work together to nullify the threat of the IRA, and finally to assist in finding a peaceful solution. I think we all agree that we need the Irish Government on our side; they rely heavily on us for their economy, which is fragile to say the least. Our suggestion we might close the borders completely and stop all their beef coming over seemed to do the trick.

159

'I am as keen to hear from our intelligence agency cousins as to how they are building up a better picture of the network in the south. If I may say so sir John, I do feel the having several different agencies acting independently may not be the most economical use of our resources and would move to suggest that all intelligence operations come under Northern Ireland Command under the GOC. That way we would be able to co-ordinate all the various assets and direct them accordingly.'

'You were asked to open the meeting Colonel, not tell me how to do my job, now sit down please.' Sir John was clearly irritated by the barbed comments made.

The Intelligence Corp Colonel did as he was bid. The GOC remained blank faced, clearly waiting to hear the reports before speaking, in the circumstances that was by far the best course of action. That's why he was a General.

For the next 40 minutes, Rosie gave a précis of their intelligence gathering activities, highlighting the success of recent operations. She left the best to last, her pièce de résistance.

She explained to the large group how they now had an agent close to the IRA Group Council and that he was providing excellent intelligence. It was the first real breakthrough in the two years of the Troubles.

She was challenged on the reliability of the source code name monkey. It was Colonel Gilbert who responded on her behalf.

'I can and I will vouch for this agent. He is of the highest calibre, we are fortunate to have him, and he has shown exemplary intuition to date and has provided us with first grade intelligence. Needless to say, that information has been acted on and proved to be 100% first grade. The tide is turning, gentlemen, we are getting off our back foot and taking this war to the enemy and we are starting to win it. If we step up our activities and expand the MRF we could all be done here within 12 months that is my personal prediction.' The GOC had heard enough.

'Yes, the fact that the UDF attacked Dublin has worked in our favour and yes we have managed to take a few more of their players off the street and yes we have been able to celebrate these small wins. But small wins they are. Across the six countries my men are under pressure and put their lives on the line every day. When I walk around the streets of Londonderry or Belfast, it doesn't seem like a war that we are winning, in fact just the opposite. The IRA is getting more and more organised and their tactics are evolving. I have already expressed my opinion to the Prime Minister and requested at least another Division should be deployed.'

The room was quiet. People knew that the Regular Army was stretched and that we already had almost 20,000 troops stationed in the Province.

'Harry, we hear you and of course would like to help you all we can of course. How do you suggest we do this?'

'Help? Then let's clear the room of all personnel except SIS and I will tell you.'

160

People took their cue and started shuffling their papers, clearing up what files they had brought and made their way towards the now open double doors.

Sir John looked across, 'Sorry old bean, I think that means you as well.' He was referring to the Senior MI5 officer across the table.'

'It's OK, he can stay,' it was the GOC speaking.

The room now only had six people remaining the GOC, Sir John, the Intelligence Colonel, MI5, Rosie and Colonel Gilbert.

'First of all, let me personally congratulate you on your recent wins, they are splendid, just splendid. Truth is they are just not enough. We are seeing a constant escalation from the IRA, they are getting better, more drilled, better weaponry and they are winning, I want you all to know that. We need a big push; we need the IRA to think this is not 1916; we are not going to just roll over. The Orange lodges won't allow us to do that. Up to now they have shown some restraint, but we believe that won't last for long. If we don't get on top of all this we could find ourselves in the middle of a very bloody civil war, the Protestants outnumber the Catholics significantly in the north, it would be a bloodbath and would force the Irish regular forces to intervene. We know they have drawn up plans to invade the north and in that event we would have to engage them. It would be a disaster; they have zero air assets to speak of. What would our American cousins think of all that? We would be pariahs, that's what.

'The only way this conflict is going to be settled is if we can rattle the IRA enough to believe it's a war they can't win and get them to the table. Your job is to find me a way and find it quickly. The PM is running out of patience. It doesn't sit well with the British public that they have to watch a war taking place on their streets. The Scottish are getting more militant too. Fund raising for the Ulster cause is rife across Glasgow, heaven forbid the bloody troubles spill over onto the mainland.'

'No, this man Monkey, we need him to find a way to bring them to the table. Can you deliver this?'

'He's the best, sir, if anyone can our man can.'

'Right, I think we are done here. Sir John and I have a few private matters to discuss, so I bid you all good day.'

In the briefest of moments, they were dismissed and exited the room.

It was now up to Rosie and Colonel Gilbert to figure a way to deliver what the General needed them to.

Chapter 43:
New Year's Eve in Boston

It was bloody cold, but Ciara didn't mind at all, this was the first New Year's Evening for many years that she had spent with a man. It felt good. In fact, it felt very good. She really liked Miller, more than any other man since she the one had been engaged too some 15 years back. She had never let anyone as close as this for a long time, she felt at ease with this quiet, broody, hunk.

She was frightened too. She was in a constant state of anxiety since her return from New York. She was having serious misgivings about her role in the movement and how she had been drawn into the spider's web of intrigue. It was one thing to raise money for the cause but now on top of all that she was directly involved in using that money to buy arms, more especially explosives.

How could she do what she was doing and still love Miller, a former British soldier who would despise her if he ever found out what she was up to?

She mused. If he liked her as much as she liked him, they would find a way, surely, wouldn't they?

They had been to one of the quieter bars in town, the others had been far too smoky, Miller detested the aroma of stale cigarettes and she didn't care too much for it either. They were now stood among the expectant crowds in Fan Pier park overlooking Rowe's wharf on the other side of the river where the fireworks were to be set off. It was exciting. She linked her arm through his and pressed the side of her body closer to benefit from the protection he gave her from the sharp biting wind which blew inland from Massachusetts Bay.

The crowd around them represented all walks of Boston life, whole families, children sat upon their father's shoulders, groups of teenagers celebrating being allowed out so late.

The children closest to them are muffled in their warm, cosy hats and gloves. Their gloves grasped the railing on the pier side tightly as the gathering, anticipative crowd waited impatiently for the firework display to begin. She hugged into Miller.

The countdown from twenty seconds on the large illuminated clock began and then the cheers went up as the first rockets screamed into the dark sky at the striking of midnight.

The crowd erupted into noise. She turned into Miller and pulling his head to her, she kissed him passionately full on the lips.

'Happy New Year, Algernon,' she smiled.

'Miller, to you,' he smiled back, and they kissed again. They were oblivious to all around them and stay locked in their embrace for a few minutes. The couple to their left leaned in and offered their hands in friendship; "Happy New Year". The crowd was in a jubilant mood.

They all watched in utter fascination at the manmade shooting stars revealing elegantly high above them in the twilight sky. The glow was illuminating the harbour as the glittering gems crackle and disperse into thin air. It looked so vibrant, as if coloured paint had been randomly splattered on an ebony canvas Beautiful, boisterous and bright. The fireworks looked like a multi-coloured spider spreading its fluorescent webs across the moonlit sky. The faces of the people in the crowd reflected the vivid colours; pink and red, pink and red, pink and red. Simultaneously, the fireworks exploded creating deafening pops and crackles. The watched as the spectacle unfolded before them, lovers entwined.

After what seemed an age, as suddenly as they had started, one large air burst signalled the display had finished. The smoke drifting from the other side of the river thickened as it drifted towards them.

The energy and the bubbling excitement are drained quickly from the atmosphere as the families prepare to go home.

'That was great, just great,' Ciara exclaimed.

'Thank you for coming with me, Miller, it means a lot, you know. In fact, you mean a lot to me.'

Her voice trailed; she was in unchartered water. They joined the throng of the crowd to start their journey back home.

They had been walking for over half an hour back to the pub mostly in silence save for an occasional banal remark.

'Penny for your thoughts?' questioned Miller. He could sense Ciara had checked out and was somewhere else.

Ciara stomach tightened; she was afraid, very afraid.

Suddenly she stopped and in the middle of the sidewalk turned to him.

'Miller, I have something I need to share with you and it's not an easy thing for me to do.'

'Spit it out girl, I won't bite.'

'No, but you may do something much more and that's what I am afraid of.'

Miller answered quickly, 'I know have my issues and I can be violent, but I have never struck a woman in my life and I never will.'

'No, I don't mean that, I wasn't suggesting for a moment, honest Miller, that's not what I mean.'

'So, what exactly do you mean? As I said, spit it out.'

'Can we sit over there,' responded Ciara pointing to a low wall.

The couple sat and after a few moments of silence.

'I have told you how I came to work over here, haven't I?'

'Yes. You met Mac in Spain and he offered you a job.'

'Yes, that's true.'

'But that was then, and this is now. My role has sort of evolved.'

'Listen Ciara, I know Mac is no angel and of course I know he's mixed up with the IRA and I can figure out where the profits to your pubs are going to, there does that help? I also know it's going to land you into a lot of trouble, someone, the authorities, are going to figure it all out and you lady, will go to jail for a very long time, you do realise that?'

Of course, he wasn't just speculating. He knew this for certain; the security services had already raided the apartment with his collusion.

Ciara's head was now resting in her hands face down, she was openly crying now.

Miller went on.

'Before I came over to Dublin, I spent time in the prison in Manchester, not long, but long enough to know it's not where I wanted to be. Prison in America, well, that would be much tougher. Is that what you want Ciara? Trust me lady, that's where you are heading. It would break your ma's heart Ciara.'

Ciara sobbed loudly, caught her breathe and managed to say;

'It's worse than that, Miller, oh, it's suddenly got much worse now.'

'How so?'

'I can't tell you, it will cost me my life, trust me, you said Mac is no angel, that's an understatement. He is capable of just about anything. If you double crossed him, Miller, you would be disappeared very quickly, others have.'

'Others?'

'Let's just say if we ever run into a problem over here, with gangster's or just chancers, it is always sorted, I don't know the details I just know the problem goes away.'

'Ciara, I can sense there is something you are not telling me isn't there?'

'What is it girl, if you don't share, I can't help.'

'I'm scared to.'

'OK, then let's head back home and stop wasting our time here sat in the cold.' Miller stood to leave; he was bluffing to push her over the edge.

Ciara was sobbing loudly now, a couple walking on the other side of the road looked in. They obviously thought for a moment about intervening, but the size of Miller probably made them think again.

Miller pulled Ciara to her feet and forced her to start walking again. The pace was slow but at least they were moving. Miller turned her and lifting her chin with his hand he could see her face clearly in the Boston moonlight. The black mascara was running down each of her cheeks making her look like some white trailer trash from Kentucky. She didn't look a pretty sight. 'What is it you're not telling me Ciara? I can't help if I don't know what the problem is.'

'New York,' she started. 'It was in New York.'

For the next ten minutes, Ciara spilled her guts. All about the fundraising, the meeting with the Libyan and with some difficulty she managed to spill the beans both on the arms shipment and the training camps they were expanding.

Miller, listened quietly, without intervening, he knew it was a very hard thing she was doing and at the same time didn't know how to respond, she was already in too deep and the US intelligence authorities had enough substantial evidence to put her away for a very long time.

They were now back in their own warm bedroom and Miller helped her off with her coat and shoes, she was so numb with anxiety she could function.

'What I can, I do, Miller; I know what it is I want to do.'

'And?'

'I love you, Miller, very much, I want us to run off somewhere, Australia, New Zealand, anywhere. I want to turn my back on this life.

'More importantly, I want to know how you feel about me, you are so deep, so quiet, I never know what you are thinking, do you even like me?'

'Of course, I do, I came over to Boston to see you, didn't I?'

'That's told me nothing.'

'Well I don't know what to say, Ciara, you are a lovely lady, the best, and I love being with you. You have two kind parents who mean a lot to me, they took a stranger into their home and showed him kindness without judging him. I love them for that. They helped me put my shit back together after years on the streets; I know one thing is certain I am never going back to that life.

'You have shown me what it is to be loved, to enjoy the love we share; you have changed me, Ciara Corcoran. Yes, you have.

'I don't want to see you go to jail but that's where you are heading for sure.'

'For sure, do you know something?' She was suddenly startled.

'No, I don't, at least not for certain, but you haven't exactly covered all your tracks, have you? Do you even know if you were followed to New York? You could be under surveillance, even now.'

'I think you're exaggerating. Yes, police probably suspect we siphon off some of the cash from the pubs, but who doesn't do that over here.'

'OK, so who else is in your team, how many of the lads from the bar know what you are up to, Ciara?'

'Only the one, Sean. He watched my back, I like him, I trust him, so does the movement too. Dia, a colleague over from Dublin trusts him.'

'Dia?'

'You would have seen him in Fagin's. He is Mac's partner, only more ruthless, I would be careful around him when you go back. He doesn't think you should be over here or around in general. He is a major threat to you, Miller. He would have you disappeared if it was up to him; he's said as much to me. He thinks you could be a British spy.'

'I am tired,' Miller changed the conversation, though it was useful to know he had a threat in Dublin.

'Let's try and get some sleep and we can talk about this more in the morning, we need a plan. Right now, Ciara, you are heading to hell in a handcart.'

'Thanks for that, Miller, that's cheered me up no end and you expect me to sleep after that?'

Miller pulled the covers over his shoulder, rolled over on to his side and within a few minutes was fast asleep; it was a different scenario for his female companion.

Chapter 44:
Miller Requests A Deal for Ciara

New Year's Day had been relatively uneventful; the pub was open for food and had seen a steady trickle of clientele from noon onwards as families of Boston celebrated their short time together. Ciara was subdued, lost in her thoughts, distant which drew attention from the Irish barman, in fact she looked totally depressed. They concluded she had been fighting with Miller.

They were wrong of course.

On the 2nd January, despite the sub-zero temperature Miller took to his bike again.

He cycled around the city and then over to the Marine base in the early afternoon. This time he wasn't seeking Chuck, he was seeking a secure line to Rosie. He spent over thirty minutes chatting to her on the scrambled line provided; he wasn't certain it wouldn't be taped by the Americans but preferred to err on the cautious side so assumed it was.

He listened to Rosie giving the highlights of her meeting with folk in London.

In turn, he gave a report on the Americans covert raid on the pub which he'd facilitated and what they had found. She would request a full report from Chuck and thanked Miller for sharing. She would also ask the Americans what had transpired down in Manhattan too.

Miller gave Rosie the telephone number of the call box he wanted her to ring. He used the simple OTP code he'd learnt in Fort Monkton to scramble the numbers.

After the brief call with Rosie, he gave some time to listen to Chuck and promised he'd back first thing in the morning to go over the next stage of the plan in greater detail with him.

After ensuring he wasn't been trailed, it was tricky for a car to follow a bike, he circled back around to the call box tucked into the side of a convenience store. It was only ten minutes of waiting when it rang, and he could hear Rosie's voice again.

He gave her the full story on Catriona's meeting in New York with the Libyan and the imminent arms shipment and outlined what he wanted from Rosie in return. He shared he suspected the Americans would have staked out the meeting but didn't know for sure.

She listened to his proposition.

To get the Americans to believe Ciara was already working with them wouldn't be easy; Miller wanted her off the hook. But who did they have left to hang if not Ciara? It was going to take very delicate negotiations to exonerate her. But not impossible Rosie sought to placate and reassure Miller.

In return, Rosie had her own agenda; Miller had to get Mac to the negotiating table. How was he going to do that without confessing he was an intelligence agent?

To start the ball rolling, Rosie committed to get Miller access to someone based in the British Consulate General office in Boston. He could then have access to Rosie independent of Chuck and the Intelligence forces team in the US. He needed to somehow get Ciara there too, that was going to be a sensitive thing to broach.

He would do it after their next lovemaking session when her guard was down.

Chapter 45:
Dublin, Council of War – The Leadership Considers It Options

Mac had called the extraordinary meeting of the IRA Council to discuss the recent events and to agree a plan of action going forward. Things had seriously escalated, and it called for a review of their strategy. As was the usual drill Tom Cullen, the bar owner of Fagin's sat next to the door controlling all who came and left the first-floor room.

David O'Conner was newly arrived back from America and he was excited to share his news.

Before he could do so, Mac called for an update on the bombings in Dublin in early December, he wanted to know who was behind them.

'Almost certainly it was the Brits.' It was one of the senior Dublin IRA players speaking.

'How so?'

'We believe they colluded with the Proddy bastards from Shank hill road.'

'Can we prove this?'

'Well, according to their own official sources it was a Brit voice who phoned in the warning, such as it was, the bombs went off in under seven minutes later. People saw the Brit fellow to, a big bloke so he was.'

Mac turned to the Derry commander.

'And what news do you have for me?'

'Same, and it's not good, at all. We've lost several loyal men over the past few weeks, some were ambushed by the Brits and others it is claimed were taken out by the Prod's, not that I believe that. They have even struck at us all the way down in Cork, which was to send a message of their intent.'

'So, what do you think is going on?'

The gloves are off, that's what I think, this new unit out of palace barrack, the MRF, law to themselves, the claims of the UDA or UDF taking us out are just a cover. It's the fucking Brits, dressed in civvies. Of that, I am certain.'

'And proof.'

They are too well informed, they hit and run, don't hang about, never talk, fit, fast, good with their weapons they are fucking soldiers believe me. Probably from Hereford, that's where.'

Mac let the fact the young man from Derry was constantly swearing go this time and looked over to his trusted partner.

'Better news from New York, I hope, Dia?'

'Great news, actually. The lead and contacts we were given from that electrical construction company in Tipperary proved very fruitful indeed. It exceeded all my expectations. We met the Libyan go-between, handed over the cash they'd asked for, very reasonable if you ask me. They don't want to ship the stuff using the contractor electrical panels as we originally thought, they are going to take reasonability for bringing a ship all the way into a port of our choice. Kinsale is what I suggested.

'When this shipment is made, we will be able get our hands-on new weapons including rocket launchers, RPG7's no less and lots of Semtex. Not only that, as icing on the cake they have offered to step up the training of our folks in their camps. They want to treble the numbers going through now. They can arrange details once our teams land in Tunisia.'

'Anything else?' asked Mac.

'Oh a few details here and there, I met with the Italians, their man in New York asked for a favour, on account he gives us free rein to manage our pubs. I promised we will take care of them for him.'

'Favour?'

'A couple actually, they wanted an introduction to the bishop in Boston and for us to broker a conversation with the Irish gangs up there. We've done both. Oh, and they wanted us to cement the relationship by removing a stone in their shoe, a gangster from Columbia who's pushing his own line of hard drugs. I've set Sean that task.

'Will there be any come back on us? We don't want to get in the middle of a turf war between the Italians and the Columbians.'

'None, that was the appeal, they wouldn't know who made the hit and he could completely deny it.'

As Dia finished his report, the Derry commander didn't wait to be asked to speak, he jumped in again.

'Mac, we are building momentum right now, we need to seize the initiative and increase the intensity of our operations, we need to bring the Regular Irish Army into the struggle too. We are on the cusp of throwing out this evil fecking Imperialist Empire once and for all.' Mac raised his finger.

'You really think the Irish Army are going to side with us, they have just rushed legislation through to outlaw us, all due to the pressure the British Government have brought to bear. Do you not realise where all our milk and beef go? If the Irish army took a single step over that border the RAF would blow them to smithereens, and they know it.'

'No, if we are going to win this struggle and unite all of Ireland, we have to adopt a twin approach. We have to get them to the table for talks.' The Derry man stood.

'Are you feckin kidding me?'

Tom came over opened his jacket so all could see the colt pistol there.

The room went totally quiet and atmosphere was immediately tense. Mac brought the room under control, that's why he was the Chief of Staff.

'We will adopt a twin strategy; we will maintain the low intensity operations of sanctioned assassinations and continue the selected bombing campaign and at the same time we will enter into discussions with the British Government. That's what we are going to do.' It was the Derry man again.

'Oh, and how do you propose we do that? Catch a ferry over to London and march up to Downing street and knock on the door?'

'Clear the room, do it now.'

Mac was incandescent his portly face was glowing red like a smelters furnace.

'Dia, not you, I would like a few moments of your time alone please.'

Tom, stood, his weapon now drawn, as he watched the council carefully as they filed past him and down the stairs into Fagin's lounge. On a single nod from Mac, Tom turned and followed them.

For the next thirty minutes as they sat alone Mac outlined his plan to Dia.

They would use Miller to open a back door to the British government, he could do that, he owed them. They would have a concerted effort to learn more about the MRF and track their movements. They would also retaliate against the Shank hill mob too; send a clear message to them.

Dia explained that the young man from Derry was highly influential in the north, they needed him and that he would insist on being present at any discussions. Reluctantly, Mac agreed. He disliked the man enormously, but he knew that Dia spoke with straight words. Dia also shared he neither liked nor trusted the broody Brit. Mac placated him.

'He's to do our bidding, we need a pawn and he is just that. If he steps out of line, I will shoot him myself.'

Chapter 46:
'Cometh to Jesus moment'

The barman Sean was glad Miller was returning to Ireland. He didn't mind the man, at least not at first, but the affect he'd had on Ciara was plain for all to see. She was a broken woman. Her normal joie de vivre had all but disappeared. When he had first arrived, her face had been lit up and she her appearance was as happy as the cat with the cream. All that had gone; whatever had transpired between them at the intimate level since New Year's Eve had changed that. Sean had tried to provide that reassuring shoulder for her, but she was having none of that. Miller was training each day for a couple of hours, either cycling or in the cellar doing pull ups on the overhead pipes. He was looking lean and mean. He certainly didn't look like a man to cross. He wondered if he was being a bully to Ciara, what went on behind locked doors was one of life's mysteries. Perhaps she had hoped for more from her man, a ring perhaps? She wasn't about to share anything with him no matter how subtly he tried to tease it out of her.

They had both taken a few afternoons off to, Ciara wanted to show him some of Boston, but whenever they did, she seemed to return in an even blacker mood. Something was troubling her for sure. He wondered if he should report it to Dia.

It would wait; perhaps her mood would lift once the Brit had left Boston.

The flight to Dublin was an overnight one so Ciara had gone to the airport to see Miller off. When she returned there was no hiding her feelings, Sean could see her eyes were bloodshot and puffy from the crying. He decided to follow her up to the room.

'I know it's none of my business, but what's with you and Miller?'

'You're dead right; it's none of your business.'

'It's just that I care for you, that's all, Ciara, and since New Year's Eve you've been like a bear with a very sore head, that's all. So, what is it with you two?'

'Listen Sean, I like Miller and he likes me. I want to be with him on a more permanent footing. I don't want to continue here working seven days a week for what? Life is passing me by. I am not a young woman anymore; I have a chance to be happy with a man I love. There I said it, I don't want to do this anymore, I want to go back to Dublin or anywhere and live a normal life, is that too much to ask?'

The tears rolled down both of her cheeks, Sean was overwhelmed, and he didn't know how to react to her out pouring of emotion. He leaned in and embraced her.

'I understand, Yes, you deserve to be happy and if I can help you do that I will.'

'Well I might need your help when I tell Mac' he needs a new accountant over here. I don't suppose you want to step up to the plate?'

'Who, me? I failed all the maths test ever set, I'm not your man, sorry, Ciara. I can't help with that, I'm afraid.'

'Well I can't exactly advertise in the Boston Globe, can I?'

'Crooked accountant wanted to siphon off funds from pubs for the bloody IRA.'

'Don't talk like that, Ciara, never. That can get us both into deep trouble and, I, for one, don't want that.'

'Talk to Mac, tell him you are burned out, and tell him how you feel, after all it's his problem to sort, not yours.'

'Hmm suppose so, easy said than done though, isn't it?' Ciara's chest rose as she took a deep breath.

'OK, I will stop behaving like a witch and put on my game face. And yes, I will pick my moment and let Mac know it's time for a change for me, a big change. Thanks Sean, I needed to sound off to someone.'

She closed the bedroom door and leaned her back against it.

Sean had no clue what was going on, or why she hadn't slept for five nights on the trot. The threat of a long jail sentence still hung over her. The spook from the British consulate had been noncommittal, despite Miller's adamant stance that her freedom was important to him. She didn't understand why they would care a lot about that. Who was he to them anyway, a street tramp with a prison record and what sway did he hold over them, none whatsoever?

Things quickly spiralled out of control the day after Miller had flown back to Dublin. It was a Sunday, she'd been to early mass and the streets were deserted as she walked back to the pub. The car with the blacked-out windows spun in front of her in a dramatic way disgorging suited well build men. As she turned around to move away, the second car discharged its occupants out to block her route. She was caught, like a fly in a spider's web. No ID was offered, and she was forcibly thrown unceremoniously into the back of the lead car to where she had not the faintest idea. Her hands we secured expertly with a cable tie and at the same time her bladder opened as she urinated involuntarily out of complete shock and fear.

Chapter 47:
Miller Returns to Fagin's

O'Donnell was genuinely pleased to see Miller as he exited the arrivals terminal at Dublin airport. Miller was expecting anyone to be there to greet him, it was a pleasant surprise. As they exited the short stay car park O'Donnell was firing questions off ten to a dozen.

How was Boston, what was it like at Christmas, what was the pub scene like, did he meet Sean. What did he do for New Year's Eve. The fusillade of questions was constant.

'Miller replied in a sarcastic but friendly way.

'Do you ever come up for a breath?'

O'Donnell laughed.

Miller addressed several of the questions by giving him a brief summary of where he'd been and yes it had been a great break.

'You look a lot better than when you went. How's the arm?'

'All mended, strong enough for me to do 30 pull ups.'

'Thirty! I would be lucky to manage five and my arm was never broken,' laughed O'Donnell.

'Can I assume we are heading for Fagin's, are we?'

'Where else?' was the response he got. 'Mac ordered me to pick you up and bring you to see him as soon as you landed.'

'So, am I in trouble?' Miller was hesitant.

'No, he just asked to see you, that's all.'

'Why, where else did he think I was heading for? I lived on the streets, don't forget.'

'How was your lady then, fill your boots, did we?' Miller didn't care much for macho boy talk.

'If you are referring to Ciara, yes it was nice to spend the time with her, but the girl's got big problems.'

'Problems? What do you mean?'

'She's totally burnt out, that's what I mean. She's on edge, barks at all the staff. She's lost the plot, I'm afraid.'

Miller lay in it on thick just as he had agreed to do with Ciara. They both needed Mac to think her time in Boston was at an end. It was the only thing that could save her.

'Really? We've never heard that, that girl walks on water as far as Mac believes, treats her like a daughter, he does.'

'Well, I'm no doctor but if you ask me, she's heading for a massive mental break down. She had been a complete bitch since New Year's Eve, in fact I was glad to be flying back, if truth be told.'

'Wow, that's some problem, Mac would trust her with his life, thinks the sunshine's out of backside. He won't want to hear this news.'

'Well it's not for me to say, is it? He needs to ring his man Sean, and he would agree with me, I'm sure about that.'

There was a natural lull in the conversation as O'Donnell negotiated his way through the busy rush hour traffic.

Miller picked his moment.

'I've a favour to ask, a very big one, in fact.'

'OK, what is it?'

'I need it to be between just you and me, can I trust you?'

'That all depends on what you're asking for, Miller, what is it?'

'I want you to get me a handgun and two full clips, can you do that?'

'Fecking no way! Are ye mad? Me get you a gun, a Brit, what the feck do you want with a gun anyway?'

'I only want to borrow it, for a couple of hours that's all, get it to me in the morning and I'll give it back to you by teatime, promise.'

'Oh, and why does a Brit need a gun, might I ask?'

'Its insurance, that's all, I want to go and clear the air once and for all with that Gypo Andy Connor's, otherwise, I will be looking over my shoulder each time I step out of Fagin's. I only need it just in case that's all; I think I can smooth things out with him if we speak man to man.'

'You have no fecking idea, do you? You took his eye out, you took down his number one enforcer and you expect him to kiss and make up? It will never happen, no you're right, whenever you step out of our place you will be prey to one of his henchman, that's for sure.'

'You're not listening, are you, O'Donnell? I need to sort it out, I don't want this cloud hanging over me, come on, do this for me, if our roles were reversed I would do it for you.'

O'Donnell chest rose and then lowered just as quickly as he let out a sigh.

'Not promising but I will see what I can do, here we are, leave your bag in the boot for time being.'

Tom Cullen was standing in the room, client side and he turned as Miller strode confidently into his pub. It was empty save for a couple of staff; it was over 45 minutes until opening time.

'Welcome back, Miller, good trip?'

Miller was taken aback by the overt courtesy shown him from a man who had only ever scowled before.

'Good, thanks.'

'Let's get you a brew, Mac is on his way, so he is.'

It was the friendly face of Catriona who brought out two mugs of tea and sat on the stool opposite him.

'So, how's my cuz, and more importantly how was Boston you lucky fecker?'

'Well, Boston was amazing, the pub was great, live music five nights a week, but I was telling O'Donnell coming over here, I can't say the same about your cousin. She's done in.'

'Done in? What do you mean? What's up with her?'

'Well she's knackered, that's what, working seven days a week and running up and down to New York and Chicago has finally taken its toll on her. She needs a break, a long one or it's off to the funny farm for her and I am not kiddin' you.'

Catriona sat upright, and her head shot back too as she took on board the information Miller had divulged. It was totally out of the blue and yet somehow not totally unexpected, she had often chastised her cousin for working so hard.

'Wow, how did you leave it with her?'

'Well she's been to the doctors, I do know that, and they have given her some sort of antidepressants and something to help her sleep. She's a wreck, she's aged five years in the past few weeks.'

Miller was painting as black a picture as he could tee things up before Ciara called Mac. He knew all his words would get back to him and quickly.

'Oh, you've really shocked me, I'm going to give her a call, I need to speak to her and she's like a sister to me.' Catriona was genuinely concerned. She had taken the bait.

'You do that, she needs a friendly shoulder, only don't tell her mum or dad, she doesn't want them to know.'

'Of course, I understand.'

'Mr Miller,' it was Mac, his overcoat was shining with the fresh rain on it.

'Let's go into the snug, I need a private chat with you.'

The chat was a long one, over two hours, Miller had been hoping for some opening to suggest the conversation with the British Government and before he could, Mac had brought up the exact same subject; he did so in a hesitant way at first but then opened up.

Bingo. It couldn't have played out any better.

Miller also told Mac about how he'd left Ciara and the fact the girl needed help. Mac was genuinely both surprised and troubled, he really liked the girl. He would speak to David about her and see what he thought.

All in all, amongst all the yawing he'd done, it had been a very successful and productive morning.

He had shared with Mac that his in and back door to the UK security forces was the welfare officer who'd managed to get him out of Strangeways' Prison, he would be the conduit for him to the government. He could trust him and wouldn't even need to share the reason; he was confident about that. Of course, none of that was true; Rosie was waiting for a call from him anyway on the exact same subject.

Miller had to play his chips well if he was to help Ciara out of the very dark, deep pit she was in with the Americans.

Mac had fixed up for Miller to return to live with the Corcoran's again, they were waiting to hear news of their daughter and Miller had brought over gifts for each of them from Ciara.

It was two days later, when O'Donnell collared Miller and showed him the piece; it was wrapped in a dark oiled cloth. A single magazine, fully charged, was with it.

'I don't know what you are up to, Miller, and Mac will be furious if he knows I've done this so let's keep it between us. Right? And I want it back in three days' time, maximum. Deal?'

'You betcha,' Miller was ecstatic.

Mac would know soon enough about the gun. It was time to get to work on several fronts, life was good, Miller was upbeat and bouncing with energy.

Chapter 48:
Miller Returns with a Bang

Miller had done the walk-by five times now over the past two days, each at a different time and from different ends of the street. The house was a large three storey Victorian detached, with a small front garden and large enclosed rear. Adorning the gate posts sat two stone lions on their haunches, tacky and tasteless.

There was a car permanently parked on the drive, a Chrysler. *Presumably not working*, thought Miller. It was quite a busy house too with lots of comings and goings. Miller reckoned that there were probably four or five people living in the house. He sat mulling it over and decided that teatime, five o'clock would be a suitable time for the visit. It would have just turned dark by then and folk would be watching early evening TV. Perfect.

He parked the car a few streets away. It was drizzling rain that was an unplanned bonus, not many folks were on the street and the leaden sky made the evening darker. He stood on the corner as if waiting for a lift from someone. He didn't have long to hang around.

The car pulled up and the big man alighted, and Miller made the positive ID immediately, it wasn't hard to do of course. Two minutes later, he made his move. He walked briskly down to the front of the house and slipped easily down the side of the parked car on the drive. He pulled down the balaclava mask and was careful to step past the empty milk bottles on the step, slowly he depressed the front door handle, it turned, and the door opened.

Miller stepped boldly into the house, as he entered the living room, a woman in her 40s was busy ironing and watching the TV at the same time, she turned at the sudden rush of cold air and the sound of movement. In the threshold of the kitchen door carrying two large mugs of tea stood Andy, the cheap gangster, his black eye patch making him look somewhat comical.

Miller stepped forward until he was less than six feet away. Training and drill took over. Double tap, centre of seen mass.

The roar of the gun in the confined space of the lounge was deafening.

The target crumpled throwing the tea forward as the overweight trunk of the body collapsed clumsily to the floor. He was dead in seconds. A voice screamed from somewhere behind. Miller turn confidently, gun still visible in his hand. No real threat present, just a woman.

He exited the room without further engagement.

The cloth bag protecting the gun was stowed into the deep pocket of the overcoat, the two empty cases trapped inside, less for the forensics to search for now.

On reaching the car, Miller climbed in and pulled slowly away so as not to attract any attention whatsoever.

After only half a mile, he pulled over. He threw the overcoat, balaclava, gloves and shoes into the dumpster he had espied during his reconnaissance. No forensic evidence now and the police would never find them. Lastly, he emptied the bag containing the two empty cartilage shells by tipping them down the nearby storm drain.

Mac was right. Vengeance was always best served cold.

Chapter 49:
Embassy Meet

It was 9:45 am as Miller walked around Merrion square in front of the Embassy as he'd been instructed to do. Midway through the second lap he discerned the footsteps of the agent contact. Slowing he allowed the man to overtake and was instructed to follow. They walked down lower Mount Street and after 300 yards the agent tuned sharp left, continued to walk and then turning he instructed Miller to continue walking as he himself reversed the route. Halfway down the street out of a shop doorway stepped Rosie to beckon Miller to follow her inside.

'Hello Miller, you are being followed of course; our man will have spooked them long enough for us to shake them off by using this route.' They walked into the rear yard of the shop and climbed into a side door of a waiting delivery van which pulled off immediate they were on board. She held her fingers to her pursed lips gesturing for him not to speak. In less than seven minutes, the van pulled up in a semi-industrial part of Dublin and Rosie led the way into an innocuous office.

Waiting for them in the room to the rear were four others, all male. Off to one side sat behind a single desk was a Stenograph operator, a crusty grey-haired lady.

Col Gilbert stood and offered his hand to Miller and gave him a firm but friendly shake. Miller smiled back at him.

'Miller, let me tell you, we are more than delighted at your work, we are positively brimming with excitement. The Prime Minister himself can't wait for our report.'

Rosie weighed in next.

'We need to resolve the trouble up north and quickly, it doesn't sit well with us to have 20,000 troops stationed on home turf, you have a pivotal role in resolving this regrettable situation, Miller. We can't understate the importance of this meeting today. Now in your own time lets go over things shall we?'

Miller sat upright in his chair and asked, 'I thought it was us that wanted to open the dialogue, if that's the case we have to give them something.'

'Only you know that, Miller, it is MacStiofain who has requested this meeting and asked you to act as the back channel.'

'Be that as maybe, but I have an agenda here too, like, what will happen to Ciara, for instance?' Miller was keeping his cards close to his chest.

Col Gilbert was immediately annoyed.

'What of a slip of a girl? Lives are at stake here, Miller, lots of them, get on with it, man.' Miller chose not to respond, and room became quiet.

It was Rosie who broke the silence and calmed the situation down.

'Listen Miller, we know you've grown fond of Ciara, but she is up to her eyes with fundraising for the IRA, gun running and now explosives, she'll go down for a very long time. There is nothing we can do, I'm afraid; it is out of our hands.'

'Really? Then were done here.' Miller stood to leave.

'Miller,' shouted the Colonel. 'Sit down or I'll have you back in jail before you can say Jack Flash.' The Colonel was on the brink of violence.

'This is how I see it playing out.' opened Miller.

'You tell the American agencies she was working as double agent all along and get her out of the fix she's in, simple.'

'And what do we give them in return exactly? You clearly don't know how the CIA works, Miller.'

'We handover to them the intercept on the boat carrying the arms and explosives, they get all the kudos associated with thwarted Qaddafi, that's what we give them.'

'You're serious, aren't you, Miller?'

'Very.'

'Let's park this idea, how do we move things forward with the IRA?'

'You want to meet, they want to meet, how hard is that to organise?'

'Where?'

'I don't know, you figure it out; there are hundreds of you and only one of me.'

'Sir, if I may suggest we have a break for ten minutes?'

It was a young officer presumably. *Another spook*, thought Miller.

The female stenograph operator stopped typing, hesitated and then took her cue.

'Perhaps I can offer Mr Miller some refreshments?'

Miller followed her to another room sparsely furnish but with a small kitchenette and the makings for a brew.

'Where is home for you?' he asked.

'London, Holland park, to be precise.'

'How long have you worked for SIS if that's not an inappropriate question?'

'I am a civil servant, joined the Home Office straight from school, many years ago, I found my way into this specialist role just over 20 years ago, I like the work its varied and interesting and often gets me out of London, like today. So, mustn't grumble as we say.'

Miller liked her immediately. She was the archetypal English spinster who had dedicated her life to the Crown. She was in her early 60s, plainly dressed but with an air of orderliness. She wore her hair in a matronly bun, keeping it away from her face.

'Who have you met in this job; anyone I would know.'

'How would I know with whom you were acquainted?' she replied. Then rather boldly she added, 'I did serve sir Winny in his wartime cabinet, perhaps you have heard of him?' she teased sarcastically.

'Winston Churchill, now that does impress me!'

'Yes, and so did the Ambassador here in Dublin, Mr Peck, he was one of his private secretary's during the war.'

It was a full forty minutes before Rosie appeared in the frame of the door to put an end to their cosy chat.

'We are ready for you, do come in.'

Miller smiled warmly at the stenographer stood and returned to the briefing room.

Colonel Gilbert spent the next ten minutes running through the details of the planned meet.

It was to take place in two phases, and initial meet in Northern Ireland, at the home of a catholic and former soldier, Colonel MW McCorkell. The retired officer resided at Ballyarnett, which lay a few miles to the north-west of Londonderry. They were to cross the border from Donegal near Bridegend, the soldiers manning the vehicle check point would be briefed and intelligence agents would be on hand to ensure safe passage. Gilbert pushed across a paper showing three dates and explained the IRA were to choose a primary and an alternative. The purpose of the meeting was to agree the agenda for the follow up meeting which would have to take place in London.

'A meeting about a meeting,' Miller commented.

'Not sure that is what Mac had in mind.'

'If you like, yes Miller, please understand, this is a very delicate matter, there is over 800 years of historical animosity between us, we need to tread carefully, very carefully if we are to be successful. You need to sell it, Miller, it's the best we can do at this moment in time, but it would be real progress. I don't need to tell you this is top secret, no one outside of this circle must know about this.'

'Except I need to share it with Mac, of course,' Miller was being sarcastic.

'And what about Ciara?'

'We can't promise you anything, of course, Miller, but we will discuss it with our cousins over the pond. She will need to give them full details of the arms shipment, in fact she will have to start work for them too, a joint asset so to speak, we've discussed this and believe this is a plausible way forward, more importantly it's all you are getting, Miller.'

Miller remained silent; he didn't know how to respond so silence was the best course of action.

'Let's get you back in circulation and across to Fagin's.' The operations team is on standby outside.

Rosie shook Miller's hand, 'Keep up the good work, there are a lot of innocent lives at stake here, Miller, you are holding cards which can alter the future of millions of Irish people.'

'No pressure here then?' He remained in a sarcastic frame of mind.

'Here is a telephone number of our operation desk in Dublin; it is OK to show it to Mac by way of legitimising your position. You clearly have remembered the emergency one by rote as you have proved already.'

As Miller nodded his acknowledgement, he looked over at the stenographer and could have sworn she offered him a small smile and a wink of her eye, but he couldn't be sure.

The operations team took him further out of Dublin and dropped him on the bus route from Swords into the centre.

Chapter 50:
The Committee Meet

Corporal Fergus McMenemy was disappointed at being excluded from the meeting. Privileges of rank he supposed. He felt it odd that of the ten men locked in hushed conversation not even one of the soldiers attending was from Ulster, they were all from the mainland.

The Committee, as they called themselves, was a leadership group drawn from the Brigade command, the MRF and the RUC Special Branch. The man running the meeting was dressed in civilian clothes looked to be in his mid-forties and yet was a soldier, a senior officer in fact.

According to Bob, they were there to discuss and collate evidence of active soldiers of the IRA, the players. All he knew that it was a long list, several pages in fact. Captain Bob loved all the intrigue associated with it. The Committee meeting went on for hours without a break and with no interruption. It was the most clandestine meeting held in palace Barracks, that much he did know. The product was always the same, a priority listing of persons of interest.

The Special Branch men attending were handpicked exclusively from the Protestant community.

No balance there, it was always biased against the Catholics. Less chance of a leak he assumed.

Captain Bob came out from the meeting, not at all tired, just the opposite in fact, he was almost skipping. Whatever had been agreed behind those closed doors clearly met with his full endorsement and made him happy.

'Care to share?'

'Sorry, as much as I'd love to, Fergus, it's not possible, it's strictly on a need to know basis. Let's just say the gloves are well and truly off and our IRA friends won't have it all their own way over the coming weeks. We've been far too lenient for far too long; we know exactly who the bad guys are so it's a time of reckoning for them; let's just leave it at that.'

'Any feedback on that ambush we helped set up? It went off well, didn't it?'

'It was mentioned in passing, only on the grounds we need to do more of them, that's all.'

'Who was the middle-aged man who seemed to be running the meeting?'

'Middle-aged? Don't let him hear you say that, he is an absolute guru on low intensity operations, decorated in Kenya for actions against the Mau Mau, what he doesn't know about this kind of warfare isn't worth knowing and by the way, he may be in civvies but he is a brigadier!'

'He has told us that we need to provide the green army with better intelligence, in order they can plan and execute more of those operations, execute being the operative word. Big Boys games call for Big Boy's rules. What I can share with you is that we will be working more with my friends: the hooligans from Hereford in the next few weeks, the gloves are off.' He laughed out loud to himself and then disappeared down to the ablutions.

At times this is such a strange job, Fergus thought to himself, so many circles within circles. What he did know was that Bob was in his element and would never have trouble sleeping that night, well, except for his obvious excitement that is.

Chapter 51:
The First Meet with Security Forces

Miller shuffled uncomfortably in the back of the car as it traversed the roads of county Donegal. Their journey from Dublin had been a long one. He noted them passing through Sligo, Donegal town, Letterkenny and as they approached to the town of Bridgend. O'Donnell who was driving gave them the warning that the border with Northern Ireland was less than five minutes ahead.

As the saloon slowed to join the queue on the A2 through the army check point, the atmosphere in the care became noticeably tense.

'This is where we discover if you have set us up, eh Miller?'

It was O'Donnell breaking the ice. He didn't think for one minute his new-found friend would have done anything of the sort. He may be British but he both respected him and more importantly trusted him.

The VCP was on the straight stretch of road close to the village of Coshquin on the Buncana road, they had been instructed to approach the Londonderry area from this direction. There were still three cars in front of them waiting to be searched when the man in the camel coat exited the portacabin and approached them. Miller wound down his window as the stranger drew alongside, 'I'm Miller,' he offered.

The stranger immediately became agitated and waved his hand at the officer standing to one side of the barrier. Several soldiers piled out a sanger close by fumbling with their webbing and adjusting their smocks. Traffic in both directions was halted immediately. The civilian in the coat waved again this time to Miller's car to pull out of the line and he gestured it forward. The barrier was raised, and their car sailed through. No search, no ID check, all as agreed.

'So far, so good,' said Mac.

The two army motor bikes appeared from the side of the road and took up position in front of their car to escort and lead them to the rendezvous. They were being given five-star treatment.

In under ten minutes, they pulled up in front of the modest detached house, owned by a former senior Army officer, Colonel sir Michael McCorkell. He was an Ulsterman, a soldier, devout catholic and a former British public servant. This house was to be the venue of this momentous meeting between the antagonists, one the one side, the British authorities and on the other the IRA. As the men disgorged from the car and stretched. It was the homeowner sir Michael who greeted them by welcoming them to his humble home. David O'Connell asked to use the phone and he spoke briefly to alert the persons on the other end they had arrived safely, and the meeting was ready to start.

The group sat in the comfort of the Colonels lounge drinking their tea to await their colleagues from the north. They didn't have to wait long, less than seven minutes in fact. A car swung into the driveway and two very young men climbed out before the car sped off its wheels spinning on the loose gravel of the drive. Miller recognised the shorter of the two men; he'd seen him both in the pictures during training and as a visitor to Fagin's. The second man, wearing glasses was unknown to him. He looked more like a schoolteacher than a terrorist.

The two parties made their way into the dining room to commence their negotiations. Miller had thought to accompany them but was asked to wait in the adjoint room. He felt miffed at fist at being excluded then concluded it was probably for the best. After all, it was him who had liaised with both sides to agree meeting venue. His work was done as far as he was concerned.

For the next four solid hours the discussions went back and forth, as the two sides danced around the major issues trying to agree some common ground.

Finally, a comfort break was called for and the room disgorged its occupants.

As Miller exited the toilet, on the landing the small young man from Londonderry, blocked the passage.

He was only about 20 but looked much older than his tender years, his hairline was already receding and what was left was a mop of unruly curly ginger hair. His face was contorted, and he wore an angry expression just about all the time. Miller was surprised that someone so young had a place at this negotiating table. The Irishman squared up to him.

'How did a fecking ex-Brit soldier worm his way into the favour of the Dublin council? I don't trust you, Brit, and for less than a penny I would gladly waste you, I want you to know that.' He gave Miller a cold stare with the eyes reminiscent of a shark.

'Really? Listen short arse, I didn't ask to be here, I was coerced by your countrymen to set this up and as for your threats, you little wanker, I could swat you like the flea you are.' The conversation became confrontational.

'Big man, are ye? I've heard about you and the pikeys, well you don't scare me, you make one false move and I will have you whacked, believe me, with or without Mac's permission.'

'Glad we've sorted out the formal introductions.' Miller's right arm swept up, catching the small Irishman off-balance and brushing him aside easily aside.

'The bog's free, bogtrotter.'

Returning to the ground floor of the house, the general atmosphere in the dining room was far more convivial; one could even be forgiven for saying friendly almost.

Miller shook hands with the British negotiators who were all smiling as their party prepared to depart.

Twenty minutes later, they were in the car, had cleared the border checkpoint easily again and were heading south back to Dublin, the poisoned dwarf from

Londonderry had already left with the man with glasses as they had been collected separately by some of their local henchmen.

O'Donnell was driving again; Miller sat in the back with O'Connell whilst Mac rode up front.

'When you came to our intention months ago after you fight outside the pub, I had a gut feeling about you, Miller. Call it instinct if you like. I never imagined that the tramp I saw before me however would be the back channel to the British authorities; never in my wildest imagination did I think that.'

His voice was friendly and upbeat. O'Donnell looked in but offered no comment.

'Nor did I, trust me. Do I take it that you were happy with the deal then?'

'No, definitely not, but it's a start, let's call it that. Our man from Derry got his assurance that your Countrymen would suspend arrests of republicans and searches of our homes, a small win, I guess. We got the promise of a meeting with your Government in London. That was the prize we were looking for. And as icing on the cake, both sides have agreed to a ceasefire. A respite if you will, from the recent cycle of violence. It's up to both sides to keep to their sides of the bargain now.'

'The man with the glasses doing lots of the talking, the schoolteacher type, who was he exactly?'

'You're referring to Gerry Adams. He is a good man, so he is. His Grandfather was a famous patriot and was his great-grandfather; he has a great mind on him, so he does. You couldn't meet a more loyal family to the cause.'

'Really, well I can't say I care for his mate though; he is an aggressive little shit if you ask me.' Mac let out a brief guffaw. O'Connell jumped immediately into the conversation.

'Don't you go talking about one of our patriots like that Miller if you know what's good for you.' His tone, in contract to Mac's was aggressive and hostile. O'Donnell shot Miller a glance into the rear-view mirror knowing he'd overstepped the mark.

'OK, OK,' Mac intervened. 'Let's drop it, we are all tired. Enough.'

Miller stared out of the window. How did he even get to be sharing a car with the Chief of Staff of the IRA? More importantly how could he extricate himself out of this total deception and with him Ciara? Shortly after crossing the border O'Donnell pulled into a pub car park where Mac and O'Connell climbed out leaving only Miller left in the car.

'Looks like it's you and me again, Rory, let's see if we can find a chippie, I'm starving.'

Chapter 52:
Ciara Returns to Dublin

Miller had borrowed a car to take the Corcoran's to Dublin airport to welcome Ciara home.

His standing with the community of Fagin's had taken a giant step up since it was learned that he was now the back channel to the British Government. Even Cullen was courteous these days.

Mae had insisted on going early, before the flight was due to land, even though Miller had explained that it would be at least an hour from the plane arriving until Ciara exited the customs. It was the least he could do was to show patience, they were very kindly folk and their daughter meant a lot to him too.

Mae had been up early and climbed into her best Sunday clothes and she had cajoled Sean to dress in a suit and tie, not something he was comfortable with, but he was happy to keep on the right side of his formidable wife. The shirt collar was too tight, so he wore the tie but left the top button of his worn shirt unfastened and the necktie loose.

The arrivals hall was full of excited people waiting for their loved ones to appear. It was quite an environment, noisy, but in a nice, almost magical, way.

Groups of families waited, some with children carrying balloons, some with signs and others with flowers. Family was special to the Irish, they had endured centuries of losing their children to far flung corners of the earth: America, Canada and Australia. The diaspora was spread around the globe and could be measured in tens of millions.

Miller watched on the electronic arrivals board: *plane landed, bags arrived and now it should be no more than twenty minutes*, he thought to himself. They had been in the arrival's hall for over 90 minutes already.

'Isn't it lovely,' Mae offered, 'all these folk reunited, it brings a lump to my throat.' She was feeling very emotional at her daughters return after so many years living away.

The number of arrivals exiting the secure area slowed to a trickle. As they passed, Miller had asked several to confirm that they had flown in on the New York flight which they had. Even the air crew had exited through but there was still no sign of Ciara.

Mr and Mrs Corcoran were becoming anxious.

'You don't think she could have missed it, do you?' She asked no one.

'No, of that I am certain; she would have rung last night if she had.' Miller did believe that too but hat the same time he was also perplexed that she had not yet cleared.

He walked to the security desk and spoke in a quiet voice to the Garda. He returned ten minutes later to share the news that Ciara had indeed landed but she had been randomly selected for a full bag search and could be delayed for a while.

Mae stood up; she was all for going to the Garda herself to complain. Miller explained that wouldn't help at all and they needed to be patient, it was just routine and unfortunately Ciara had been selected. It was nothing to worry about. They should go and get a bite to eat he suggested.

It was over an hour later that Ciara eventually appeared with her two worn large suitcases.

Miller was totally taken back by her appearance. She looked completely dishevelled, with bags under her eyes surrounded by large dark patches, she looked retched. He was shocked.

On seeing her precious daughter Mae couldn't hold back the tears any longer. 'Oh, our Ciara what's happened to you, sweetheart? You look awful.'

Ciara locked herself into a hug with her mum as Sean and Miller looked on not knowing what to say and do. The few remaining people in the hall looked in on them as they had done for the past two hours.

'I'm not feeling well mum, that's all, can we go now please, get me out of this airport,' she pleaded. She pecked her dad on the side of the cheek, but never spoke. She offered no form of greeting whatsoever to Miller.

The drive back to the house was strained.

'I've told you mum, I'm not myself that's all, I'm tired and can we just leave it please?' Mae had asked her so many questions. Sean had the common sense to stay out of it. As they walked down the garden path, Miller was left to struggle on his own with the two cases. Mae had prepared lunch, but Ciara was having none of it. She took herself straight off to her room.

'I expect she's very tired,' Sean offered, 'that's all, it's a long flight, best she gets some rest.'

'There is something seriously wrong; I am telling you, I know my own child, now get out of my way, you big useless lump.'

Miller was witnessing the first row between the Corcorans, he felt awkward and out of place.

He decided to make tea.

After Mae's telephone call, Dr McGrath arrived in less than thirty minutes. A heavy smoker and an even heavier drinker of the Jameson whisky, he had been the family practitioner for over thirty years. His nose was large, bulbous and glowed red. He was only with Ciara for less than five minutes before he returned downstairs and suggested they go into the parlour to talk.

Miller pretended he was reading the paper, which he had already looked over from back to front at the airport.

After he left, Mae climbed into her coat and made to leave the house. Miller stood, 'I still have the car outside, Mrs Corcoran, can I give you a lift somewhere?'

'No, I'm not going far,' was the reply. She never offered to explain to where and Miller was not about to ask. He could take a hint.

When she left, he waited until Sean had gone into the back garden and then climbed the stairs two at a time.

On seeing him alone, Ciara burst into tears, the sobbing was uncontrolled and so loud.

'Come on now, Ciara, you can tell me what the matter is.'

'I'm done for that's what the matter. I'm a goner, I am either going to jail for a very long time or worse still I'll end up with a bullet in me and a shallow grave.'

'No, you won't. I won't let it come to that,' he tried to comfort her.

'Oh, Miller, how did I ever get mixed up in all this, I have been so stupid and naïve.' Miller heard the front door close; it was Mae returning.

'You don't share anything with my mum, Miller, promise me and swear on it, now.'

'Of course, you have my word.'

Miller was about to descend the stairs as Mae started to climb, he back pedalled he knew it was bad luck.

'Is she still awake?'

'Yes.'

Miller could see that Mae was carrying a chemist's white bag with medication inside, no doubt something prescribed by Dr McGrath.

Miller decided to make him-self scarce. He popped into the garden to let Sean know he was off to return the borrowed car.

He stopped at a call box just off the main road. He called his special number and made arrangement to meet with Rosie to share with her that Ciara had been interviewed by Irish Special Branch on arrival and to find out if she knew anything. She owed him that much.

According to the National news the ceasefire he had been instrumental in brokering was holding, that, at least, was a positive.

Chapter 53:
M.V. Claudia

Guenther rose from his lying position on the wooden slatted bench of the sauna as his wife entered, she never acknowledged him and neither did he admit to knowing her. It was a game they liked to play in public.

He wasn't the only man watching her as she laid her towel carefully onto the wooden panels and sat down. All three male occupants of the sauna watched as her lithe naked body leaned back onto the wall, her head tilted toward the low ceiling. It was the normal custom and practice of all Hamburg sauna clubs that swimsuits were not required, why would they be? They were not prudish like the British or the Americans. Here nudity was the norm.

In her hand was a small white soft cotton flannel. Marlene firstly brushed off the excess water from the shower she had just taken from her pert breasts. At only 32, she was fit. With no children to her name yet, her beautiful body was completely unblemished. The onlookers looked at her with admiration of the beauty of the naked form. Next, she parted her legs exposing her quim to all and diligently mopped the inside of each thigh slowly and provocatively. There was no visible pubic hair, it had all been removed by waxing. Her hand movements were slow and deliberate and designed to arouse the three men watching her. It was just as if she was putting on a show to deliberately stimulate, excite and tease the men.

After a few more moments, she stood upright and walked across the room to the bucket in the corner, she gracefully bent over without bending her knees, exposing her firm buttocks and small neat posterior to the men as she lifted the wooden ladle, turning her head over her right shoulder she enquired;

'Does anyone mind?'

'Nein,' was the choked response from one of the men. She scooped several ladles of water pouring them slowly and carefully over the coals. The steam rose from the top of the sauna heater in white plumes like the exhaust of a locomotive and there was a sharp, immediate increase in the temperature in the already hot room. The three men sat mesmerised at the scene being played out in front of them. Her tanned lean naked body was reminiscent of a Greek goddess. Her movements were graceful and balletic, hardly surprising as she had spent her formative years attending dance classes. She returned to her bench to return to her sitting position opposite the men.

'Are you visiting our city?' asked Guenther, pretending to the audience he had never met his wife before. She looked up, 'No, not really, I keep a small apartment here but spend most of my time at my villa in Cyprus.'

'Oh, and if I may ask what business you are in that keeps you in Cyprus?'

'Shipping,' she replied, 'I am the owner of a small merchant vessel which I contract out.'

This part, at least, was very true: Merchant Vessel Claudia was indeed registered in the name of Marlene Leinhaeuser but really owned by the man asking the questions, Guenther.

One of the other men took the short silence as his cue to join in the conversation.

'Really, how interesting Frau, how is it living in Cyprus?'

'Oh, its fine I guess, not ideal, I would sooner live in Monaco but for business reasons Cyprus works for me.'

By asking her the question the stranger was able to look at her at the same time, he liked what he saw. She was truly beautiful. She was ultra-confident, her cheek bones framed her symmetrical face; she was quite simply an Adonis. His train of thought was interrupted. The door to the sauna creaked open and they were joined by another lady, this time in her early 60s, her boobs were sagging almost to her navel and she was ungroomed in all the places she should have been. The men shuffled around to make room for her.

'You look very fit, if I may say so.' Guenther continued his flirting of the Adonis.

'What's your secret?'

'Thank you, yoga I guess and my appetite.'

'Appetite, you're never hungry I take it?' He asked.

'No, I am referring to my sexual appetite,' she responded provocatively.

'It burns off lots of calories, don't you know?'

The three men shuffled uncomfortably on the bench, clearly both startled and aroused at her explanation. The older woman looked in and tutted disapprovingly at the suggestive remarks of the younger woman.

After a short pause, Guenther stood, smiled warmly at the young woman and reached across to her.

'If it pleases Frau,' she accepted his hand, stood and they exited the room. Leaving their towels in the sauna they walked hand in hand naked across to the shower room and closed the door behind them.

Curiosity got the better of one of the men and he stood to peer out of the small window in the door, he could clearly see the outline shape of the woman facing him, her hands were pressed against the large glass door of the shower room leaving their imprints whilst she was clearly being ravished from behind. The scene was an erotic one. Sitting back down, he turned to the other male stranger on his right and out of the corner of his mouth, he whispered, 'Lucky bugger, he's scored.'

Meanwhile, many thousands of kilometres away in the Mediterranean waters, the employee of the promiscuous couple from Hamburg was busy at work.

Captain Hans-Ludwig Fleugal, was the master of the vessel, the 289 tonne Cyprus based M.V. Claudia. He watched from his ship's rails as the soldiers of the Libyan Army staggered under the weight of the heavy boxes of arms and equipment they loaded onto his vessel. From the bridge he could just about make out the flag fluttering from the Embassy building, which was close by, it was the Union Flag, the symbol of Great Britain. *Ironic*, he thought to himself. He knew this cargo was heading for a rendezvous with the IRA and it would be used against the forces loyal to this flag. He cared not a jot. He was going to get paid very handsomely for this cargo by his good friend Guenther. It would be enough for him to retire if he chose to.

Following the completion of the loading into the hold, the Irish stranger he'd met briefly earlier, known only to him as Joe climbed the sloping aluminium gangway onto the vessel to join the precious cargo.

The world of illegal arms procurement was truly a global business and a cache of this magnitude had many moving parts. The voyage had commenced from its home port in Cyprus proceeded to Tripoli and from here they had legitimate cargo drops to do: first at Tunis, onto Gibraltar and then Cadiz. From this Spain port they would then head north across the turbulent Bay of Biscay to their final destination, Cork.

Two Libyan naval vessels cruised alongside as the Claudia chugged out of the port at twilight, they would escort it on the first leg of its journey and its highly illegal voyage to Ireland.

Bill Casey had flown into Shannon airport with his team and the cavalcade of cars from the Irish Special Branch picked them up direct from the tarmac, no prying eyes of over keen customs official could be allowed to compromise this mission.

From Shannon, the intended operations room was over two hours' drive away in the naval base situated on Haul bowline, a small island in Cork harbour, away from any inquisitive locals.

Already present in the Ops centre were the representatives from the British SIS and a Naval Commander as well as a large contingent of the Irish navy. The three countries were carrying out this joint intelligence operation, the origins of which Bill Casey had instigated with his surveillance of the IRA in the Iroquois hotel in Manhattan several weeks ago. He was going to be calling the shots, this had been agreed up front and he wanted to remind the team of this.

The Irish naval operations team was in half hourly contact with the British submarine that had been tasked with shadowing the M.V. Claudia. These regular situation reports allowed them to track the vessel along its journey from Libya. Cruising slowly in the cold dark waters of the Atlantic Ocean several miles offshore Ireland the three coastal minesweepers of the Irish navy lay in ambush. They had only recently been purchased from the British navy for fisheries duties and this was their first real operational task. The crews of the ships were excited to be part of this momentous action.

The ops room was tense. They were playing a waiting game of cat and mouse which would be played out over several days. The go ahead with the final intervention was going to be Bill Casey's call. He had insisted on that. He originally had wanted to use a US naval vessel and its Marines to make the boarding, but legal teams had thwarted that. Once the Claudia was in Irish territorial waters the vessel could be legitimately boarded by Irish officials and they would have a cast iron case in any court in the land, but especially so in Ireland.

When the call was finally made after four days of patient waiting, Claudia was almost home and dry. Some 50 miles east of the operations room and less than two miles off Helvic head in the county of Waterford the three Irish naval vessels closed in and ordered Claudia to weigh anchor and make ready for a boarding party. Armed Irish naval ratings lined the railings of each of the vessels.

On orders of its captain, on the leeward side of Claudia, a side door on the vessel was opened and several of the crew worked feverishly to throw as much of their cargo overboard as they could. It was too little too late, far too late, they were caught red handed disposing of the weapons. Just before the boarding, Captain Fleugal had managed to get off a short message to the vessel owner, Marlene, informing her of the intercept.

The Irish sailors boarded the merchant vessel and took over its command, they were accompanied by civilians dressed in overalls and wearing buoyancy aides and unknown to all was that these men were all field operatives from the American CIA tasked with searching the vessel for further evidence.

Under Naval escort the vessel was steered back to the Haul bowline naval base.

When the news reached them of the successful boarding, it was high five's all round and total jubilation in the operations room. An intricate intelligence plan spanning several countries had been executed with precision. It was quite an achievement, mission accomplished.

When the inventory of MV Claudia was finally made, it would reveal they had intercepted over five tons of weapons destined for the troubles up north. A whole armoury in fact: over 250 pistols, 250 Russian rifles 200 antitank mines 500lbs of Semtex explosives and 25,000 rounds of ammunition, they had hit the jackpot.

The intercept coordinates were noted and over the next few days Irish naval divers were tasked with attempting to recover the weapons poured overboard during the final assault. They were to prove unsuccessful; the waters at that point in the Atlantic were deep and the seabed crisscrossed with hidden fissures that would never give up their treasures. The operation was aborted after a few days.

Marlene was shocked to the core when the telex arrived. She stared at it for a few moments before calling out in panic to her husband. They needed to move quickly. Hamburg was not the place for them to hide out, she and her husband would have to fly immediately to somewhere in the Mediterranean which didn't have extradition arrangements with the western powers. Time was of the essence. They quickly scooped up their important belongings and prepared to drive south in the hour. They would have to assume that the immediate Airports would be on the lookout for them. They would motor down the 1200 kilometres to Milan, here the security was lax and if necessary, customs officials could be persuaded to turn a blind eye with a donation. From there too where? They would have to figure that out on the journey, the imperative now was to get out of Germany.

The Spanish evening was mild for this time of the year. In the quaint restaurant called El Faro, located in the ancient district of Cádiz that is called "La Viña", the two men looked across the eatery at each other. Joe Cahill then walked across the room and warmly embraced his long-time friend.

Xavier Izko de la Iglesia was a passionate and committed member of the outlawed ETA terrorist movement in Spain. The two men shared the struggles against oppressive governments who refused the will of the people. They had spent many months together in the training camps in the Middle east many years ago. The camaraderie and trust they had built in that period had only grown over the years not lessoned. When his friend Joe had reached out to him for his help a few weeks ago, Xabier could not refuse and true to his word he had provided the wherewithal and resources to unload the majority of the important cargo of the MV Claudia onto two other smaller vessels off the coast of Cadiz. part of the load they left for the authorities to find, eventually.

Their girl in Boston, Ciara, had provided the warning and the vital intelligence of the CIA plan which had allowed them to sacrifice a small part of the consignment to save the rest.

In payment the two men would share the spoils dividing the cache between them and have of the inventory would be shipped over to Ireland over the next several months in much smaller cargos under the noses of the slip shod Irish navy and the incompetent British intelligence agencies.

It was a job well done. It was a time for celebration; the two men clicked their wine glasses to toast together, 'Sláinte.'

Chapter 54:
Chelsea Morning

It was only few days after their trip to Londonderry that Miller had passed on the type written detailed arrangements to Mac in Fagin's. Miller was not to be included in the delegation to go to London for the upcoming talks. O'Donnell had shared with him privately that the Derry man McGuiness had insisted on this. Clearly their minor altercation outside the bathroom at Colonel's house had struck a nerve with the IRA brigade commander. Miller was unperturbed at this, totally.

It had been arranged that the Irish negotiating party would be met at the Air force base to the west of Dublin. Somewhat ironically, this facility was called Casement Aerodrome in honour of the nationalist Roger Casement, executed for treason by the British in 1916. They were to be collected by a VC 10 aircraft from ten Squadron RAF and flown in comfort to RAF Northolt near London and then transferred to a discrete hotel in Chelsea. The meetings were scheduled to take place close by the next morning at the home of a Government minister, Paul Channon, who owned a period home on Cheyne Walk, just off the embankment and Albert Bridge in Chelsea. Rosie's team had worked hard on the minute details for the meet in the past few days, there was such a lot at stake.

The Prime Minster had committed the Home Secretary William Whitelaw and a small number of other interested parties to represent the British point of view. Any mistake and that would be Rosie's career over, and she wasn't about to let that happen.

After some internal discussions within the council, MacStiofain had opted to take quite a large delegation, in addition to the team who had met the British in Londonderry he added the leadership of the Belfast Brigade of the IRA which was largely in the hands of Seamus Twomey and Ivor Bell two seasoned soldiers and experienced commanders. The surprise inclusion was Myles Shevlin who was a Dublin-based solicitor and a member of Mac's church congregation, he acted as the IRA's legal adviser.

The meeting differed completely from the preliminary discussions held at Col McCorkell house, this time it was Mac calling all the shots whilst other members of his entourage listened in. They had pre-prepared a list of their demands principal of which was for the Government to issue a formal statement that demanded that the British recognise the right of all the Irish people to determine the future of Ireland. Whitelaw pointed out that legislation lay in place which countered this by suggesting the future of the northern six counties could only be decided by the Ulster community. It was to prove a major hurdle. MacStiofain also laid out the roadmap for the phased withdrawal of all British troops within three years.

It was as well that MacStiofain was running the show, whenever the Belfast man Bell made comments, no member of the British party could understand a single word he uttered.

His Belfast accent was so strong and guttural.

By the end of the day, Whitelaw confided with his contingent privately that he had found MacStiofain the most unpleasant individual, adding the meeting had left him feeling depressed and emotionally exhausted.

Under pre-agreed instructions, the Irish contingent returned to their hotel for dinner and never discussed a single issue between them-selves all evening assuming all their rooms and the common areas would have been bugged. They were right to think and do so because they were 100% correct. A team of over thirty MI5 operatives had been assigned to gather each available snippet of information. Individual profile files had either been created or in the case they already existed added too. Over 700 photographs of the Irish team had been taken too. The meeting itself had made use of a trusted stenographer, totally unnecessary, she was for show purposes only as the whole of the meeting had been recorded for the intelligence teams to sift over at their leisure.

The very next day was a Saturday and Mac had arranged with his team to stay over to visit with friends and relations. He himself had many as he was, of course, born in London. The early summer weather was warm and the days long and the negotiating team made the most of their time in the capital. Their flight back to Dublin was not scheduled until Monday morning in any case. Mac reflected on their meeting, it was real progress, they were talking turkey now and the British Government clearly wanted to find a way of ridding themselves of the problem that Ulster caused. It was significant to that there were no representatives from the Unionist or Loyalist community; no doubt they were probably totally unaware of taking place.

It would take patience and skilful negotiations, but he was confident he was up to the task he had no self-doubt. He would become a legend in Ireland, the Englishman who created one Ireland. He smiled to himself, that was a prize worth being patient for. There might even be a statue or two in it for him. Now wouldn't that be something he mused.

Chapter 55:
Secrets and Lies

Sean Corcoran, could count on one hand the number of times he had stepped foot over the threshold of Fagin's pub. He was not a frequenter of such establishments, but he wanted to have a quiet talk with his long-time friend Tom Cullen. He was worried for his daughter and wanted to understand why her health could have deteriorated so quickly in only a few months. He also wanted her release from the employ of MacStiofain. He believed that this was ultimately the root cause to his daughter's problems, and of course, he was right to think this. He was no fool, he knew of Mac standing in the Irish Nationalist community and the reasons why. The fact his only daughter worked for him meant that she was also involved in some way with the movement. It was never discussed at home, but it was plain for all to see.

Sean had no quarrels with the British, both himself and his now deceased brother had served in the British army in the Great War like over two hundred thousand other Irish men. There was little or no work in Dublin in 1914 and the chance of decent of pay and three-square meals a day seemed an offer too good to refuse. Little did he realise what he had signed on for and the horrors he witnessed after his division had landed at Suvia bay in Gallipoli in August 1915 and the tough fighting with the Turks would stay with him forever.

Cullen could not have been more cordial or pleasant. He listened over a glass of Guinness to this concerned father with the deepest respect and genuine admiration. He knew this quiet unassuming man had served in the Irish contingent in the War and that he had been awarded a medal for his conspicuous bravery in rescuing a comrade under heavy enemy fire without any consideration for his own safety. *He was*, thought Tom Cullen, *the salt of the earth and the sort of man who was the backbone of real Ireland*. He committed to Sean that he would do all within his power to see Ciara was taken care of and that her employment in Boston could be ended.

As Sean walked back to his home, he felt better, he wouldn't mention his conversation with Tom to his wife Mae, he didn't like to keep secrets but sometimes things were best kept to oneself he decided.

He has also chatted to Tom about this English man Ciara thought so much of. Tom couldn't help him much there beyond what he already knew. What he could share was that despite Miller's violent track record he was very confident that he would never lay a hand on Ciara and the first time he did would be the last. Sean was still uneasy about his daughter's choice of a man; he would have

199

to find a way to discuss this with her and use his persuasive skills to suggest she found herself a new feller. Something about Miller was off putting but he just couldn't put a finger on it.

Back in the Corcoran's house Miller had never found himself alone with Ciara since her return from Boston. This afternoon the opportunity presented itself. Mae was at a parish meeting and Sean had taken himself off for a long walk, where, he hadn't shared.

'I have a surprise for you, sit up and I will help you out of your nightdress.'

'Go away, Miller, I am not up to having sex with you, I don't even feel like breathing at the moment.'

'Who said anything about sex? Sit up, Ciara.' Reluctantly she struggled to lift her head off her pillow to stare at him.

'What?' She asked.

Miller pulled back the blankets and sheet covering her.

'Lift up your arms.' Miller helped her out of the bri-nylon nightie.

'Here lay on this.' He rolled a large bath towel under her now naked torso and encouraged her to lay face down on top of it.

'What are you doing to me Mr Miller?'

'You'll find out in a minute.' He was fully clothed. As Ciara collapsed down onto the bed again, he covered her up with a second large bath towel.

'I am going to give you a Thai massage,' he said, 'Not like the one you gave me in Boston, but something I experienced in my time in Asia, it will help you sleep and make you feel better.'

'I don't want any massage, Miller, go away,' she argued feebly. The medication she was taking made her feel constantly drowsy.

Over the next hour, Miller set about diligently lightly massaging each single muscle of Ciara's body and to her surprise, she loved it and didn't want it to end. It was sheer bliss. She didn't even mind him massaging her breasts, it all just felt so nice.

He rolled her back off the towel and lifted the covers back over her now naked frame.

'Come back to me soon, Ciara, I miss you.'

He leant over and kissed her gently on her forehead like a parent would do to a child. Ciara closed her eyes and drifted into a peaceful and deep sleep.

Chapter 56:
The Future Looks Bright

The room over the bar in Fagin's was crowded. Apart from the usual members of the council there were representatives from all four provinces: Connacht, Leinster, Munster and Ulster as well as two active soldiers from Kilburn in London.

Folk were in good spirits, the ceasefire in the north was holding, and they were all eager to hear how the meetings with the British Government had gone. Mac opened the proceedings before handing over to Dáithí Ó Conaill (David O'Connell).

Daithi issued out a copy of the pre-conditions set ahead of the meeting and then passed out the formal declaration of intent they had drawn up and shared with the British Home secretary.

None of Irish contingent had truly expected great things to come out of the face to face but collectively agreed that the fact the meeting had taken place, dialogue was commenced that that it was a giant step forward and represented a momentous opportunity to unite their country once again. They believed the British Government was intent on returning the six northern counties but had to tread softly to persuade the Ulstermen in was in their long-term benefit to do so. They had never experienced such a window of opportunity since 1924. It was that significant, in fact it was monumental.

The Derry man was somewhat less enthusiastic.

'It's OK for you to talk this way, it's our women and children who suffer daily under the jack boots of this Imperial oppressive regime.' His sentiments were totally out of kilter with the general mood. His compatriot Gerry Adams sounded a more optimistic note.

'Listen, it's a good start that is for sure, we have a long way to go and much work to do but yes, it is a good start.' He went further.

'We need to legitimise ourselves, if we can set up a meeting with the British Home secretary then we need to do the same here in Dublin with the Taoiseach and again in Washington too. We need to play a long game, keep on the high ground and exert pressure where we can. We need all our supporters to get the message over that only when Ireland is whole again will justice have been served. It is our destiny to be whole again and it is up to us to achieve it.'

For such a young man he had a good grasp of politics and a keen understanding of how to influence others.

The debate went on for a further two hours, factors such as how the south would finance the Policing and social services, how the education system could be integrated, how jobs could be created and exports to the mainland could be increased. There was no shortage of passion or enthusiasm in the room. It was agreed that alongside the military wing it was time for the IRA to create its own political wing to legitimately press home its position and negotiate the best possible terms for the return of the six counties.

Mac closed the meeting and invited all the attendees to supper and a drink in the rooms below. The festivities carried on long into the early hours of the morning with much singing and jubilation.

It was not the end of the struggle, but it could be legitimately considered to be the beginning of the end of the struggles.

Chapter 57:
Dark Night of The Soul

Ciara was slowly returning to normal. It was helping that she was reducing her dosage of the tranquilizers she had been prescribed by Dr McGrath. She was sleeping less during the day now and managing to get out of bed for a couple of hours at a time. The colour was also slowly returning to her face improving its pallor. Miller had become her constant companion these past days. They were limited to how open their conversation could be as Mae was never far away, fussing her daughter. Today was a major milestone in the process of her recovery since her breakdown.

It was Sunday; he would drive her to the Velvet strand, a wide expanse of beautiful clean sandy beach located to the north of Dublin in Portmarnock. Running for over five miles long, the Strand stretched all the way up to Malahide. They could have a bite to eat in the White Sands hotel and walk as far as she felt able to along the beach. There are so many health benefits to being by the crashing waves and Miller was confident it would help Ciara feel better and sleep better hopefully without the use of her tablets.

'How did I get into this state?' She asked as the two of them stared through the window of the hotel restaurant.

'It was more than one thing Ciara, it always is and running between New York, Chicago and Boston these past months can't have been easy.'

'It wasn't that, Miller; it was that bomb at Christmas in town. I realised that I had become part of that cycle of violence, it could have been my own mame blown up; I hate myself for it now. I hate myself so much I don't care if the bloody IRA or the UDA bump me off, it's better if they do.'

'Please don't talk like that, Ciara, I don't like it, you worry me. Anyway, you are over all that now; Mac has found someone to run the books in Boston, even if it's just temporary for now. You are not on the CIA's most wanted list anymore and even though you are banned from visiting the country again, so what? There are plenty of beautiful places in the world nicer than Boston, trust me.'

'How did you get them not to arrest and charge me, Miller?'

'I didn't, you managed that all by yourself,' he lied.

'Giving them the details of the arms shipment was very brave and no one here suspects you had any hand in it at all. Mac just thinks you had a nervous breakdown by over working that's all.'

'You don't really believe that, do you?' she sounded confident in her response.

'Surely, if he did think you had anything to do with it, you wouldn't be here now would you and nor would I. He would have retired us both to a shallow grave, wouldn't he?'

Ciara wasn't about to tell him the arms cache discovered by the CIA was only a token sacrificial amount to hide the real deal. She was sworn to secrecy and her life would be at risk it that leaked out to the authorities. Mac knew she had given the details of the shipment up and had made the necessary plans to thwart the authorities. No, regardless of where her relationship was going with Miller, she needed to keep some of her past a secret.

'The gypsy boss, the one who had the big funeral, Catriona said she suspected you had a hand in his murder. Did you?'

'Well its very true there was bad blood between us, it was his gang which killed my Pilgrim so I guess people can see I had a motive, but no, as much as I hated him, I didn't kill him. Where would I get a gun from anyway? I assume it was carried by one of the many other gypsy families he'd cheated over the years. I'm just pleased he got what he deserved.'

Lying had become second nature to Miller these days, he did it so well he would have passed any polygraph.

After lunch they took a walk down the beach, not far as the weather was chilly and the wind cut through them, but Miller was right, it was somehow uplifting all the same.

After a short while spent almost completely in silence they returned to the car.

'What about you, Miller? Are you going to continue working for the enemy of the British, MacStiofain and the IRA?'

'No, my work is done here, Ciara. I did as Mac asked and brokered the meeting outside of Londonderry, he doesn't need me now and he's proved that by not taking me to London. There is nothing to hang around here for now?'

'Nothing, really? Is that true, Miller, and what about me?'

'I thought we were talking about work. Of course, I am here for you, what do you think we are doing today, or do you think Mac is paying me to be your nurse?'

'That's not enough for me, Miller, I want you to be here for the same reason I want you here. I love you, Algernon Miller. What I need to know is do you love me?'

'Yes, I believe I do, Ciara, I can't bear it when we are away from each other, I just worry some times that we are on different sides of a war, can we ever feel safe or will either be free of the shackles of our past. That's what I am concerned about.'

'I need you, Miller, now more than ever. I want you to take me away from this place, as far as we can possibly get.'

'Where to, girl? Are you forgetting I don't have any trade or skills to speak of? Who would want a washed-up former soldier who until recently was content to beg on the streets?'

'We can't let the past define our future, it's up to us to carve out a new life, as you say, our work is done here, let's just go away, just you and me.'

Miller pulled the car over into a bus stop. He leaned over and kissed her passionately on the lips.

'OK, madam, you want to leave, then let's do just that. We can start by me showing you the part of England where I grew up, warts and all.'

'I'd like that,' she smiled. 'I'd like that very much.'

They finished the car journey holding hands all the way as they headed back to the house.

They stopped off and picked up a fish supper for the four of them, it was still only 4:30 and Mae wouldn't have started the tea yet. It was never before six on a Sunday.

Mae could see by the look on her daughter's face that the trip to the beach had been the tonic she hoped it would be.

'Fish supper, ma, from your favourite chippy, fetch some plates, I'm starving.'

The four of them sat around the square dining table in the top of the room tucking into the supper. Mae had buttered some sliced bread.

'What do you think? They are good, aren't they?' Ciara asked.

'Oh, I have always liked the way he cooks his fish,' Mae added to the conversation.

'Sorry to burst your bubble but I've tasted better,' Miller responded.

'No way, and where would that be exactly?'

'Care to place a bet on it? A few miles south of where I was born is the fishing village of Whitby, it is famous for two things: firstly, Captain James Cook sailed from here in his ship the endeavour to discover Australia and secondly, it serves the best fish and chips in the world, bar none!'

He laughed out loud as he finished his tale. They all smiled with him.

'I'll take that bet, Mr Miller, and furthermore, I would love to see the village where ugly British brutes like you are bred from. When can we go?'

'Then we should as soon as you feel well enough, there is nothing stopping us, Ciara.'

'I love you, Algernon Miller. What I need to know is, do you love me?' It was the same question she had asked an hour ago but now it was in front of her parents.

'Yes, I do, Ciara Maria Corcoran, I believe I do.'

Ciara reached across the table with both hands and took hold of Miller's with them.

The two lovers were silent, drinking in the moment. Mae smiled at them both, made the sign of the cross to give thanks to almighty God for answering her prayers. Her treasure was returned from the dark night of the soul.

She had only been telling the priest after mass that morning that she could she a little improvement. *What a difference good honest pray made*, she thought to herself. God was always willing to help those who believed in Him. She would return tomorrow and offer a rosary in thanks for the recovery of her daughter.

Sean was silent, somewhat uncomfortable at the outpouring of emotion at his table, he could see his daughter was happier than she had been since she returned. Her choice of suitor still sat well with him. His earlier idea to talk his daughter into dumping the lodger clearly was no longer on the cards. *One good thing at least the boy was a Catholic*, he thought.

'Daddy,' Ciara started hesitantly, 'I am feeling a lot better today, I'd like to ask you if Algernon here can move into my room tonight, is that OK with you?'

So startled was he that Sean's tea dribbled down his chin, he was clearly embarrassed by his daughter's request and shuffled on his seat.

'Best you ask your ma about that, not my department.' Mae looked and just smiled her approval; she just wanted her daughter to be happy and she would offer a penitence for the sin later.

Ciara looked longingly into Miller's striking blue eyes; she was lost in her own world of happiness. She had turned a corner and exciting new adventure awaited them both. Miller looked across the table at this beautiful Irishwoman with magical green eyes and thought to himself, *we have a chance, I can feel it, I want to marry this lady.*

Still feeling a little uncomfortable Sean broke the silence.

'Look at the time, we are missing the early evening news,' he got up from his seat and walked across to the TV to turn it on. It was the release he needed from the awkward few moments he had just found himself in.

Chapter 58:
Snakes and Ladders

As the TV sprung to life, Sean retired to a more comfortable seat closer to the TV. He had his own chair, with a little table beside it for his newspaper and glasses to sit upon. No sooner did he make himself comfortable when he unmistakable and distinctive clipped tones of the BBC news reporter filled the room. They all stared in silence with utter disbelief at the scene unfolding before them. The correspondent was speaking live, direct into the camera against a background of several cars on fire and black smoke could be seen rising into the early evening air, it was a scene of utter chaos.

'In Londonderry this afternoon, what had started off as a peaceful march by thousands of civil rights protestors from the Catholic community objecting to Internment, had quickly spiralled out of control as a breakaway group of a few hundred people had confronted the watching Security forces.

'The British army had responded, first by using water cannon and then tear gas to disperse the group. This had been going on for several minutes. The resident Army battalion had been reinforced by units of the parachute Regiment drafted in from Belfast earlier that morning. Shortly after having suffered a fusillade of bricks and petrol bombs thrown at them the army had deployed snatch patrols from behind the temporary barricades to surge into the crowds to make arrests. It was then, according to reports from officers on the scene, one of the Soldiers, who are from the crack Airborne unit: the 1st Battalion parachute Regiment, opened fire with his rifle on a suspected nail bomber.

'The snatch teams in front of the barricades then came immediately under direct fire from gunmen hiding in the blocks of flats which towered over them. For several minutes pandemonium and confusion reigned. Almost 60 rounds of the lethal 7.62 calibre bullet were fired into the innocent crowd of men, women and children. A priest identified as a Father Daly holding up his white hankie as a sign of peace escorted a small group who were trying to carry a wounded teenager out of the melee and onto one of the many waiting ambulances.

'Latest reports have confirmed 13 dead and another 16 people are receiving treatment for gunshot wounds, some of the injuries are life threatening. The situation is unclear, and the death toll could easily rise as the severity of the injuries is established. Because of this terrible and unfortunate turn of events, riots had quickly flared up across the Province in Belfast, Lisburn, Newry and Omagh. This Sunday evening, as the world looks in, Ulster is ablaze.

'Dublin too had not escaped the backlash, many thousands of protestors on hearing the news have surrounded the British Embassy in Merrion square and have set it ablaze.' The cameras were switched in the studio to another BBC reporter this time in Dublin.

It was another BBC reporter with the same polished monotone accent.

'As a direct result of the riots in Londonderry and the subsequent shooting of innocent civilians by members of the Parachute Regiment, hatred of Britain in the Republic has now reached a fever pitch.

'As our embassy's interior is blazing fiercely, watched by a crowd of several thousand. Burn, burn, burn, this angry crowd shouted as chunks of masonry and woodwork fell blazing onto the street. The crowd redoubled their cheering whenever they saw the fire breaking through into new parts of the recently refurbished building. police and the fire brigade are standing by helplessly, overwhelmed by the size of the crowd and the magnitude of anger and who could blame them?

'It is a very dark day for Anglo-Irish relations and who knows where we go from here?'

The front room of the Corcoran household was silent, save for the TV. They all stood save for Sean and stared at the square screen speechless.

Ceasefire, Peace talks, progress?

They had just gone up in flames in Merrion square and along with them were the hopes and dreams of millions of Irish people.

Miller looked to with disbelief, 1 PARA, his parent Regiment, they had lost the plot, the red mist had risen, and they were doing what they did best, dish out gratuitous violence.

THE END OF BOOK ONE